At the Crossroads of Terror

By Lenny Emanuelli

Special Message from the author Lenny Emanuelli:

Although this book is fiction and a story I made up somewhere between a childhood fear and a winter's nightmare, the violence described in this novel is unfortunately real, and occurs someplace in the United States every two minutes. I hope this book brings to the forefront some of the real life violence that takes place in every city in America today and that we as a civilized nation, have the means to put an end to it.

What would you do if.... You were being hunted by a gang of killers? These vicious killers are holding your childhood sweetheart captive. You are also being hunted by the police for a murder you did not commit. Would you run? Would you fight? Would you seek revenge? Who do you turn to for help? Surely not a person you don't trust? A person you believe has ulterior motives. These are just some of the situations that haunt Charlie Johnson that he needs to answer. What he does to overcome these and many more obstacles might surprise you and are answered in this new suspenseful romantic thriller.

Charlie Johnson, a man suspected of killing a local merchant, reluctantly teams up with a television street reporter, Sherry Mann, trying to prove, he is innocent which takes them both deep into the world of an organized Asian street gang, who is on the verge of making their biggest stride, in their drug business.

Published by:

E.P. Publishing
101C North Greenville Ave
Allen, Texas 75002
www.EPPublishing.com

ISBN - 978-0-615-35979-3
ISBN - 0-615-35979-5

Cover Design: Dnicoart Company (www.dnicoart.com)
Cover Artist: Danielle Nicotri
Final Cover design: Nancy Starkman

Published in United States;
Printed in United States
Second edition
July 2010

Book Edits: Lisa Velarde and Carl Esposito
Final Edits and Corrections: Steve Berent from StarMemoirs.Com
Special thanks to StarMemoirs®

This book is dedicated to;

　All victims of a sexual crime;

　All victims of gang related crimes;

　Ms. K. Buller - A true survivor

　A place to get help 1-800-656-4673

Cast of Characters;

Charles P Johnson (CJ)
Michelle Kelly Robinson (Chelly)
Sherry Mann - WWNJ Street Reporter
Frank Johnson – Charlie's Dad
Renee Johnson – Charlie's Mom
Kym Nguyen – Female Gang member
Long Ngô – Leader of Flying Dragons Philly
Jeong Kim (Nhat-Quo) – Flying Dragons Leader
Hung Vuong- The Street Prince
Rudy Van - Bartender
Kwan Tran – Philly Gang member
Duc Pham- Philly Gang member
Phuong Le–Female Gang Member
Ly Linh– Female Gang member
Phuc- Philly Gang member
Quang Dang- Philly Gang member
Trung Duong- Philly Gang member
Sa'ng Phan- Philly Gang member
Sinh Tran- Philly Gang member
Thao – Philly Gang member
Danh Duong – Chicago Gang member
Huc Le – Chicago Gang member
Khan Min – Chicago Gang member
Dac Kien ('Doi-Moi') – Chicago Gang member
Danh Duong – Chicago Gang member
Quoc Bao Gia Xuong – New York Gang Member
Canh Huynh - Leadership Council Member
Hoc Pham- Leadership Council Member
Binh Phan- Leadership Council Member
Dat Vu- Leadership Council Member
Hung Dang- Leadership Council Member
Thinh Ho- Leadership Council Member
Sing Choi – Owner Choi Funeral Home
Ms Thuy Dang- Owner Thuy Dry Cleaner's
Jim Sweeney – PDD Detective
Ralph Inzerillo– PDD Detective
Allen Kennedy – PDD Officer
Doug Burke– PDD Officer

Frank Torteresi – Moorestown Officer
Richard Ng – Owner Ng Auto Collision owner
Sing Choi – Owner Choi Funeral Home
Robert O'Hara – Cherry Hill PD Detective
Ray Forster - Cherry Hill PD Detective
John Fennick Philadelphia Police Captain
Clyde Berkshire - Chicago Police Captain
Helmut Krause – A friend of Charlie & Chelly
Chester A. Wright - News Chief WWNJ - Philadelphia
Kevin Scotsman – News Chief WGNTV Chicago
Steven Bailey – WGNTV Cameraman
Arte Bridges – Maple Shade High School Student
'Kieu-Be' – House Madams
Suzanne Davis – Cook County Hospital Nurse
Jason Cornwell – WGNTV News Reporter Chicago
Gloria Stewart – WGNTV News Reporter Chicago
Jonathan Baker – WGNTV News Reporter Chicago
Robbie Jones – Comfort Inn Desk Clerk
Tony Pellegrino – Good Samaritan
Jeff Andrews – Fire Chief Cherry Hill NJ
David Farley – Fire Marshall Cherry Hill
Corby Ryan – Fire Marshall Cherry Hill
Steve Laper – Cherry Hill Police Chief
Dennis Manley –Sherry Mann's Father
Marie Manley – Sherry Mann's Mother

At the Crossroads of Terror

Prologue; Tuesday August 25, 1992-1 AM

They threw the woman to the ground, naked, on top of a pile of dirt at a construction site on the corner of Front Street and Noble Avenue in Philadelphia. Her hands were bound behind her back as she lie there slowly dying, her chest throbbing from the pain of multiple stab wounds, her body aching from the brutal rape the four Asian males standing around her committed.

She knew she didn't have much time left before her eyes closed forever and hoped that she and her husband had done a good job raising their only child, and that she would be able to cope with her parent's murder and the painful road ahead. Lying there dying, she could see her husband's body twitch in pain from the beating the men had given him. When they slashed his throat from ear to ear, she heard him cry out with pain like never before. They forced her to watch while they tormented him and made him beg for mercy.

They ended his pleading by holding his head, while another man reached into his swollen blood filled mouth and pulled out his tongue. With one flick of his knife, one of the bastards had the dying woman's husband's tongue in his hand and held it high in the air like a trophy, laughing and joking above their victim. He then tossed the bloody tongue towards the woman as they continued to laugh and joke.

Writhing in pain, she thought about how quickly the attack had happened and struggled to understand the brutality and sadistic way they had been overpowered. She knew her husband was almost dead. His moans became soft gurgling sounds as his heart pumped the last pints of blood out of the gash in his neck. Finally, she watched from a haze of pain and confusion as one of the men pulled out a gun and fired four shots into the man she had so loved.

Tears flowed down her face, her cries only heard by the men who just raped her and killed her husband. Her eyes started to twitch uncontrollably and her vision dimmed as her body started shutting down from the substantial blood loss.

Everything around her began to darkened, fading into history. As she struggled to stay alive, fighting against the darkness, trying to cling to the idea of avenging her husband's death, watching those bastards suffer the way they made him suffer, she then gasped for her last breath of air. Her final exhale took all her energy as she forced the air into a scream. "Oh My God!" she stammered with her last exhale before everything went dark. She was dead.

The four Asian men looked over the scene enjoying their work, their masterpiece. The one standing next to a black Cadillac Deville, the leader, lit a cigar like a victorious champion. Then he walked over to the other three, congratulated them on a job well done. As quickly as it began, it was over, and the four men got into the Caddy and drove away.

Three hours later, Maple Shade NJ;

When the phone rang, detective Frank Johnson looked over to see the time, trying to blink himself awake and shake off the tequila and beer from earlier that night. He and his wife had been out celebrating their 30th wedding anniversary; now she slept beside him as the phone continued to ring. He knew it couldn't be good news at 4 in the morning, so he prepared for the worst.

"Hello," he said, still trying to blink himself to full consciousness.

"Frank, its John," the caller said excitedly. "You have to meet me at the construction site at Front Street and Noble." The caller, his partner John Fennick, was a homicide detective for the Philadelphia police department. "You need to get down here right away; we've got a double murder," John continued before hanging up. This would be their first homicide case together. John's promotion became official a week earlier and he became Frank's partner just two days prior. It didn't take long for new murders to take place, especially not this year in Philadelphia. They were on pace to hit more than 400 murders, surpassing the 1987 record of 418.

[2]

At the Crossroads of Terror

1 year later; Wednesday August 25, 1993

Frank and John spent a year pounding the pavement, trying to generate leads, interrogating neighbors, friends and, relatives of the victims, Dennis and Marie Manley. The case soon went cold and was put into the unsolved case files at the Philadelphia PD, where the case remains today. The case continued to haunt detectives John Fennick and Frank Johnson as one of the most brutal and sadistic they'd ever witnessed in their careers.

The Dragon Awakens

Chapter 1

14 years later- April 17, 2006

" . . . Just a man and his will to survive. . . it's the eye of the tiger" ,blared the alarm clock instantaneously, and ever so abruptly ripping Charlie from his peaceful slumber; as he recklessly reached out for the snooze button, launching everything in its path. Oblivious to the world, Charlie attempted to gain some composure – at least enough to get him to the nearest tub of hot, flowing h2o. Little did he know, today, unlike any other ordinary day, would prove to be the first day of the rest of Charles Peter Johnson's life as he would know it.

A 35 year-old native of New Jersey, Charlie a.k.a. CJ, was born in the small town of Cherry Hill, named for its beautifully landscaped hills. He grew up there, along with his older sister (by a mere three years), and currently resides there today. In fact, his apartment is less than ten miles away from the very yard where one of the best tree houses in the whole world was painstakingly conceived.

At the Crossroads of Terror

A typical Jersey guy is what most everyone that knew Charlie, which was just about the whole town, had pegged him for. He spent most of his time either at work or on the sunny Jersey shores for some surf, sun and fun. His folks owned a beach house in Point Pleasant, and at the ripe age of twenty-one, he and his lovely sister Anna, were given inclusive access to all its wondrous amenities with the gift of their very own key. That key, suspending from Charlie's keychain, became a permanent fixture, reminding him of his youth, and all that that implied.

Married with 3 children, Charlie's only sibling, the outspoken Mrs. Anna Renee, lived just east of Cherry Hill, a mere 10 miles, give or take, within the historic district of Maple Shade, NY. To her brother she was known as the neighborhood newspaper, always in everyone's business, except her own. In fact, she was voted president of the school newspaper club and quite proudly proceeded to conceive the very first edition hot off the press.

Their devoted father, Frank Johnson, the renowned homicide detective, made a good living for some 40 years with the Philadelphia PD. Apart from the numerous awards and commendations, his unrelenting loyalty, superb devotion and impeccable service sky rocketed him to the pinnacle of his career.

Their Mother, a.k.a the neighborhood Samaritan, worked part time at Shane's retail department store, was head of the PTA, led the church choir, and volunteered for any good cause. Known as "mom" to everyone, she never complained, even when the stress of her husband's job was great. She worried about Frank, with his line of work, and never knew if he was going to come home alive and in one piece. He constantly had to reassure her that he absolutely never entered a crime scene until the police had given clearance. She knew him better than that though, as courageous as he was, and she'd put nothing past him when it came to his job.

Reflections of an otherwise wonderful childhood often play a recurring beat within Charlie's mind, though unfortunately, not every experience lived up to his expectations. Apart from the constant dedication to his family, Charlie's father was ever so enthralled in cracking the next big case. Surely when holidays rolled around, they were absolutely splendid with everyone present. Due to his lovely mother, the family was extremely close knit, sharing momentous times together. Charlie and Anna experienced a grand childhood and till this very day their unbreakable relationship is rock solid.

Charlie led a more diplomatic, moderately reserved, existence for a bachelor. Opposing commitment, enjoying a lifestyle with few, if any demands, having the ability to come and go as he pleases, and practically with whomever he chooses. Having been awarded most eligible bachelor in high school was by any means no exaggeration, as he was blessed with movie star looks, and a rugged surfer dude appearance that definitely gave him an edge in the dating scene. His contoured, fine sandy blonde locks, and piercing ice blue eyes, seemed to stop women in their tracks.

Charlie's bank account was by any means the perfect example of hard work and perseverance. Being touted as quite the workaholic, he'd earned numerous awards in the field of computer software, as he was the senior project manager at a highly reputable business which designed, engineered, built, and operated large constructed assets such as roadways and railways, with an exceptional arrangement of software solutions, later known as Barley Systems.

Charlie's latest fling, or so it seemed, was with a woman from Maple Shade, a childhood companion, though in fact they grew up together in Cherry Hill. Michelle Kelly Robinson, to be precise, as a child, was personally nicknamed Chelly by none other than Charlie himself. With a terminology all his own, the inclination of merging words to form one unique expression or phrase, had always been his biggest vice. Which just so happened to be quite contagious, as everyone around him tended to pick up on his slang. "The best form of flattery is imitation", Charlie's famous last words.

As a child Chelly was a real tomboy, preferring to cling to Charlie due to the simple fact that not one of the neighborhood girls ever interested her. She would much rather play games that were significant to boys than with baby dolls, or any other girly possessions for that matter. Mrs. Renee ever so adored Chelly, with her long silky dark brown hair. In fact, one Halloween she had sewn Chelly an Indian princess costume, inspired totally by those lovely locks, which become almost an everyday outfit as she and Charlie played cowboys and Indians recurrently.

With puberty's arrival, Charlie looked at girls in a whole different perspective, especially Chelly. Despite the fact that they were truly best of friends, practically inseparable, it wasn't till prom night that he realized what a beautiful young lady Chelly had become. As graduation day had finally come and gone, college was all anyone ever spoke of. The old neighborhood inevitably became a phantoms graveyard. Chelly was accepted to a renowned University out of state and Charlie attended a community college in Philadelphia. The internet had become their only link to one another and through e-mails they kept each other in the know. Eventually that was taken to a screeching halt, in fact ending bitterly with an argument that Charlie immensely regretted, being his fault entirely.

Chelly's beauty blossomed beyond compare, with a stunning, silky straight, luscious, dark brown main framing her perfectly heart-shaped face and rosy cheeks, amidst her porcelain skin, delicately sun-kissed with freckles. Her enormous eyes, how they'd sparkle and reflect, resembling beautiful amethysts, all leading up to the piece de resistance, her perfect, 36' 24' 36' drop dead gorgeous figure. A young woman like that, left to wander amidst a bunch of testosterone jocks.

Charlie had become extremely insecure. He struggled to gather his thoughts, and to understand his feelings. He knew, beyond the shadow of a doubt that he needed Chelly now, more than ever. Through the frustration, he'd lost control of his emotions and exploded with anger when he finally decided to let Chelly in on the feelings he had harbored for quite some time. Unfortunately, Chelly had grown tired of waiting for him to make the first move and eventually accepted a date from the brother of one of her sorority sisters. Charlie felt jealous and entitled, an argument ensued, and that inevitably wedged a knife into their relationship, severing all contact for many years.

One picturesque, sunny day, while downtown during the usual lunch hour rush, when everyone in the city seemed to be trudging the sidewalks looking for a bite to eat, amidst all the hustle and bustle of commuters and venders, Charlie found himself as usual, right in front of the Philly cheese steak vendor., "Order up Louie, hit me with ya best shot!" shouted Charlie, speaking over the noisy crowd. "Oh my God CJ is that really you?" gasped Chelly as she caught her breath, chocking on the last bite of her sandwich. Recognizing the voice, he quickly turned to look over his shoulder when all of a sudden, their eye's met and it seemed as though everything else in the world just disappeared.

Entranced in her eyes, Charlie turned to go to Chelly and tripped over someone's briefcase, losing his footing, almost falling onto an elderly lady, before being pushed backwards into the Philly cheese steak vendor. Without an apology or anything Charlie bellowed out, "Chelly, where are you". "I'm here", she replied, and as she reached out to grab him around the neck, Charlie wrapped his arms around her body, and proceeded to squeeze her ever so tightly. He wasn't quite sure of was happening and sensed by the look on her face that there may have still been a connection lingering somewhere all those years. After all, she called him "CJ", and only true friends called him that.

Charlie knew as a child that Chelly was into him and secretly, at least in Charlie's mind, he was into to her. "I was just over visiting with my second mom and dad they told me I'd probably find you here," exclaimed Chelly. "So I took my chances". As the crowd slowly diminished, they were faced once again with the reality of having to part ways. At this point Charlie was willing to take the day off for their long-awaited chance meeting. "CJ, I really need to talk to you", Chelly tenderly explained in an angel's voice. "I know it's been way too long, and I'm so very sorry Chelly", interjected Charlie, suddenly remembering he had a meeting scheduled back at the office concerning a major project.

"Chelly you must forgive me, but I have a very important meeting today that I just can't bang in", "Oh my God CJ, you never cease to amaze me with that slang of yours. I figured that would go during your years in college, I should've known better", Chelly chuckled. "I would definitely like to see you again, Chelly, maybe

[8]

dinner. Would that be okay?" questioned Charlie as he watched the expression on Chelly's face go from somber to elated. "Yes, yes definitely, CJ, it would be wonderful; there's so much lost time we need to catch up on and I know the perfect place," exclaimed Chelly.

They set the date for Monday at approximately 9:00 pm, to meet at The Dragon's Den in downtown Philadelphia for a few drinks, and then, unbeknownst to Chelly, head out to Chinatown for dinner. The Dragons Den served exceptional Chinese cuisine that unfortunately just happened to be a tad overpriced for Charlie's palate. He didn't perceive himself as cheap, rather a sensible guy who will not allow himself to succumb to such impracticalities. Besides, with Chelly's obvious beauty, the classy lady she had surely become, in all probability frequented refined establishments such as The Dragons Den.

He wanted to impress her with a stroll down memory lane, to the very restaurant in Chinatown they'd run off to many times while in high school together, just the two of them. This would be their first date as a couple and not just best friends, at least that's what he perceived it as, and he hoped the feeling was mutual. Bright and early Monday morning, Charlie left his apartment at precisely 7:30, headed east on North Kings Highway as he had repetitively done every morning for the last ten years or so, to catch bus #22. It was his daily commute to work, as it was significantly cheaper, quicker and less stressful for him. All of a sudden he heard a loud bang, sort of like a car when it backfires, but only louder and more resounding. That's when he noticed a beautiful Asian woman walking out of Chang's Cleaners. He couldn't take his eyes off of her. She was simply spectacular, a real stunning woman, the kind that guys only dream of, knowing they'd never be lucky enough to actually be with her. As he scanned every inch of her body from head to toe, he couldn't help but notice that she was dressed to kill in a sexy, black silk dress with a slit cut all the way up the side, right to her hip, and her gorgeous legs seemed to go on forever, with those sizzling strappy stiletto's that glistened in the morning sun. Charlie thought it a bit odd though for such a classy woman to add a pair of short, white silk gloves to such attire, in April of all months, but he didn't care because the rest was so very good.

Enthralled in this amazing woman, Charlie could not for the life of him take his eyes off of her. It was as if they were the only two people on the sidewalk, and as she stared right back into his eyes, they locked into each other, and for a moment in time the whole scene began in slow motion. It was as if something inside of him had taken control, and as he looked deeply into her eyes, her image seemed to singe right into his retina. Her seductive smile, the way her body moved with every breathtaking step, he'd be able to recognize that gorgeous physique with his eyes closed. As she got close enough to touch him, without losing eye contact, she placed something into his jacket pocket. As he tilted his head down toward his pocket, with one finger, she gently pushed under his chin, lifting his head to keep eye contact, and said, "Ah ah . . . not yet". At this point Charlie felt invincible, sensing that she was totally digging him. As she lowered her body to enter the idling Chrysler 300M, she paused before breaking eye contact, and that's when Charlie noticed the strange tattoo high up on her thigh. With a smile she blew a kiss, and vanished.

Slowly regaining his composure, as if waking from a trance, engulfed in curiosity to see what treasure awaits him, Charlie immediately looked down towards his jacket pocket. As he reached in, jolted by a veritable bolt of lightning, sending a shock right up his spine, instantly bursting his bubble, there in his palm was a pistol. "Now why would such a beautiful woman be carrying a pistol, let alone give it to me", thought Charlie, as he suddenly heard sirens in the distance, getting louder with their approach. Putting two and two together, he ultimately realized the sound he had previously heard was a gunshot, and he was possibly holding the evidence. "Oh great, this is just great. Damn, why me, of all people, why me? My dad would've thoroughly enjoyed this. Hell, he would've relished just the thought of this", sobbed Charlie as he paced back and forth with his hands in the air, as if holding something up above his head. Suddenly an idea entered his mind, stopping him in his tracks as he said to himself, "Wait a second. I can handle this. This could be my chance to prove to the old man that all the tight lip about his work didn't keep the natural detective in me out in the dark". As a little beam of light began to appear at the end of his tunnel, Charlie was momentarily paralyzed as police cars, medics and detectives engulfed the area.

At the Crossroads of Terror

As Charlie headed toward the approaching police vehicles to clue them in on what had transpired only moments earlier and to give them what may possibly be the one and only form of evidence linked to the case, it dawned on him, his fingerprints were on the gun. He panicked, not knowing how to deal with the situation; it seemed like fleeing the scene presented as the best option, so he quickly placed the gun back into his jacket pocket. Knowing he had previously interacted with the beautiful woman who was currently the last person to leave Chang's, peaked his curiosity a bit more than he'd expected. Consequently he decided to take a closer look. What if this was a homicide, he thought. After all, every indication pointed in that direction. As he slipped past the officers, he attempted to enter the store, when all at once he was abruptly pulled back.

"Close enough, this is a crime scene," exploded the officer. As he was pulled, the pistol fell out of Charlie's pocket to the sidewalk. With all the commotion as cops and bystanders flooded past, neither Charlie nor the officer were aware the gun hit the pavement. More patrol cars were arriving by the minute with reinforcements. Even a television news crew arrived on the scene to film a live breaking story. As Charlie turned to walk away, he kicked something that went between the officer's feet. He looked down, it was the gun.

His heart began to pulsate, "Oh my God," he thought, "What am I going to do now?" Out of nowhere, someone in the television crew from station WWNJ spied the gun. As the cameraman recorded a close up, Sherry Mann, the reporter, spoke swiftly into the microphone, the camera panned Charlie in the shot as well, and to make things even worse, Sherry came up to him, "Sir, please be careful, this just might be the murder weapon." In an instant the police officer looked down, and noticed the gun lying there.

"Oh Damn", thought Charlie. Now that he knew this was a homicide, he believed the gorgeous woman was the killer. If the fingerprints found on that gun are proven to be mine, I'd be an innocent person, convicted of a crime I didn't commit. I could be thrown in prison for life, or even face the death penalty. What will my parents think of me? What will I leave behind as my legacy? All the Philly newspapers, right on the front page will read: Charles P. Johnson, Detective's son, convicted of murder", pondered Charlie.

"Did you hear anything?" asked Sherry.

"Did you see anyone running out of Chang's Cleaners?" she asked again. For the life of him, Charlie couldn't understand, out of all the other people around him, why the reporter had chosen him for answers.

"How about the gunshot, did you hear it Sir?" She continued in that *fake* television tone that Charlie loathed, acting as if she were a concerned citizen, when in reality it was all about the spotlight and the money.

"Did you hear it sir?" she asked again.

Charlie looked right into the camera, and answered as blunt as possible, "No, I didn't see or hear anything."

In a matter of minutes, Charlie had practically witnessed a crime, bungled the murder weapon, and ended up on television. The police backed everyone away from the weapon, when Charlie realized Sherry was starring straight at him with a rather strange expression on her face. He imagined somehow she read his mind. She understood what he was thinking. Could she? As he hurried to flee the scene and the crowd that continued to grow, not far behind Sherry had been trailing him, Sherry in a soft voice said, "I sense you know something." Charlie turned, Sherry continued, "I may be a reporter, but I'm also a woman, a woman with a strong intuition and If you don't talk to me, maybe you would like to talk to the police. Your face will be all over the news tonight and I'm sure somebody in this neighborhood will recognize you. It won't be hard for the police to find you."

"I know what you're trying to do," retorted Charlie.

"What do you mean?" she replied.

"You're just trying to give your career a little boost, and it isn't happening at my expense", he snarled. "The gun fell out of your pocket," she said. The blood in Charlie's head rushed out and his face appeared white. For someone like Sherry Mann to notice the gun fall out of his jacket meant bad news.

"Why was it in your pocket?" Standing with one hand on her hip, and pointing a finger at him with the other, "Who are you, and what do you know?"

At the Crossroads of Terror

Charlie's heart pounded in his chest harder than ever before. When he left his apartment that morning he felt fantastic, while looking forward to a special night with Chelly. Never did he think anything like this would happen to him. Just then the cameraman came over to talk to Sherry.

"Let's get closer. The police are going to make a statement." Sherry looked at Charlie, handed him her business card and said, "We need to talk. Do not leave or I will tell the police everything I know."

As Sherry and her cameraman rushed over to the scene, Charlie figured it was time for him to leave; he couldn't wait around for her to turn him in. He felt he couldn't win against someone of her community status and clout. The first thing he had to do was phone his boss to inform him he had a family emergency and would not be in today. Then he could go home to decide what he needed to do to get out of this mess. As he was walking back home, bus #22 pulled up along the sidewalk, the doors opened, and Bill the driver yelled out, "CJ hop on."

Startled Charlie replied, "Oh hey Bill, I decided I'd bang in sick today, thanks anyway."

"OK, just checking," said Bill. "I figured you couldn't get by the crowd to get to the stop. Have a good day and I'll see you tomorrow."

"Yeah, tomorrow", interjected Charlie with his head down as he kept walking towards his apartment.

"Hey you", bellowed Sherry Mann, standing like a mother calling her child. "I thought I told you to wait for me!" she continued, "Did you think I was kidding and that I wouldn't go to the police?"

"No," replied Charlie, "Oh I do believe you would go to the police, but I have to consider my options. I have your number and I was going to call you later." By the look on her face he could see she didn't believe a word he'd said. "Well, the conference is over, it was quite brief, and predictably uninformative," as she continued, "I told Joe, my cameraman, I'd meet him back at the office later this afternoon." They both looked at each other for a moment, and then she sped up to walk next to Charlie as he was heading in the direction of his apartment.

"Hey, what's your name anyway?", out of breath, Sherry asked.

"Charles Peter Johnson; some people call me Charlie, but to my friends I'm known as CJ," Charlie replied in a hasty manner with his head down.

"Well my name is --", replied Sherry, as she was rudely interrupted by Charlie. "I already know." As he continued to walk, trying to keep his distance from Sherry. Hesitantly, he unloaded on her in his words what had transpired, from the gunshot to the Asian woman.

"Whoa slow down Charlie, just look at me honey, I want you to relax, and slowly exhale," Sherry said in a calm manner as she reached out and placed her hand on Charlie's shoulder. He stopped and turned to look over at Sherry and can't help but think, "Oh no, is this really Sherry Mann, the same cold hearted bitch that has reported for WWNJ for the last ten years and known for shooting from the hip? What if she's just playing me for a story and didn't even see the gun fall out of my pocket."

Sherry asked, "Have you ever seen her around the neighborhood, Charlie?"

"No I haven't, but she had an odd tattoo on her leg. Something with the word 'sisters' and a letter F", Charlie replied, confused. At this point Sherry realized Charlie was unaware of the Asian crime organization in the area known as the Flying Dragons.

"Come with me" Sherry said. "Maybe I can help you, and together we can come up with a plan". After pausing to catch her breath she continued, "Besides, I have an extensive database on the Flying Dragons as I've followed them from day one of my career, and believe me Charlie, your life is in danger!"

"No", retorted Charlie, "I just want to go home and pretend this never happened, if only just for today", and as he pointed at Sherry he yelled out, "This happened to me, remember, I'm the victim!"

"There is no way I'm leaving your side, buddy, no matter how long this takes," Sherry interjected.

Eventually Charlie followed her back to her vehicle, a large black SUV, and as they drove away she began to tell him all about the Flying Dragons.

"Charlie, they are a highly organized Asian crime syndicate, with their members consisting of immigrant Asian youths who consider themselves born to kill; they are mostly Vietnamese, although lately they've expanded to include the Chinese, Koreans, and Taiwanese. Members are usually Asian runaway teens. Most of the members were the children of the American servicemen of the Vietnam War era, but over the last ten years they've joined forces with almost all other Asian American immigrants. The women are used to get into places the men can't. They are also used as sex slaves in massage parlors as part of the Flying Dragons' prostitution ring. Except for a few, most of the women are transported from one city to another every couple of weeks and work the massage parlors. When the Vietnam War ended, the children that remained were treated harshly by the local villagers in their native country. They were forced to leave the towns and villages to roam like wild animals. The US gathered many and brought them back to the States. Once here they were brought to military bases in Kansas, Iowa, Nebraska, and Oklahoma. They were taught English, and helped to adjust to an American lifestyle. They were sent to American schools and fostered to Asian families to help them to adapt to the change. Those children who couldn't adapt ran away to find themselves. The runaways were picked up by local Asian gangs, such as the Flying Dragons. Children with similar backgrounds who befriended the runaways were eventually recruited as well, into a life of criminal activities like prostitution, gambling, robbery and drug trafficking.

"While the Flying Dragons were in their early stages, robbery was their main source of income. They started to become more of an organized gang, when three runaways, Jeong Kym, Hung Vuong and Long Ngo wanted more out of their lives than the streets could offer. Jeong Kym is the top man in command. He is a rich and powerful person and is feared by the entire Asian community, ruling the gang from Chicago. Hung Vuong is known as the street prince within the Asian communities. He travels around to all the sectors of the Flying Dragons throughout the US. The third man, Long Ngo, is the leader of the Dragons here in the Philadelphia metropolitan area. Mr. Ngo is one of the most respected of the three, especially here in Philadelphia. When he enters a room, Asian immigrants stand and bow to him to show their respect. None of the three men have criminal records. They've never been arrested or investigated. The trio, that's what I like to call them, makes huge donations to all city-sponsored charities. In turn, the mayors of these cities treat them as model citizens. It wasn't long before the three started to organize their crime sprees and target their victims more carefully. The revenue increased and they became highly organized. When the gang started drug trafficking, their revenue increased to what it is today. I estimate the Flying Dragons gross millions of tax-free dollars every year and recruit thousands of Asian youths back in China,

Korea, Thailand and Vietnam for their prostitution ring. Because of their great business savvy, and the greed of the trio, they train their gang members in martial arts and military tactics. The Flying Dragons recently expanded and now have syndicates located in Dallas, Houston, and Portland, and I believe the main branch of the Flying Dragons is still located in Chicago where Jeong Kym resides."

The ride took a mere 30 minutes or so but seemed like hours to Charlie, before they arrived at Sherry's condo.

"This is freaky," Charlie said to Sherry. "Is this all real? Am I in a James Bond movie?" No sooner than they'd pulled into the driveway, Sherry's cell began to ring, with Charlie being so preoccupied with all that Sherry had told him regarding the Flying Dragons, and what had taken place just that morning, he didn't hear a word that was said. When she hung up the phone, she explained to him that she had told her boss and cameraman she would approve the edit for tonight's news broadcast from home. She told them something had come up and that she was following some leads; that way they'd have all day to put a plan together.

"You know, Sherry, after many years of watching you on the television, I can honestly say that I do believe I've harshly misjudged you", reasoned Charlie.

"Oh yeah, in which way, if you don't mind me asking?" Sherry boldly inquired.

In a swift attempt to change the subject, Charlie nervously replied, "Why me, Sherry; obviously I'm just an ordinary guy with no actual knowledge in crime."

"Charlie, you give yourself no credit; as far as I'm concerned, you are a very interesting guy; besides, I do believe you can help me help you, and possibly everyone else along the way."

"What do you mean by that, everyone else, like who?" Charlie inquired, insecurely.

"You know Charlie," explained Sherry. "Crime organizations like the Flying Dragons are the reason I made news reporting my career. I'm revolted with the way these scumbags seem to get away with murder right under our unsuspecting noses, and it's people like you and I, that end up paying for their crimes. Oh, but not on my watch baby, no siree. I want to exterminate the bastards", so passionately she replied.

[16]

At the Crossroads of Terror

Awed and amazed Charlie was taken back by the unexpected burst of courage; it was extremely sexy. At that moment, in a sudden glimpse, they make eye contact, and share a mutual connection.

"Charlie, I'm writing a book on the Flying Dragons and the Sisters of the Flying Dragons, and I need your help."

"Why would she need my help?" Charlie wondered.

Moorestown, NJ:

Sherry lived in Moorestown, New Jersey another Jersey suburb, 6 miles east of Cherry Hill. Moorestown is your typical suburban city where the neighbors take pride in their home's appearance. The lawns are well manicured with fantastic gardens, fountains and walkways. All the cars are high-end SUVs, Cadillac Escalades, Lincoln Navigators and BMW's. Its 10:30AM when they arrived at Sherry's condo. To enter her complex a code is needed on a keypad to open the gate. There are covered parking spots for guests, and each tenant had their own double car garage for their vehicles. They entered her condo through the front door, instead of through the garage, stating she has a tremendous amount of unpacked boxes there. Charlie trying to make conversation, "I learned from a professional organizer if you can live three weeks without what's in those boxes, you don't need them."

Sherry smiled and laughed, "You're kind of cute."

"Is she laughing at me or what I said," Charlie thinks to himself. "I wonder?"

Charlie entered her condo, in awe of the décor, although he realized she was not as manicured as she appeared on television. "Home, she is a bit messy and into the arts, similar to me." She had oil paintings on the walls, lots of books on book shelves, and stereo. It was his type of place and he felt welcomed. Sherry showed him where the TV and computers were.

"Go ahead and make yourself comfortable; I'm going to get comfortable myself," she said.

Charlie took off his jacket and threw it towards the sofa so he could get to her computer. He didn't notice at the time, but his jacket flew over the sofa and landed on the floor behind it. With access to the newsroom's server, Charlie couldn't believe all the research and facts he was able to obtain. He read almost everything he could on the Flying Dragons and the Sisters of the Flying Dragons. What he was reading started to horrify him. The things they got away with -- the killings, the shakedowns, the prostitution, the drugs, but most of all, how they were able to fly under the radar of any law enforcement was the mystery.

[18]

Evidence against them always disappears without a trail. The crime statistics in Cherry Hill was ranked in Money magazine article one of the 'Best Places to Live' in America in 2005 and 2006, with Cherry Hill listed in the top ten for being in the lowest crime risk category. Yet the Asian population was one of the highest.

Sherry came out wearing designer blue jeans and a light white sweatshirt. Charlie couldn't believe how relaxed and refreshed she was. "Damn, Sherry is one hot looking chick", thought Charlie. With her stylish strawberry blonde hair, her full lips which emphasize the beauty of her pretty face, she was more like the girl next store type, a real healthy and wholesome looking woman. "I'd better stop thinking about her and continue to do my research."

As he continued, Sherry informed him more of what she knew, "The latest is they became more involved with drug trafficking, importing drugs from South America and Asia. Their youngest members distribute them to teens across the country."

Charlie, who researched for hours, realized the time. "Just my luck, as soon as I schedule a date, this happens", he thought. He just couldn't be late, not tonight. He had always been late for everything Chelly and he did together. He wanted tonight to be different.

Sherry got up from her chair and put on the TV for the evening news. She had an internal alarm clock, Charlie surmised. Her story is the lead story of the night.

And now let's go on the scene with Sherry Mann.

"Good evening Ladies and gentlemen. I am Sherry Mann, WWNJ reporter. This morning, the owner of Chang's Cleaners on North Kings Highway in Cherry Hill was shot and killed. Police are investigating, but gave no immediate information. Let's go to the action as it unfolded this morning."

Charlie couldn't figure out how she managed to tape that intro scene, unless she recorded it that morning before they left. He had to admit, he was impressed. As disturbing as the story was to him, he was impressed with the way Sherry handled it; other than that phony TV voice of hers, she was factual and honest.

Now a replay of this morning's crime scene video:

"I'm Sherry Mann, for Eyewitness news. I am standing outside Chang's Cleaners where neighbors reported hearing a gunshot. There is a lot of chaos as police and medics try to get inside the store."

Just then you get a close-up of the gun, and Charlie.

"Look at that", this could be the murder weapon. Folks, we might be witnessing key evidence, the murder weapon."* With the camera back on Charlie: *"Sir, please be careful, this just might be the murder weapon."* The cameraman gets another close up of Charlie as Sherry asks, *"Did you hear anything?"*

"Did you see anyone running out of Chang's?"

With a slight pause; she asks, *"How about the sound of the gun being fired?"*

"Did you hear it sir?"

"No, I didn't see or hear anything," blares Charlie. The cameraman filmed Charlie as he turned, and started to walk away.

"Oh my God", Charlie moaned, "This looks worse than I thought. Am I the star of the news?" He was sure his mother, father, and sister watched.

Meanwhile at the Dragon's Den, Kym, the beautiful woman who was walking out of Chang's cleaners, yelled out, "Long come here, the guy I gave the gun to, Long, come quick", as she pointed to the TV, "Come, come look guys, this is him."

Long Ngo, the leader of the Flying Dragons in Philadelphia, which includes parts of Jersey, Cherry Hill and Camden, to name a few, is a Vietnamese immigrant, muscular in stature and in his late twenties, somewhere around 29. He is the brains behind the operation. He came to the US in 1986 when his older brother Tran, who lived here since 1972, went to Vietnam to retrieve him due to their mother's death. Long was 9 years old at the time.

At the young age of 13, Long had caused much dishonor and grief for his brother's family, hanging out with juvenile delinquents and getting into all kinds of trouble. His brother tried to help get him acclimated to living in the US, but it was futile. When Tran realized Long would not adjust, he threw him out to fend for himself. A tough decision, and even tougher for Long, but at 13 years of age Long Ngo became tougher. Not only did he survive, he became one of the most powerful gang members alive. Long is considered third in command under Jeong Kym, and Hung Vuong.

"We must find this guy," Long said in anger, to the gang. "We must find this guy. He has seen Kym and now is in possession of my property. Kwan!" Long yelled, "get your boys in here; we need to discuss something." Kwan Tran is Long Ngo's right hand man. He is in charge when Long is not around. He is shorter than Long, about 5'5" and muscular for his size. He can bench almost twice his weight, and is an expert in martial arts. He has black hair and a dark complexion, due to the fact he is Vietnamese and Korean mix. Kwan is the type of guy who thinks everything is a joke. He gets a kick out of someone else's pain and suffering. He committed many crimes for the gang, but somehow no police record. Evidence and witnesses seem to disappear. Without hesitation Kwan opened the door and yells to his gang, "Come in guys, we are having a meeting."

"Boys, we have a problem," Long clamored, "This morning, after we paid a visit to Chang, Kym bumped into a passerby and handed him the gun used to kill the bastard."

"Great, Kym", Kwan said, "You found a patsy". Everyone seemed to agree.

Long explained, "With the gun, she also gave him the glove right off her hand." The gang starts chattering amongst themselves. "Quiet down", Long retorted, "We need to find out who this guy is, where he lives, and where he works. We must do away with him quickly and quietly. We need to get the glove back, and this round eyed white man turns up in the city morgue." Laughter breaks out, "Let us start with Chang's family. Maybe one of them knows this guy. He must live or work nearby. He was there when the shooting took place. Now let's also find out everything we can from WWNJ. They must know something about him," Long ordered.

Long received a call from one of his gang members, everyone can hear, "What? When? Where....?" "Ok," Long said, "I'll have someone meet you." Long is a little distraught and in disbelief.

"What's wrong boss?" Kwan asked.

"Thao and Giang were busted downtown with the shipment in the van." Angrily he shouts, "You know what needs to be done!"

They all replied in unison, "Yes, Long, Yes."

Back at the Condo:

"Once again at Chang's Cleaners where inside a few moments ago the owner was shot and killed. I'm Sherry Mann for Eye Witness News, WWNJ, in Philadelphia."

Charlie turned the TV off and retorts, "Now what am I supposed to do?" After a slight pause he shouted, "The entire Philly-NJ area saw me; I was in the picture more than you! Who's the star of the show anyway?"

"I'm sorry", replied Sherry, "but until we can prove your innocence in this matter, the people should be aware of as many details as possible. I'm a reporter," Sherry continued.

"Yeah, I know that for a fact!" Charlie replied as he looked down at his wrist watch; he cannot believe where the day has gone. It's 8:45 pm, and he still has his date set with Chelly.

"Where are you going?" Sherry asked, as Charlie begins to walk out the door.

"I have a date tonight. I can't believe what time it is, wow! Time sure does fly when you're having fun," with a sarcastic sigh. "We've been here all day. Now it's time for my date," explained Charlie.

"You're not going anywhere without me, Mister," grunts Sherry. "I am not letting you out of my sight. Do you want my help, or what?"

"What kind of a date would it be if I brought you along; she'd think I was insane", replied Charlie.

"Well aren't you?" In a playful voice, "I mean you could have spoken up, and proved your innocence this morning, but no Charlie decides to leave the scene of the crime with his fingerprints on the murder weapon; you must be crazy."

"Okay, but please stay far enough away until I can make up an excuse to reschedule," Charlie moaned.

"Deal", Sherry replied. They get into the SUV, Charlie realizes he forgot his jacket in Sherry's living room and murmurs to himself, "Forget it, I'll get it later." Meantime, little did either one of them know, The Flying Dragons hang out at the Dragon's Den on a regular basis. In fact, the place is owned by Long Ngo and several other gang members under aliases. The Dragon's Den is just that . . . the Dragon's den.

Meeting the Dragon

Chapter 2

*T*he Dragon's Den, a designed structure set amidst two lush acres of extraordinary landscape which enhance its Vietnamese Tran Dynasty architecture, setting apart from all surrounding acreage. The manicured gardens lend an astonishing feature to the customary Asian architecture, which reflects the concept of the Orient. Upon entering through an immense golden gateway and being saluted by duel towering golden dragons as if standing guard, defending all that waits within, you will be overtaken as subtle oriental music plays. The ambience is in a class all its own, with the lovely addition of a dreamy waterfall accented with Bonsai trees and other lush tropical plants. The white noise from the water flowing down the wall of stone will lull you into a world unknown, as you are greeted by a massive golden statue of Buddha. Set high atop the building itself is a representation of a Vietnamese royal palace and is featured in Philadelphia's tourist guide pamphlet as a must-see for visitors and tourists because of its unique architectural design. The restaurant boasts a five-star review. The structure has a large kitchen surrounded by three main rooms catering to over a thousand guests and provides employment for about 200 people, all Asian descent.

The Dragon's Den is designed with upper floors allocated for business-end employees only, catering to the elusive organization of The Flying Dragons. The main floor has an efficient system of corridors connecting all the rooms to the kitchen, consisting of the red room, the green room and the white room. A layout which is convenient for the type of businesses conducted within. The elite restaurant and lounge is popular with young couples as the reception halls bestow an elegance all their own. The Dragon's Den received the highest reviews from numerous local food magazines. Apart from its astonishing beauty, The Dragons Den is, in an unsuspecting way, the main lair for the notorious Flying Dragons in the Philadelphia area, who bear a reputation of having obvious disregard for life and all that it entails. The rush they acquire from intimidating their victims is insatiable, like the cravings of a heroin addict. A typical spring night in Philadelphia, the temperature is quite nippy, around 45 degrees with clear skies. On this Monday night, only the red room is open, unless of course a huge unexpected crowd shows up. Chelly entered the main floor and is overtaken by the décor. She sauntered past the waterfall, making her way to the bar. She sits upon a barstool at the far left corner, as to have full view of the entryway.

The bartender on duty is Rudy. He is an Asian American.
"Whacha havin' lady?" Rudy asked, while enjoying her beauty.
Chelly is sporting a hot pink miniskirt, silky sheer nude stockings and a tight, white knit sweater, tight enough to show off the curvature of her upper body, allowing everyone to enjoy her voluptuous shape. She is the kind of woman men turn around to get a second glimpse of as she passes. Being as English as they come, as Chelly's great-grandfather was born in Bournemouth, England and came to America after World War I, she resembles an Indian princess.
"Is your clock right?" asked Chelly, as she glances down at the elegant wristwatch she is wearing, alternating with the large Asian style clock on the wall.
"Yeah lady, why?" asked Rudy as he continues to eye Chelly over.
"I'm supposed to meet a friend of mine here tonight at nine," replied Chelly thinking, "late as usual."
"If he doesn't show, he is a fool," Rudy said smiling.
"I never said I was meeting a man . . . I'll take a sloe comfortable screw."

"I bet you will lady," Rudy mumbled to himself as he chuckles.

Meanwhile on the other side of the bar, Chelly was aware of three young Asian guys staring at her as they talk amongst themselves in a promiscuous manner regarding her body. Sporadic outbursts of laughter can be heard. In a boast of bravado, one guy marches over,

"What brings a beauty like you here tonight?" he said as he groped her with his glaring eyes.

Looking at his reflection in the elegant mirrored wall behind the bar, she replied in a low deep tone, "Waiting on my 'guy' friend to arrive," emphasizing guy, as she turns her head in his direction to make eye contact, and with a sarcastic expression adds, "and I'd like to be alone."

"Whoa, cool it bitch, you don't know who you're talking to", as he snatches her wrist, constricting it within his grip. She lets out a yelp; his two buddies on the other side of the bar, quite amused, begin laughing. "If you want to stay out of trouble lady, you'd better get the hell out of here," threatened Kwan.

"Quit it Kwan", snaps Rudy, and as the laughter continues, "We don't need any more trouble here tonight." In a friendly gesture he says with a smile, "Here my friend", as he passes a beer to Kwan, "on me", placing his hands together in front of his face, in a slight bow.

Kwan pushes Chelly's arm away, he gives an angry glare at Rudy and takes hold of the beer. He turns to Chelly, and with a sneer he threatens her once again, "Make sure you and your 'guy' friend watch your backs tonight," emphasizing as to mock Chelly.

"No need for trouble now, Kwan", a strong voice echoes from the other side of the barroom and the laughter comes to a halt. Long Ngo, with Kym on his arm approaches, points at Kwan, "Understood?!" Kwan nods and walks away.

"Thank you Mister," Chelly says with an inquisitive look.

"Long." he replies. "My name is Long Ngo, and this is the lovely Kym Nguyen. I am one of the owners here, and Miss Nguyen is a good friend of mine. I'm sorry for any problems my --," and in a sudden choke, clears his throat and continues, "These boys have caused you Miss?" Long rolls open his hand in Chelly's direction.

"Robinson, my name is Chelly Robinson," she replies, coincidently noticing the nasty expression on Kym's face.

"Ah, Miss Robinson, I can assure you this will not happen again," Long says turning to the bartender, and with a wink he continues, "This lady drinks for free tonight; are we clear?"

"Yes boss", Rudy replies, "crystal."

"Why, thank you Mr. Ngo," Chelly responds.

"Long, call me Long." In keeping eye contact with Chelly, he takes a hold of her right hand, lifts it to his descending lips, as he gently places a kiss on it.

"Why, thank you Long," replies Chelly, holding back a big smile. "I hope to meet you again sometime," with her eyes opened wide and a naïve smirk about her face.

"I'm sure we will, Miss Chelly, I'm sure we will," as he reaches for Kym's arm. Meanwhile Kym turns back around to flash Chelly another nasty stare as she walks away with Long Ngo.

"Here you go, miss," Rudy says. "Here is your Sloe Comfortable Screw," chuckling as he places the glass down in front of her. "Hope you enjoy it."

"Thank you Rudy", Chelly adds with the same naïve smirk. "You are one hell of a comedian." As she takes a sip of her drink, in the mirrored wall behind her, Long and Kym walk up to Kwan and his buddies and she thought to herself, "How odd, seems Kwan and Long are friends. Maybe he wanted to impress me, but why when he had such a beautiful woman on his arm?"

"Come with me boys. We have a lot to discuss tonight," insists Long as they all follow him up the stairwell.

Meanwhile, outside the Dragon's Den, Sherry and Charlie enter into the designated parking lot.

"There," breaks Sherry, "right under that gorgeous colossal tree." Upon exiting the car Sherry is hit with a faint aroma of the Delaware River. "I hope that's not you?" kids Sherry, as Charlie trudges on, in deep thought. "Oh so now you choose to ignore me?" asks Sherry. "What?" Shaking his head, "Did you say something Sherry?"

They reach the front door and Sherry says, "Remember what we talked about now?"

"Of course, I will cancel the date and reschedule my whole life." Charlie responds, "So we can continue on with this quest, rather our quest and maybe save my butt."

"'Our' does sounds better," assures Sherry, "I'm not leaving your side," as she paces a few steps behind. "In saving your ass, you might make my career as well," she says as she chuckles to herself.

"Was that supposed to comfort me?" asks Charlie in a concerned manner. "Wow," he mumbles, "I'm getting another chance to gaze into those enormous amethyst eyes, and maybe hold her hand as I . . .'sigh' . . . cancel our date." Charlie couldn't stop thinking about Chelly since last Tuesday when they'd met during the lunch. How she'd matured, how much of a woman she'd become since the last time he'd seen her back in 1991. *My heart is pounding with anxiety. Okay CJ you can do this, yes you can, and get out as fast as possible.*

"Slow down, you don't want to be desperate; try to relax Charlie, and whatever you do, act natural." reasons Sherry.

Charlie enters The Dragons Den and is startled by the massive waterfall with the Buddha staring right down at him. His eyes seem to follow every move. In an attempt to locate Chelly he precedes to the bar, not long before Chelly's beauty catches his attention. She is breathtaking. He gazes at her from afar and says to himself, *"Wow what a woman, what an absolute knockout."*

"CJ", Chelly yells out as she stands up and waves.

"She still considers me a good friend because she called me CJ."

"Late as usual; I guess you will never change," Chelly says with a big smile on her face. "Oh my God CJ, I saw you on the evening news. Isn't Chang's cleaners right by your apartment?" she asks.

"Yes, what a crazy day . . . 'sigh,' I hate to tell you but, I'm going to have to cancel tonight. I'm quite shaken up with this morning's events," as he scans the room for Sherry.

"Ah CJ, I'm sorry, I sensed you'd be a bit rattled after what happened today," she begins stroking his arm in a circular motion with her fingertips. "I figured we could go somewhere relaxing and maybe hang out for a while, the two of us, like old times?"

Charlie could sense his body heat rising, as Chelly caressed his arm and hearing her sweet voice. This is the moment he'd awaited since 1991, and he finds himself in such a predicament. *What am I, insane? I woke up this morning, I was so pumped about this date, how could such a fantastic day turn so bad?*

"Chelly, I would love to spend the entire evening with you, but I wouldn't be much of a companion, and I do not want this to ruin whatever we may have in the future." Without a word she placed her hands on his shoulders as she gives him one of the sweetest, most passionate kisses. Her eyes closed, her lips puckered, reaching behind his neck as to pull him closer to her. As their lips meet, she caresses Charlie's tongue with hers, squeezing harder as her tongue massages the inside of his mouth. This causes Charlie to get rather excited and for the moment, he forgot about all his troubles. As he reaches for her hips, he squeezes her tight while pulling her body closer to his; he sticks his tongue deeper almost down her throat, caressing her with his hands up her back, concentrating on her bra strap, and as he playfully pops it against her skin, slowly moves down as his fingers slip under the elastic of her silky thong on his way to her perfectly round, plump butt cheeks. When he hears someone shout:

"So this is your friend?" the voice says in a heavy Asian accent. It was Kwan; he'd come up from behind, as he precedes to viciously pull them apart, knocking Chelly to the ground.

"What are you doing pal?" yells Charlie while pushing Kwan away.

"Kwan, please go back where you were" sobs Chelly.

"You know this joker, Chelly?" demands Charlie. That's when Charlie notices the tattoo on Kwan's arm, the Flying Dragons tattoo. At that moment Charlie nervously scans the room; the mysterious woman from Chang's that morning is behind him. She's talking to some huge guy, as they both head for the exit. The door was locked, trapping Chelly and Charlie inside; everything became silent.

"Oh my God," thinks Charlie, "I'm dead."

Meanwhile Chelly screams out, "Long! Long! Please help us! Why aren't you helping us?"

"Because your friend is the guy we've been looking for, bitch. He has something of ours and we want it back," interjects Kwan as he pushes Chelly back down to the floor with his foot.

"What?" Chelly screams, as she gazes over at Charlie, and in a panic yells "What the hell is he talking about, Charlie? What do you have of his?" Charlie was speechless. He stood silent and realized his vulnerability. Like the time the two of them were in high school and a bully had pushed the books right out of their good friend Helmut's hands. Charlie just stared and did absolutely nothing. He was hopelessly helpless. That's what he was then, and that's what he is now, only this time, these guys are vicious killers. Chelly stands up with fists at her side, looks at Charlie and with clenched teeth yells, "Charles, are you going to say something, anything?" Engulfed with fear, she hunches over and begins to sob. Charlie realized at that moment Chelly didn't consider him her friend anymore. Instead of calling him CJ, she called him Charles, and that was one step below being friends.

"I am so sorry for getting you involved. I never meant for any of this to happen to you, Chelly".

"Why must you involve Chelly? Let her go and I'll give you whatever you creeps want," implores Charlie, sounding quite defeated. Now Long Ngo orders Kwan to seize Chelly as he saunters over to Charlie, followed by two of his thugs; with force they grab him by the arms, holding him erect.

Long slowly looks him over, shakes his head in disgust, and strikes an awesome blow into Charlie's stomach, and as he doubles over in pain, Long shouts, "That my friend is for looking at Kym the way you did this morning." As Charlie gasps for air, he is jerked up. With Long's cronies holding him, dazed and in excruciating pain, Charlie anticipates another hit, as he tenses his stomach muscles by holding his breath, with teeth clenched. Long delivers another devastating blow. Upon impact the air is plunged from Charlie's lungs at such magnitude his mouth explodes open, and some vomit heaves out. As his body doubles over in agony, his legs go limp, so Long's cronies let him fall. While lying gasping for air, moaning in pain, Long yells, "And that one is because you had the audacity to show your miserable face in public, let alone come into my club. You are in deep trouble my friend," rubbing his hands, "very deep trouble."

"Stop it, please!" Charlie can hear Chelly sobbing as she yells out.

"I want Kym's glove!" Long shouts as he is pumping his body at Charlie, as if to hit him. The gang's laughter echoes throughout the room like cackling hyenas, mocking. Long raises his hand and instantly everyone shuts up. "I also need you to pay a visit to Chang's family, to hand deliver a note that I will give you. Then, and only then, will I let your girlfriend Chelly go."

"What Glove? I have no glove," Charlie replies in obvious pain.

"Ah, my friend, think back to this morning. You see a beautiful young lady walk out of Chang's Cleaners. She was wearing a pair of white gloves, and when she placed the gun into your pocket the glove was accidentally placed there." Long shouts, "I want it back!"

"Why?" moans Charlie, as Long pumps his body at him as if to hit him again. As Charlie cringes, the gang's loud laughter echoes miserably in his head. He clenches his teeth in anger as he peers around the room getting a good look at each of them. Sensing the disadvantage he was in as he lie in agony, he figured if given the chance to walk away he'd hunt them down and make sure they get what they deserve.

"'Why' is none of your concern. Your concern is to do what I say or your sexy friend will not get out of here alive." Long walks over to Chelly, violently gropes her breasts, moving up to her neck, takes a hold of her chin, pulling her face closer to his, eye to eye, "Do it or she dies". Instantly he pushes her away, like yesterday's trash, Chelly's body drops to the floor. Another gang member enters the room with handcuffs and a rope, Long orders Kwan to hand Charlie the note. As Kwan stands over him, he teases Charlie, holding the paper just out of his reach, pulling it farther from him as he tries to grab it. With a loud moan Charlie attempts to get up, as he is kicked in the backside by another gang member. As his body lunges forward, Kwan, along with the rest of the gang, begins to ridicule him with laughter. Kwan just tosses the note at Charlie's head.

The worst feeling Charlie can ever have is people making a mockery of him. Charlie's mind takes him back to his school days, he begins thinking about an old friend. The day Mrs. Dorr, his fourth grade teacher, introduced Helmut Krause to our class. His family had moved to Maple Shade from Connecticut. One of the kids in the class yelled "Louse, everyone, its helmet the louse" and everyone started to laugh. As Mrs. Dorr tried her best to calm everyone down, the entire class started chanting "Krause is a louse, Krause is a louse!" repeatedly, and that's when Charlie noticed the expression on Helmut's face, and right at that moment he sensed the poor guy had been through this before, and hoped things would be different here in Maple Shade. It would only be a matter of time before things got even worse.

As Chelly and Charlie grew tired of the way Helmut was being treated, they befriended him. He was teased everyday about one thing or another: his name, his weight, the color of his hair -- everything. Many times when they were together the teasing brought tears to Helmut's eyes, and as it was happening, Charlie never defended him, not even once. Lord knows it wasn't because he was a coward; he feared the teasing would turn away from Helmut towards him, and Charlie couldn't handle that.

Over time the teasing became more than Helmut could bear, and one day he cracked, he went totally ballistic. It happened when they were all seniors in high school. Arte Bridges was his name. A bully back from Mrs. Dorr's class decided to make a scene. Helmut was gathering stuff from his locker when Chelly and Charlie arrived to meet for lunch. They witnessed a terrible scene. Arte and several of his bullies surrounded Helmut as he had his head in his locker, unaware of what was about to take place. No sooner than Helmut closed the locker door, Arte was in a stare down with him. Helmut was holding three textbooks, a loose leaf binder, and a brown paper bag with his lunch in it. Arte pulled that brown paper lunch bag out of Helmut's hands so fast, with many students in the hallway. Arte opened the lunch bag and named each item in a sadistic fashion and threw them at Helmut. Shouting things like "Here's your sandvicth Helmet Krause the louse", a different saying for each. As students passed they ridiculed and laughed along with Arte and his buddies, as if they were gaining a free pass from being bullied.

Again as usual, Charlie stared at the entire situation and although he wanted to beat the crap out of Arte, he didn't. Charlie kept thinking to himself "Thank God it isn't me."

Chelly began to yell at him, "Charles when are you going to say something, anything?" She'd always become frustrated with him, as if he had something to do with it; she just never understood his feelings on the situation. As Arte ceased with the final contents of Helmut's lunch, he got right in Helmut's face, keeping eye contact, knocked the books right out of his hands. As they drop to the floor, loose leaf papers seemed to scatter everywhere. Arte started chanting the exact demeaning phrase he did back in Mrs. Dorr's class: "Krause is a louse! Krause is a louse!" repeatedly in a German accent, while he danced around like a fool. All the students in the hall seemed to laugh hysterically.

Helmut lost it emotionally and was no longer intimidated by Arte, or anyone else for that matter, and it was like pure magic. Enduring twelve long years of being the focal point of Arte's teasing had finally taken its toll on good ole Helmut. He'd become so infuriated that the color of his face developed into a dark shade of red, with squinted eyes and clenched teeth. Charlie could sense anger building within, the anger he'd been holding inside all these years. Helmut exploded like a bomb; it was odd, especially since he never fought back or gave any resistance. His actions took Arte and everyone else at the scene by surprise, and what happened next was right out of a Hollywood movie. Helmut's hands were balled in fists, and as he raised them, his eyes locked on Arte's. Helmut's fist flew into Arte's face, knocking him clear across the hall and into the lockers on the other side of the hallway. Arte spun around from the impact of Helmut's punch, and as his head hit the locker, his right eye went into the combination lock, splattering blood everywhere. Helmut turned and gave a nasty stare to all Arte's bullies and yelled, "Who's next?" They all ran away as fast as they could, but it didn't stop there. In his rage, Helmut took a pencil from his shirt pocket and uncontrollably started to stab Arte in the face and chest.

Chelly looked at Charlie with such anger, anger that in all our years of friendship had never come out. She takes it upon herself to help Helmut. She tried to calm him down, but it was futile, a hopeless but valiant attempt. Between Helmut's strength and his pent up anger of twelve years, one wave of his arm and Chelly went flying at least a yard away, ending up right at Charlie's feet.

All shaken up, with tear-filled eyes, at the top of her lungs, Chelly yells: "Stop Helmut, please stop!" She looked up at Charlie, and as their eyes met she flashed him the most hateful look. At that point, all her anger seemed to be aimed at him. She was so angry they didn't talk for weeks. That was the longest three weeks of Charlie's life, as she wouldn't return any of his phone calls. She even passed up going to the Eagles football game against the Giants, something they waited for every year. Charlie thought she'd hated him.

"Go!" Long shouts, "be back in two hours, or else!", as Charlie suddenly comes too. With a loud grunt, he heaves himself up holding the note, and staggers to the door.

At the Crossroads of Terror

In the parking lot:

Charlie pushes open the massive double doors, the night wind strikes him in the face, sending a chill right up his spine, and as the little hairs stand straight up on the back of his neck, he takes in a deep breath, becomes lightheaded and loses his balance. In falling forward, with a reflex he catches himself before plummeting head first into a cement pond, filled with exotic fish and turtles. He let his body drop to the ground without realizing the note for Chang blew away. Hunched over like he'd been struck with a sledgehammer, he experiences agonizing pain, unfamiliar to Charlie, and scared the hell out of him, as he led a sheltered life. Dazed, his mind filled with thoughts of what happened and what was still to come.

In a faint voice, a sweet voice whispering out to him like an angel, "Charlie psssst, Charlie hey, over here". He lifts his head and everything was a blur, but he did recognize Sherry's SUV.

"Oh my God, I'm getting out of here!" gasps Charlie, as his heart started palpitating as if to come out of his chest. He staggers, making his way to Sherry, as she yells, "Jump in!" In a lunge, Charlie's upper body hits the backseat and rolls down to the floorboard. As Sherry hits the gas, Charlie grabs hold of the legs of the seat, with his legs dangling out of the vehicle, flopping about like a rag doll, but manages to hold on.

Sherry yells, "Charlie as I make this right turn I'm going to try to swing you in. Pull up your legs, okay? NOW! Ok Charlie!"

With a heave he exhaustedly flips over himself, "I'm in... I'm in!" Out of breath and in pain, in one moment Charlie thanks Sherry for saving his life, but next he begins to yell, "Oh my God, Chelly!"

He is obsessed with the horrible thought he'll need to face The Flying Dragons once again in two hours if he wants to free Chelly. His mind kept alternating from thoughts of Chelly as a childhood friend, to her body dropping to the ground. He becomes furious. In a rage he starts to utter thoughts as they come into his mind.

Sherry shouts, "Get a hold of yourself, man!"

Charlie tries to contain himself by taking deep breaths; he begins to start over as he tries to explain the events as they'd occurred. His mind keeps going back to the vision he had of Chelly dropping to the ground limp, the way she'd fallen, was, as if she --.

"Oh my God, every second counts until I return with a glove!" yells Charlie. Up until now the glove was obsolete in his world. He tries to pull his thoughts together and begins to explain to Sherry what transpired from the time she'd left The Dragons Den till she crawled out. Charlie lets out another scream, "The note.... where is it...OH MY GOD!"

"I do not believe you are getting a hold of yourself Charlie", explains Sherry. "First things first, forget the note CJ. It is 9:45pm, we have until 11:45pm to be back. We must retrieve your jacket from my condo. The glove should be in the pocket, okay CJ?" As Sherry peeks through her rear view mirror at Charlie, with a strange smirk on his face as he stares off into the distance with swollen eyes from crying.

"What?" Sherry questions, "You're smiling?"

"Huh, I was?" Charlie replies.

"Uh, yeah you were," Sherry says with a smile.

"Oh my God Sherry, I was lost in a moment. You called me CJ."

"Okay, I guess?" as She rolls her eyes as if gesturing to herself that he was acting loony.

"Only my friends call me CJ. I sure need a friend."

With a comforting smile Sherry quickly glances at Charlie through the rear view, "CJ, I'm here for you, like it or not". Focusing her eyes to the road reassures him, "I promise you CJ, I will do whatever it takes to get Chelly back alive, and to clear your name of any fallacies."

"Thank you Sherry, I can't imagine what I would have done without you", as he grasps his abdomen. "I must help Chelly, I knew her all my life, and to leave her with those guys, that breaks my heart."

Sherry hits the dash with her fist and yells, "Damn you Long, you always seem to find a way to get what you want!"

"Long?" Charlie questions.

"Yeah, Long . . . He's the coward who struck you twice while his cronies held you. I caught the action through a tiny decorative window. As I told you CJ, I'm not leaving your side, and I damn well mean it."

"So that's his name, Long", Charlie moans, "I hadn't caught his name, only his fist in my gut. Is he the same Long Ngo that you talked about earlier this morning?" with a slight moan.

"Yes, and lets go to the police." Sherry says as she races towards the ninth district police station on north 21st street.

"No!" Charlie shouts, "We can't. Chelly's life depends on it, and if we go to the police, Chelly's a goner."

"She's a goner if we don't!" Sherry fires back. "Why are you so against going to the police and avoiding them? Do you have a record?"

"No", Charlie says, "I am familiar with how these things work. If we involve the police, Chelly will vanish."

"We need to go to the police with the glove", demands Sherry. "That's the best plan of action, CJ"

With a slight smile, "Wow!" as he looks over at Sherry. "You called me CJ again. I am flattered and in a lot of pain, but definitely flattered." They arrive at Sherry's condo. Charlie's anxiety seems to get the best of him; as he stumbles out of the SUV, making his way to the front door, he can't help but realize how confident Sherry was, and in some way, it comforts him. "Aside from the fact Kym's DNA is in the glove, I'd bet my life there's more to this story," explains Sherry, "So if indeed we find this so called glove, we'll decide what to do, whether we go to the police or not.

"Let's take some time to figure out some sort of plan CJ." She reaches for the keys and begins to open her front door.

"Okay mom", Charlie moans with a smirk on his obviously distraught face as he looks right into her eyes. She fires back with a smile on her face, "Give it a rest, Romeo." Sherry opens the door, with Charlie a few steps behind thinking to himself, "Romeo?"

They enter the condo and the place has been ransacked. Everything is everywhere, not one untouched.

"What happened here?" mumbles Charlie, while taking in the whole scene. In shock, they turn to each other and Charlie yells in a strained tone, "What the hell?"

"Oh My God, Oh My God!" Sherry cries out in disbelief, "This is the work of the Flying Dragons. But why would he believe the glove is here? He must want this so-called glove bad to act as he has; it's unlike him. Kym's DNA is in the glove, not his, and if she was linked to the murder, he'd let her take the whole rap. Long is a dangerous man, he cares for no one but himself. If he loses a gang member, they get replaced. "Oh my god!"

Charlie reaches over and pulls Sherry close to him. Hiding his fear, and pain, he gives her a consoling hug to try to calm her down, as he softly whispers in her ear, "I'm so sorry Sherry, I am truly so sorry. Everyone I am in contact with is in trouble because of me. This is one hell of a nightmare, one big nightmare," as he squeezes her a little tighter. He moves away from her a bit, and tears streaming down her cheeks. "Why? Why has everything in my life been so hard? Why God?" mumbles Sherry.

As Charlie grabs Sherry by the shoulders and positions her body as to make eye contact with him, he says, "Never question God. I am sure plenty of people would love to be in your shoes and trade places with you, even at this very moment. I'm positive." He wipes the tears from her eyes with a napkin he had taken from The Dragon's Den. Looking into her eyes he says "No need for tears. I will make sure everything turns out right for you. Everything will be back to the way it was before I entered your life." Charlie starts realizing he is getting poignant and wishes they'd met before all this happened.

"You're not getting emotionally attached to me now, are you?" she says with a smile, while looking into his eyes. "I have a strong women's intuition." Sherry senses Charlie *is*.

Charlie's eyes begin to tear and he wipes them with the same napkin he used on Sherry. This time the napkin had a beautiful scent, Sherry's scent. She reaches out, grabs his face, pulling him closer to her. She passionately kisses him, opening her mouth just slightly enough for him to massage her tongue with his and vice versa. This kiss is better than the one Chelly gave him earlier.

"Chelly", Charlie says aloud as he breaks his lips away from Sherry's. "We got to find my jacket; the clock is ticking."

The furniture is thrown everywhere, papers all strewn about, and Charlie spies the sleeve of his jacket in between the desk and the sofa. He struggles to free the jacket. He pulls harder and the sleeve starts to rip.

"Shit," he says rather annoyed, "I just ripped my good jacket."

"Hey, no need for that kind of language", Sherry shouts angrily.

"Sorry again, mom," Charlie says, emphasizing the word mom.

"Forgiven, now let's get a move on." She says anxiously, "We have to help Chelly." Charlie manages to free the jacket and Sherry walks over to him, puts her hands over his, and with a warm smile, "Remember what we decided?" She continues, "We'll examine the glove and try to make the best decision possible, promise me CJ?" "But if we go to the police I will be arrested, suspicion of murder."

"Promise me?" she asks as she stares even deeper into his eyes and gently rubs his cheeks with her soft, beautiful hands.

"Alright, I promise", he reluctantly answers, as she places a kiss on his lips and says, "Thank you." Charlie hesitantly reaches for the jacket pocket thinking, "Will the glove still be here? Did I drop it on Kings Highway when the gun fell out?" As he places his hand in the pocket, all the blood rushes to his head. His heart begins to pump rapidly as he is sensing the impact the glove has on the situation. He grabs hold of something and quickly pulls it out. With a loud sigh he yells, "The glove!" A little relief realizing he still has the glove in his procession, he begins to examine it. Nothing, he cannot find anything. Getting more nervous, he hands the glove over to Sherry. She doesn't find anything either. "What the heck?" Charlie yells, as he now took the glove back from Sherry's hand, anxiously trying to figure out why Long wants the glove back so desperately.

"What's inside the glove?" Sherry says. "Look inside CJ!" Charlie turns the glove inside out to expose what they both believe is the reason Long Ngo wants it back. Asian symbols and writing are written inside the glove, invisible from the outside. Sherry says to Charlie, "Now let's go to the police." Frustrated from hearing the same words come out of her mouth repeatedly, he snaps out at her.

"No! Stop with the police," as he stumbles over her desk chair. At that moment, a fear comes over Sherry and he can sense she was afraid of him. He bows his head down in shame, upset knowing she is the last person he wants to frighten. He sincerely apologizes to her for the outburst, and with a hug she offers him her forgiveness and together they turn their attention back to the glove.

"It is written in Chinese, Vietnamese or another Asian language. What is the purpose for the writing? Is it a code? Is it just for The Flying Dragons here in Philly? What could it mean?" He questions Sherry. "Why, why would he have this writing on the inside of a glove? Maybe Long Ngo is trying to hold back something from his gang or trying to protect himself from another gang member." Charlie is thinking, "Either way this is what he wants, and what we need to free Chelly."

"No, you promised," Sherry says sternly. "We are going to decide what is best for Chelly and you . . . now let's talk about this."

"You're right", Charlie replies, "Let's talk. Okay, here is what I think. We play Long's game, the glove for Chelly. We choose a place where Chelly and I can make a fast getaway without being followed by his gang. It should be a public place where he would not attempt anything funny, not that trying to kill me is funny. A place where I, or should I say we, have control. He knows nothing of us, so you can just be yourself," as he continues, "Sherry Mann, Street Reporter doing a live spot in the place we choose to make the trade. He wouldn't try anything on live TV, would he? Could he?"

"Here is what I believe we should do. First off," she adds, "how do you know he doesn't know about us?" She sighs and raises her voice, "Just look at this place. Do you think this is a coincidence?"

"Yes I do." Charlie proceeds to explain, "If he knew about us, why then was my jacket still here?" Clumsily pacing, and breathing heavy, "Why?"

Sherry replies hesitantly, "Because . . . maybe?" Her eyes roll toward the ceiling; she thinks, and in a yell, "He was just looking for the 'unedited tape' of this morning's news, in an attempt to find out more information about you!"

"Exactly", interjects Charlie, "He has no idea I was here." They both turn towards the computer, practically knocking each other over, fighting to get to the tape. Suddenly a loud knock at the door startles Sherry and Charlie. Charlie becomes alarmed, fearing the worst. He decides to be the strong one and walks over to the door. He peers through the peephole and whispers to Sherry, "Two police officers." He motions for her to take a peek for herself. She looks out and says, "I have to let them in Charlie. I promise not to say anything since we didn't make a decision yet. I have to let them in." That's what he likes about her; besides being so beautiful, she is so faithful and honest.

"Alright, go ahead and let them in," Charlie mumbles and goes into another room.

"Moorestown Police Department, open up!" one of the officers shouts.

"Just one minute." She moves back away from the door to give Charlie some time to hide. "I'll be right there." Sherry opens the door as the police officers enter. "What happened here, lady?" one of the officers asks as they both begin looking in the condo seeing the place in disarray.

"Are you alright Ma'am?" asks an officer as they both draw their weapons and enter. "Is anyone else here?"

Charlie walks out into the open and says, "Just me officers, Charlie P Johnson."

One of the officers says, "Isn't he the guy that was outside Chang's murder this morning?"

"Yeah I think so Joe", the officer replies. "Yeah he definitely is the guy from Chang's."

"Get down! Get Down! Put your hands behind your head!" shouts an officer. With their guns drawn, Charlie with no other choice but to listen, gets down on the floor and puts his hands on his head.

Sherry shouts "No! No! He is Okay. He is a friend of mine officers", as tears begin to flow. She begs, "Please, please leave him alone. Please let him up."

"Well ma'am, we had a complaint called in from one of your neighbors. They said loud noises were coming from this condo and thought a robbery was taking place. Then they mention they heard screams coming out of this condo," the officer says while he put the handcuffs on Charlie, looking around the room, "and it certainly looks like that's what happened." Sherry tries to explain the best she can, which isn't believable to the officers. They arrest Charlie for breaking, entering and attempted robbery and read him his rights. Charlie is escorted out to the patrol car and seated in the backseat. Sherry's neighbors gather outside, with curiosity and concern.

One comes over to the car and asks, "Is that the man from tonight's newscast? Are you alright?"

Charlie is taken to the nearest station on W. Second Street, Moorestown, New Jersey, and bail set at $1250.00. Sherry follows them down to the station to try and explain to their superiors, with little success. The clock is ticking away and the booking process takes an hour, leaving them ten minutes to save Chelly.

At the Moorestown Police station:

$\mathcal{C}$harlie, overwhelmed with stress, was being booked for breaking and entering. He was mocked while being fingerprinted by some of the officers, normal procedure for them. The smaller they made Charlie, the more powerful they became. Charlie, starting to feel a little like he was back at the Dragons Den being laughed at, only this time it was legal. The officer who made the arrest begins typing the police report. He is typing so very slowly, one finger at a time, making Charlie more uneasy knowing the clock is continuing to tick. With each tap of his fingers hitting the keyboard reminds Charlie of water slowly and steadily dripping, like Chinese tortures. His heart is pounding, his mind is running rabid. "Will this ever end?" His heart thumping harder and harder, thinking about everything -- the murder scene, seeing Chelly at the Dragon's Den, Sherry's condo, and now this. "When will this end, this continuous nightmare?" He wants this mess to have a positive ending; he needs to make sure Chelly is saved. His mind wanders, "When will I get to make my call? Anxiously he waits for that moment. Then he asks himself, "Who will I call? A lawyer, my father, who?" He is a little unsteady. The stress is beginning to take its toll on his body. He has a sharp pain in his chest. He is hoping it is due to stress and not a heart attack. The acids in his stomach from Long's punches are making him nauseous. Since the murder this morning, his heart has been pounding with no let up. Between the fear, anxiety, stress and the nervous tension, his heart hasn't had a chance to beat normal. He realizes he is not in the best physical condition anyway, and it would not be unbelievable if he has a heart attack. He's had a stressful desk job the last 10 years and does not exercise. "What'll happen if I do have a heart-attack?" His mind keeps running radical. He is losing control. "Am I going crazy? Why can't I take control of the situation?" At that point, something snaps in his head, Charlie decides he is going to take control.

After being booked he is taken down to the holding cell. The cell was large, empty and he realizes there is no toilet. "What'll I do if I have to go? Just yell?" Charlie begins to pace back and forth in a panic mode, thinking and worrying. All alone in this large empty cell, alone to think, to meditate, trying to come up with the perfect solution to this dreadful situation. He is now pacing furiously back and forth. He can hear Sherry's voice, like an angel sighing. Sensing she is getting closer, realizing he will be released, Charlie feels a sigh of relief. Sherry is talking with someone. Sounds like they know each other, or she is befriending this stranger.

Sherry comes into view with this stranger, leans into the bars of Charlie's cell. With her chest against the bars, she displays concern about his well being and she in a playful tone says, "Are you okay baby?" She reaches out, trying to hug him. "Well are you hon?"

Charlie is thinking, "I kind of like this", as he pushes into the cell bars himself to make it easier for her to get a better hold of him.

"Honey", Sherry says and quickly backs up, breaking up his thoughts about her, "This is Officer Frank Torteresi, he's the officer I did a live interview with several months ago," she sighs. "He is going to try to help us get you out of here. Doesn't that sound great, baby?"

"Hi Frank," as Charlie reaches through the bars to shake his hand. "Hello", Frank replies, as he returns a hardy handshake. "Give me a few minutes. Let me see what I can do for the two of yez," in his typical Jersey accent.

"Thank you", Sherry and Charlie both say in unison. Frank walks away and Charlie gives Sherry a devilish grin and says *"Hon? Honey, are you ok? Baby"*

"Oh quit it," she says as she is smiling. "The only thing I could think of." Charlie believes not only was she acting to get him out, but she is actually starting to feel something for him. She enjoys calling him hon and honey. He begins smiling inside even though he is actually falling to pieces. "We're down to less than 10 minutes." Sherry says, "Not to rattle you up anymore than you already are but time is running out and we haven't decided yet."

"Decided yet?" Charlie raises his voice, "What do you mean?" Louder he says, "You are not going along with my plan about the trade?"

"No I didn't say that. I said we haven't finalized the plan," in a hurried voice.

Charlie looks directly at her. "You are beautiful. You know that?" With a smile, Sherry blows him off. Charlie wonders why she's being so wishy-washy. She kissed him back at her apartment, now this? She must be fighting her emotions like I am.

"Even though I think you are rather sexy and someone I would like to get to know better, I must wait until this is over before getting involved. Have you ever heard of someone falling in love with a person who is all wrong for them after a bad break-up? Love on a rebound?"

"Yeah, but...", as Charlie is trying to get the words out and thinking she is informed on this subject.

"Well, this is the same thing." She shoots out, "So forget about it for now." She pauses a bit and continues, "We're on a quest."

Charlie's self confidence starts to sink thinking, "Maybe she isn't starting to like me. She might still be acting, playing me for a fool to benefit her career." He'll have to wonder.

At the Crossroads of Terror

The Dragon's Den:

𝓞n a back room at the Dragon's Den, Chelly awakens and finds herself handcuffed to a cot. She can sit up as only one arm is cuffed. Being groggy from passing out, she proceeds to compose her thoughts. She shuffles through the events that had taken place. "Oh My God!" she yells out, realizing the reality. She is overheard by Kym in the next room.

Upon nosily entering the room, "What's your problem? I got the impression you do your best work in bed," snarls Kym. Chelly glares at her without saying a word. "Well", Kym sneers, "Do you or don't you, do your best work in bed?"

"What is wrong with you?" Chelly scowls back, "besides being a jealous bitch who hangs with the wrong crowd?"

At that moment Kym yells, "Bitch!", as she slaps Chelly, with a swift lash to the face, staining her left cheek with a crimson handprint. Her cheek swells instantly upon impact. Chelly tenses up as she endures the fiery sting as Long Ngo enters the room.

"What the hell is going on in here?" Long demands, in disgust. "You", speaking to Kym, "go, leave the room. Leave us alone for a while," as he gently rubs Chelly's cheek with the outside of his hand where she'd been slapped. "I have some business with Chelly." No sooner than Kym leaves the room, Long begins to disrobe. Quite groggy from her last drink, Chelly realizes what he's about to do.

"Oh my God, you can't do this, no", Chelly cries frantically, as she begins to tremble uncontrollably. Long continues to disrobe, ignoring every word she'd said. In a desperate attempt to impede him, she begins to beg, "Please don't do this to me! I'm bleeding! I'm on my period!"

Fear engulfs her and tears roll down her distraught face. With an obvious expression of disregard, he pulls off his last article of clothing. The sight of Long Ngo's naked body repulses and terrifies her. He saunters over, flexing his muscles while glancing at them; he stoops down to grasp her arms as he forcefully pushes her body down to the cot, overpowering her as he holds her teary face to his.

"You can make this easy or hard. Either case you are going to have the pleasure of me inside of you."

Inside Chelly's Mind:

Ꮛyes tightly shut, mouth closed with teeth clenched in anguish, "Oh my God, PLEASURE! This bastard is a thief! I hate him! Oh my God, what did I do to deserve this? Why God, why? I am nothing without my gift! Oh my God, my chest hurts, my heart is beating uncontrollably and I'm out of breath. I can't even see his disgusting face with all my tears; why am I so weak? My head, I'm dizzy. Oh God, HE'S RIPPING MY CLOTHES OFF! I will not let him, I WILL NOT LET HIM! I WILL NOT LET HIM! Long, please stop. STOP! STOP! STOP! YOU BASTARD! Get off me! I can't BREATHE; PLEASE GET THE HELL OFF ME! I HATE YOU! I HATE YOU! YOU WON'T GET IN ME, BASTARD! YOU WON'T! NOOOOOOO! NOOOOOOO!*

Thank you, God, he's finished, but what is he doing, he's hurting me! HE'S HURTING ME! Oh God, he's hurting me, STOP! NO, NO, NO! Oh my God, ouch ouch ouch ouch. . . He can take my body, but he will never take my soul.

What seemed to last for hours in Chelly's mind has ceased. She has now become a victim of a sexual assault. She begins to question herself, asking why? How? What? She also begins to blame herself for this horrible crime committed against her.

Am I going to die? If I am not, please answer me why? The warm blood dripping down my legs seems to comfort me. I am shivering, I am so cold. My body is in a fetal position, I need to hide my face from him, from the world. He is now getting dressed, I sense he is. I am still naked. I don't deserve to cry, I deserve to die. I hate myself for letting him inside of me! Oh no, my tampon is still in!

Chelly is left lying in tears. All she can concentrate on is that dreadful nuisance of a tampon as she attempts to remove it in vain. She remembers something the school nurse had told her about 17 years ago during a Sex Education class. She explained to her, along with the other female students in her class, how to get a tampon out if ever in too deep. Irrelevant she thought, but now Chelly realizes otherwise. Hoping her memory is correct, the nurse's advice was to press and push as if you were having a baby. Chelly presses until the tampon moved. Being fit and somewhat flexible, she can reach in far enough to grab a tiny corner and pull it out of her distended cervix. With a sigh of relief, she falls limp with the extreme release of pressure. She is confused with the reality of what transpired; sadness now encompasses her, as she lies in shock.

Meanwhile Kym, Kwan, along with several other members of the Flying Dragons, are fooling around in the conference room. They're all drinking, smoking, and getting rowdy when Long Ngo walks in.

"Does anyone realize the time?" Long says as he peers down at his watch. "Seems to me our friend inside has less than an hour to live. Kym, I want you to keep an eye on our friend; she is bleeding quite profusely all over my snake skin rug. I want you to look after the evidence for me", Long says, as he rubs her shoulders. With Kym's back facing him, she rolls her eyes at what he'd asked of her. Another woman gang member Ly sees the eye movement and chuckles.

"Okay," Kym replies, "I'll tend to it." She walks out.

"Gather round everyone, I want to discuss our next move!" Long commands. "I want to set up our strategy when lover boy returns. Here's the plan. Kwan, I want you and your boys hanging by the front door and make sure . . . what's his name?" Long asks.

"Charlie," Kwan replies, "Charlie Johnson."

"Yeah, Charlie, let's make sure Charlie doesn't drop and run. I do not want him getting out alive," Long says firmly and points towards Kwan. "You have my permission to get rid of him by whatever means you want." With a look of excitement Kwan replies, "Yes, boss." The events of the day begin catching up with Long. He is starting to get riled as he ponders the shipment that was lost, Charlie, the glove with his next instructions, and Charlie's girl Chelly, in the back room. He becomes extremely stressed out.

Kym befriends Chelly:

 $\mathcal{K}$ ym enters the room to find Chelly in a fetal position lying in a small pool of blood. She can relate to Chelly's rape. All the ladies in the Flying Dragons have been where Chelly is. Kym, trying to console Chelly, sits on the bed next to Chelly and begins to rub her shoulder.

"Be strong, it's not a catastrophe." Kym says, "I've been sent here to keep an eye on you. I heard you're bleeding on Long Ngo's rug." Chelly in pain, quiets to listen to Kym. "I'm sorry for what happened to you and that is the way it is around here." She hands Chelly a towel to wipe away the blood and continues with her own story, informing her how the gang treats their women. She explains that women are treated differently in the Asian cultures. Most Vietnamese Americans' lives will never be complete. Their lives are described as 'dust' because they are ever-flowing with the wind, dust which has no beginning or end. They are unwanted children in Vietnam, so they wander around the country. That's what the Flying Dragons are made up of. The females are treated extremely different than the males. Women are a lower form of life.

Chelly is astonished as Kym continues to tell her story:

In Vietnam the women, as in many other Asian cultures, are used as sex slaves. They are raped and are victims of physical violence. The men remark that women 'talk too much' and this justifies all the violence. The women experience a deep sense of shame and blame themselves. Since we consider the Flying Dragons as our family, much of the violence is tolerated. I will admit a lot of violence goes on within these walls, as much as on the outside. Chelly notices tears rolling down Kym's face as she continues about a story of her best friend Phuong, who was violently gang-raped one night right in this very room while Long and the rest of his friends partied in the next room.

"Phuong and I were out in the public area of the Dragon's Den. We had a few drinks and were a little lightheaded, so we decided to come back here and rest a bit. What seemed like a matter of minutes, Kwan and several of the boys, Phuc, Quang, Trung, Duc, Sa'ng and Sinh entered the room. They started slapping us around and yelling nasty things. I was slapped so hard I went flying against the wall next to the

[46]

door and fell to the floor. I was still conscious but faint when the violence began.

"Phuong, lying on the bed, was semi-conscious from getting slapped around by the boys. Kwan shoved a ball gag into her mouth and cinched the strap securely. Sa'ng and Sinh cuffed her wrists and her ankles to the bed posts, while they were shouting and laughing. Her skirt raised up her thighs revealing her white laced panties. They soon will have their way with her. As I watched, I wondered, 'What could she be thinking?' Little did I know I was going to be next.

"I watched as she lay on her back, her legs bent, her hands turned red in the tight handcuffs. She was fully alert now, and her eyes were wide open with the look of fear. Her skirt somehow managed to be up around her waist. I yelled, "Stop. Please leave her alone!" when Duc came up to me and slapped me again. I tried to help my best friend. I couldn't move. She struggled to keep her legs together, but having her ankles cuffed to the bed posts made it impossible. The side of her face must have throbbed as big red marks where she was hit several times by each of the boys. She must have seen a couple of them begin to undress, and at that moment I realized she understood what was going to happen. Soon a gang rape would begin. I saw the terrified look on her face, and yet I just sat there thinking I am safe for now. There was no telling what they might do to her.

"That's when Kwan yells, "Let's strip her." Her teeth sank deeper into the ball gag, as Kwan pulled out a straight razor and flicked it open. Her eyes widened, fixed on the gleaming surgical blade. She made a gurgling protest deep from within her throat and tried to roll away from him as he grabbed the hem of her skirt; but it was futile. Other hands held her in place while the edge of the blade made a faint ripping sound.

"I was positive she was aware of her skirt parting from her hips, then her waist. He jerked at it, forcing her buttocks roughly up off the bare mattress, pulling it from her and flinging it on the floor next to me. She cringed as his hands fondled her through her lace panties. He prodded her roughly, then after a moment began stroking her softly. Duc, Kwan's closest buddy had already taken off his clothes and stood

[47]

at the foot of the bed slowly stroking himself, wincing as if he was a stud horse, ready to cover a mare. Soon she would be forced to take him on while the rest of the boys held her down. No escaping, Kwan jerked her blouse open, pushed her bra up to expose her breasts.

"Man, hurry up," Duc said. "I can't hold back much longer."

"Patience," Kwan replied. "We must not rush," as he fondled her breasts between his fingers. "The bitch wants us all. That's what she's going to get."

He pinched her breasts, causing her to squirm in pain and make a whiny sound buried within her throat. Her back arched up off the bed, thrusting herself upward toward Quang as he was holding her shoulders down. Kwan let go of her breast and lowered his hands between her legs. He pulled her panties off, exposing the rest of her to everyone in the room, while everyone cheered as if their favorite sports team had scored. He leaned over and bit her breast, leaving the imprint of his teeth.

"Okay," Kwan said, standing up. "Who gets to her first?" Chuckles and cheers within the room. Sinh and Phuc released her legs and moved back as Duc hustled himself to the bed. She tried to close her legs, but Kwan placed the edge of the razor against her throat as a warning. Duc positioned himself between her thighs and pushed his manhood against her. With a quick thrust of his hips, he was inside of her.

Another moan blared out, from deep inside her throat. Quang held her earlobe between his teeth and began biting into the tender flesh while Kwan circled the straight razor around each of her breasts, made crisscrossing cuts on each one, enjoying the sound of her smothered cries. Her writhing body only served to bring Duc closer to a climax. Blood trickled down the sides of her breasts to the mattress. Duc's body moved up and down on her in an ever quickening motion. He finished in a few minutes. To Phuong, it was an eternity.

"What do you mean?" Chelly says. "You've talked with her since then haven't you?"

"Quiet!" Kym says through her tears, "and let me finish the story."

When he was done with her, Duc pulled out and her resistance finally ceased. Her rigid body sank back against the mattress in defeat. The first rape is accomplished. Sinh, Phuc and Sa'ng all decided that they would finish with a three-on-one rape. So Kwan went next. He had her cuffs and gag ball removed so he could roll her over and proceed with his preference of torture and rape. Long lets things like this happen to break the soul of the women in the group. We have to obey any male member's orders.

Phuong looked up at Kwan's face, but she could see nothing human or merciful behind the cold glint of his wire rimmed glasses.

"Please don't hurt me," she whispered hoarsely. "I'll do anything you want."

"I know you will," Kwan replied. "But I know you want some more."

"No, please, no," as she shook her head back and forth. "I'll do anything you want. Anything," she added, significantly.

Kwan dropped to the floor on his knees and pulled her by the hair to the edge of the mattress so that her mouth was positioned in front of his manhood. With a powerful push, he was inside her mouth. As he pushed deeper, she gagged. Her shoulders hunched forward and her stomach sunk in as her body convulsed. Her cheeks drew together, and then parted as she tried to squirm back, but he held her face pressed to his sweaty belly, clenching her hair in his fists.   Occasionally   he would give her buttocks a whack or two with the flat of his hand. Flesh against flesh resounded in the small room, and soon Quang penetrated her from behind causing smothered grunts of anguish to escape from her. This continued for several more minutes, the sounds of flesh against flesh as Phuong's moans resounded in the darkened room. As soon as Kwan and Quang were done, they both stood posing. They were arrogant with their chest held high like warriors, proud of the conquest. A triumph, a victory for them, and soon they got dressed and left the room.

Two finished, with three more to go. Phuong's eyes rolled, with a defeated look on her face. She became numb; she wasn't fighting or squirming as much anymore, she gave up. Let them have their way with her, each with their own different style of torture as I sat there helplessly watching.

Phuong looked at me and with her eyes I heard her say, 'not to worry it will soon be all over.' Through the door next to me, I could hear the sounds of voices and laughter with the smell of stale cigar and cigarette smoke. After two more hours of torture, Kwan came back into the room carrying his straight razor in one hand and a long neck beer in the other. He stood over her for a moment letting his eyes take in her nudity. Then it got uglier than ever. Kwan began to insert the beer bottle into her vagina. He started pushing it in and out slowly, then he got crazed, shouting, "Do you like that Bitch?" Over and over he was yelling moving the bottle faster, as hard as he could. Blood started to fill the bottle and began oozing out of her on the mattress and spilling to the floor. She screams violently in pain, screams so disturbing to me. Kwan continued to move the beer bottle in and out as fast as he could. None of Phuong's screams seemed to make Kwan let up. It seemed his excitement only grew as he was cheering himself on. The screams that came out of Phuong went through my head like a dagger. I held my hands to my ears and started yelling "STOP, STOP! PLEASE MAKE IT STOP!" Then there was this uncomfortable pause.

The room grew silent, no more screams of pain or Kwan's cheering. It felt like I was the only one in the room. My ears started to ring with the silence. All the sounds of torture just stopped. I opened my eyes to witness Phuong's body go limp. She didn't move nor make a sound. Kwan stands up and calls for Duc and the rest of the boys.

"She's dead!" Duc yells, "Phuong is dead!" The tears began to roll down from my eyes; my heart sunk to a new low. To think I was in the room and did nothing to save my friend from what she'd endured.

"Will I ever forgive myself for that? My best friend, in fact, my only friend is no longer around. She is dead."

Finally the rest of the guys came in, as Duc says, "What'll we do now?"

Dead silence for a moment until Kwan says "Kym's still here."

Now it was my turn. Unfortunately, I wasn't as lucky as Phuong." She pauses as the tears continue to stream down her face, "I survived," as she begins to sob unbearably.

Chelly just sat in unreserved shock. Being a compassionate person she said, "It's ok, Kym." Chelly believes Kym has grown tired of her gang life and would love to escape. As Chelly tried to comfort her, they both end up in tears in each other's arms.

Two Dragons are caged

Chapter 3

Around 7:30 PM the same day, on Washington Avenue in downtown Philadelphia, four people are arguing in front of Bao Hao's restaurant. The people involved are a Caucasian couple and two members of The Flying Dragons, Thao and Giang. They seem to be fighting over a parking spot in front of the restaurant. In Philadelphia the streets are so crowded and parking spots are hard to find, most people have to pay to park, or illegally double park down a side street. The argument escalates, Giang says to Thao, "Let's just forget about it." Thao acted as if he didn't hear Giang. He ignored him because he was overcome by road rage. With sirens blaring, the two men continue to argue when Thao pulls out a 9 inch switchblade. He viciously jabs his unsuspecting adversary and Giang struggles to impede him. He was unwilling to stop and a fight ensued between the two gang members. Giang manages to get a solid grip on Thao when the other man lunges out with a sharp right hook striking Thao in the face, damaging his bare cheek. Thao stumbles, causing Giang to lose his grip and balance, ultimately striking his head against the pavement. As Giang lies in obvious pain, Thao becomes irate and with a swift hurl of his

switchblade the man falls to the ground. The man is bleeding from a gash in the right side of his stomach. His girlfriend begins to scream profanities at Thao, as her boyfriend moans in pain. The police arrive with guns drawn shouting, "Drop your weapons, lie on the pavement and put your hands on your head!" Thao and Giang oblige and the arrest is made.

The officers call for an ambulance and backup squad to the scene. Thao and Giang were handcuffed and read their rights. The van was impounded and the boys were taken down to the station for booking. They were fingerprinted and mug shots were taken. Thao and Giang were thrown in the holding cell. Drugs were soon discovered and detectives from the Philadelphia narcotics squad were called in to investigate.

Detectives Jim Sweeney and Ralph Inzerillo were assigned to the case and begin interrogating the two gang members. They put them in two separate interview rooms. The Philadelphia PD uses the good cop - bad cop routine, which causes the detainee a sense of connection with one of the officers. Once a suspect starts talking, they find it hard to stop. When they start telling the truth, it's even harder for them to lie again. This type of interrogation doesn't work with Asian Street gangs and not with Thao and Giang. Due to the gang affiliation, their loyalty lies only within the gang, their leader Long Ngo. From the moment they'd entered the interview room, it was, as if they had been connecting head phones. Both men repeatedly asked the same question, "Where is my phone call?"

After two hours of grueling interrogation, to no avail, a third detective enters the room. He whispers into detective Ralph's ear, Ralph immediately turns to Thao in an attempt to inform him of what he'd been told.

"The street value of the cocaine found in the van you and your friend was driving is valued at $2,000,000 and the van is conveniently unregistered with no clear title. These charges warrant a lengthy prison term, perhaps in a federal prison without the possibility of parole. Today with tougher Drug Laws you could be facing life. That's without the attempted murder charge." Ralph becomes enraged, "Who the hell are you guys working for? Give me a name." Ralph turns to Detective Jim Sweeney then walks to the door. "Since he doesn't want to talk to me, maybe he'll talk with you." He shuts the door behind him.

[52]

At the Crossroads of Terror

The next tactic Sweeney uses is the lying strategy. Detective Sweeney presents the facts of the case, and informs Thao of the evidence against him. Some of the evidence is real, and some fabricated. Sweeney moves around trying to invade Thao's personal space to increase his discomfort. Ralph reenters the interrogation room and whispers something into Sweeney's ear.

As Sweeney's eyebrows become raised, he nods his head and reasons, "Aha, really now!" He turns to Thao and says, "We won't need your confession, your buddy Giang is singing like a bird."

Thao doesn't believe a word Sweeney says and apprehensively asks, "What is he saying?" as the detectives purposely ignore him. Thao is becoming agitated, "I have my rights. I want my phone call!" In a yell, "I am supposed to get one phone call, and I want the phone now!"

"Now don't you fret 'bout Giang . . . you'll get your call", Ralph replies in a chuckle. "About your friend Giang? He is seeking a lighter jail term. Looks like you're out." Ralph and Jim both laugh as they exit the room.

"Where's my phone call?" Thao shouts. "Where's my phone call?"

The two detectives Sweeney and Inzerillo have little evidence, but were informed about The Dragon's Dens flyers about an upcoming Memorial Day event found alongside of the cocaine in the van. They figured they'd go down to the club to investigate.

"Let's make the connection," says Jim. "Alright, yeah, let's go," says Ralph. They have the suspects put into different cells to keep them apart until their interrogation is complete. Thao and Giang get their calls as they both end up phoning Long Ngo at the Dragon's Den.

Charlie makes the Phone call:

Sherry and Charlie are leaving the Police Station when Sherry's phone rings. Chester A. Wright, Sherry's boss, is on the caller ID. She turns her head towards Charlie and says, "My boss, I got to answer it." On the phone Sherry asks, "When?" Then she replies, "No, I am not involved. I can't do that at this time." As she fumbles for her car keys, "I'll explain when I can." She hangs up and turns to Charlie, "We got to get out of here quick. Let's hurry to my car."

"Why? What happened now?" questions Charlie.

Sherry appearing startled, replies, "Your prints!" They get into her car and she floors it. "You had your prints taken about 30 minutes ago."

"Yeah, and what's your point, what's your story, what's your angle?" Another one of those infamous phrases he likes to use. As he notices the distressed look on Sherry's face, he asks again, "What, what seems to be the problem now?"

Focused on the road, Sherry nervously replies, "They've managed to match up the prints in the database with the murder weapon found at Chang's," gradually getting louder with each word.

"Oh Crap!" Charlie rolls his eyes, "What now?" At this point Charlie is ready to scream his bloody head off. *"Come on CJ you can deal, calm down, hold yourself together, concentrate on something soothing; besides, I don't want Sherry seeing me in a tantrum, he ponders."* As Sherry continues to drive, CJ tries to meditate, but he can't calm himself down enough to think of anything except the anguish he's going through. His mind shuffles through the events of the day. He can't help but become frustrated. He asks himself, *why? What's the reason for this? Why me?* Why not me? Charlie's mind wanders, he begins thinking, *what's with this glove, and message? What I know is it must be important to Long Ngo. He doesn't want anyone outside of his domain knowing I have the glove. The Flying Dragons main sector is in Chicago, so that's the best place to make the trade. We got to get far away from all this commotion, the Philadelphia, Cherry Hill, and now Moorestown police departments. Yeah that's what we should do. Go to Chicago, Illinois to make this deal.*

"Sherry!" Charlie shouts. "Turn the car around we are going to the airport."

"What?" answers Sherry.

"Yes, the airport to catch a plane. We are going to Chicago, the main sector of the Flying Dragons," as he gives her the saddest puppy dog eyes, "Please, I have a good plan." After a few minutes Charlie convinced Sherry this was the best thing for them to do. They head towards Interstate 95 to Philadelphia International Airport, Chicago bound. First he needs to call Long Ngo to give him the news. He is tired of being pushed around and threatened. Now Charlie takes over making the rules and the demands. He begins sensing his courage, something he has suppressed for some time. He realizes it is up to him to save Chelly and protect Sherry and himself from The Flying Dragons. Their only hope depends on it. Once fearful and afraid, seemed implausible at this point of the game. This isn't an option, as he boldly asks Sherry for her phone to make the call. She reminds him about Caller ID, then explains to him about *67 and how it will block her phone number. Charlie, still a little paranoid, decides it's best to use a pay phone.

"Okay Sherry, there's a pay phone at the 7-11 on Kings Highway North, the closest one I can think of". They head in that direction. As they pull into the parking lot, Charlie jumps out of the SUV and heads toward the pay phone. He dials 411 to get the phone number of the Dragon's Den. He begins to feel tense and hangs up the phone, trying to decide on his verbiage. *"What'll I say, what tone should I use, what is the actual plan?"* He looks over to Sherry and realizes no questions, only answers. He picks the phone back up, dials 411 for the phone number to The Dragons Den. He still has 5 minutes left to meet Long Ngo's demands to save Chelly's life.

"City please," the ATT recording says. "Philadelphia," Charlie responds. "The Dragon's Den in Philadelphia"

"The number you are calling '215-629-2388' can be automatically dialed, press 1"; he presses the number one to get another recording, "Please deposit fifty cents."

He yells out to Sherry, "I need fifty cents." The seconds turned to minutes before she came running up with two quarters.

"Thank you for calling the Dragons Den, my name is Rudy, how can I help you?"

"Uh yeah, this is Charlie, let me speak with Long Ngo."

"I'm sorry he is not taking calls at this moment; is there anything I can help you with?" Rudy replies.

Charlie fires back, "Well Rudy, you better tell Mr. Ngo, I have his glove, the one he wants with the message in it. So it would be wise for you to put him on the phone NOW! "

"Hold on one moment". Rudy yells for Kwan to get Long, "Charlie is on the line, sounds important." CJ hears the hold music on the line and realizes he's being transferred.

Charlie, worrying about what tone he should use, his verbiage, but the satisfaction of getting the chance to defend himself and his best friends seemed to spark the strength to suppress his avoidance he'd processed most of his life. Soon he was about to ignite the fire against the most powerful man in the area.

"Hey Charlie", Long says, "Where the hell are you, only 4 minutes left. I'm preparing Chelly for the party we're going to have."

"Well, Long", Charlie says in a demanding tone, "you better get her unprepared as I am taking your glove to Chicago. I want to meet with one of your friends, Jeong Kim." A name Charlie remembered Sherry telling him this morning. Silence on the other end of the phone. Charlie imagined Long's face drop; Long was stunned. A man like Charlie threatening him seemed unrealistic. ·

"That's nice Charles, why are you going to see him?" Charlie realizes he has Long's attention, he was now listening.

"Long, you are no longer in control, I am. You are going to meet me in Chicago. I will call you in the morning with a time and a place where I want you to release Chelly alive, if you ever want your glove again. Long remained silent on the other end. Charlie continues, "I am going to let your boss in on how you've messed things up here in Philadelphia. It's about time The Flying Dragons had a new leader. I want to speak to Chelly and I need her to come to the phone, ASAP." In moments Chelly was on the phone.

"Oh Charlie", she says in a frightened voice. *She called me Charlie, I guess that's better than Charles.*

"Chelly are you alright?" Charlie asks with a concerned tone and can detect labored breathing with a hint of sorrow in her voice.

"I'm alive," Chelly replies. "I need to get out of here Charlie, please help me, please."

"Chelly, please be strong and hold on a little longer, I promise you, I'm a different guy today. I will not sit back and let these guys hurt you. I am working on a plan to get you out tomorrow night," Charlie says, wishing it was sooner, but he needs to ensure their safety. "Chelly, I need to speak to Long again, be safe, and believe I'm here for you. I will not let you down." Once again, Long Ngo is back on the phone. Charlie makes it clear to Long he is upset and going to fight them.

"If one hair on Chelly's body is harmed, you will be sorry." Charlie says.

Long replies, "I'll be waiting for your call, Charlie" In an angry tone he adds, "And if I do not hear from you, Mother Fucker by 11:00am tomorrow, Chelly will be executed." He yells, "Got it Charles?"

Charlie hung up the phone and realized he riled up Long enough to get him to go along with the plan. Charlie felt a sense of accomplishment, and a small victory in a huge war. Now he must follow through, put his plan in action, and it must be foolproof. At least he was able to add 24 hours.

Sherry and Charlie head for the Airport and book US Airways Flight # 3247, 11:30pm, the last flight out of Philadelphia. They are scheduled to arrive in Chicago at 12:46 am. Once in flight they had a chance to relax as best they could. They sat next to each other and Sherry managed to fall asleep. She was physically and emotionally exhausted. While she was asleep Charlie couldn't help but notice how beautiful she was, as her head tilted towards him with her pretty eyes shut. He notices her eye movement beneath her eyelids, in a wild dream; who can blame her with all she's been through today. Her mouth was open and her sweet breath blowing against his neck gave him a sense of security and comfort. *"Is this how married couples feel?"* he asks himself. *"That sense of security and comfort, Hmm!! I like that, especially with Sherry. She is the complete package, a beautiful person inside and out. She is a caring woman, a good conversationalist, sincere, funny at times, and self assured."* He couldn't help himself, but the more he looked at her his desire for her grew. He reached over to grab her hand, which was soft and tender. His emotions made him squeeze a bit too hard. She opened her eyes for a moment; still being a little groggy, she gave him a smile, squeezed his hand and fell back asleep. "Wow!" Charlie wanted to yell, but he didn't. With her eyes closed, she flashed him another smile. Charlie was hooked, as they both fell asleep.

Inside the Dragon

Chapter 4

$\mathcal{A}$t 10:45PM, prior to Charlie's phone call to Long Ngo, at The Dragon's Den two Philadelphia detectives walk through the double doors. They walk past the waterfall and are greeted by a beautiful Asian woman.

"Welcome to the Dragon's Den, my name is Ly, I am here to enhance your dining experience." As she lifts both elbows, inviting the men to take hold, she escorts them to their table. Ly asks, "Smoking or non Smoking?" Ralph opts for the non-smoking section, as the two detectives are seated at the east end of the red room. The table is in the vicinity of the bar, offering the men a clear view of the entire inner perimeter. "May I take your drink order?" Ly asks.

"We'll take a Miller Light Draft, if you please", says Jim.

"Okay," Ly replies, "and would you like some spicy wings to go with your draft? They are rated the best in town," as she is peering down at Ralph with a big smile and pets his shoulder in reassurance. The men decline. In an attempt to dismiss Ly, they begin looking around the room, if anything is suspicious. Duc, Quang, and Kwan enter the bar from the backroom. Kwan is holding an intense conversation with each of them, while pointing out certain areas of the dining room. Police officers for over 40 years between them, they sense an ambush is being set up. It seems as though he's trying to put them into position for something, which sparked both their curiosities.

"Here are your drinks, can I get you anything else?" Ly places the drinks down. "Do you want to run a bar tab?" Ralph quickly motions as he reaches for his wallet, which he keeps in the inside pocket of his sports jacket.

"That'll be $6.50 please." When Ralph pulls out his wallet, he accidently exposes his Philadelphia police Badge. "You are policemen?" Ralph then identifies himself and Jim as he continues handing Ly a ten dollar bill.

"Keep the change."

"Thank you", Ly replies, wearing her beautiful smile. She walks back to the bar, hands Rudy the money, and whispers into his ear. He closes the register and hands her the change. Rudy peeks over at the table. He senses the men are not here for pleasure; he smiles and waves, with an obvious expression of guilt on his face. He quickly vanishes to another part of the bar.

"Isn't that funny," explains Jim with a smirk, "he was trying so hard to be inconspicuous, he wasn't."

Ralph replies, "He should have been an actor." Realizing they also made a major mistake exposing their cover, with the appearance of Ralph's badge, they get back to their agenda.

"The way they are motioning, seems as though they are talking about us," Ralph says to Jim, when the phone behind the bar rings.

"Thank you for calling the Dragons Den, my name is Rudy, how can I help you?" He sneaks another peek over at the detectives, and continues, "I'm sorry he is not taking calls at this moment; is there anything I can help you with?" Rudy, beginning to get tense, takes another glance over at the detectives and says, "Hold on one moment". He calls for Kwan to come over as he whispers in his ear. Kwan glances over at the detectives, and rushes into the back room. Jim decides to talk with Rudy. He walks up to the bar, identifies himself and his partner as police detectives and asks to speak with the owner or manager. Rudy tells him the owner is on a long distance call. "Would you mind waiting?" Jim nods in acceptance then begins questioning Rudy. In showing him pictures of Thao and Giang, he asks Rudy if he'd ever seen the two guys before. Rudy examines the pictures and replies, "Yeah I've seen these two around here every once in awhile. They come here to booze it up and try to sell their drugs to some of our patrons. I usually have the bouncers throw them out."

"For real," Jim asks, "Can you tell me why they have several boxes of The Dragon's Den Flyers in their possession?" He hands one over to Rudy.

In a stutter he replies, "N-n-no-err Why?"

Jim replies a bit louder, "That's what I asked you."

"I guess you need to talk with Kwan, the club manager here. He is walking over to us now."

Kwan re-enters, "Can I help you guys?" He boldly walks straight up to the men, motioning to Duc and Quang to come. As Kwan approaches the officers, Duc immediately pulls out his switchblade and stabs Ralph in the back. Ralph immediately falls to the floor with a loud moan. Kwan pulls out his gun and points it at Jim. Without ample time to draw his weapon, Jim is left vulnerably at Kwan's mercy and his buddies'.

Kwan says, "What do you guys want from around here?" pushing the gun into Jim's head. Quang disarms him while holding a switchblade to his back. "Answer me", Kwan says as he is emphasizing pulling the trigger by poking Jim's head repeatedly with his gun.

"You won't get away with this, you know", Jim says in a nasty tone, "We've already entered your location in our police log before coming here. This'll be the first place they'll come investigate." At that moment Long enters the room and wants to talk with the officers. He can see one officer on the floor, when he walks up to Jim.

"I want Thao and Giang." Jim replies with a 'who cares what you want' by shrugging his shoulders, gesturing to Long, "Not his concern", as Kwan angrily nudges Jim in the head with his gun. Long repeats his demand, "I want Thao and Giang." Jim responds the same.

Kwan yells, "Fuck you cop", pulling the trigger. Upon impact Jim's body plummets to the ground as his blood shoots out the other side of his head and spatters Rudy.

"Shit", Rudy yells, as he is covered with Jim's brain matter and blood.

"Check the fat guy", Long says to Duc. "Is he dead?" Duc gets down next to Ralph and fires a shot into his head. More blood shoots out everywhere.

"He is now," Duc replies and again everyone lets out a cackle.

"Okay, let's get rid of the bodies and get rid of their car. I do not want either to be found, ever!" Long Ngo demands.

The boys know exactly what to do and whom to call, like a fine-tuned military operation. The gang takes the vehicles they need to dispose of to Ng's Auto Body on North 31st Street, owned and operated by a Taiwanese immigrant by the name of Richard Ng. He has been working with the gang ever since he'd taken over the business from his father. He now follows Long's orders, because 10 years ago when he'd refused and threatened to report them to the police, his 15 year old daughter was kidnapped and raped until he complied. He has been their puppet ever since. His job is to strip down the vehicle entirely into parts. Anything that has a serial number that can be connected to the Vehicle's Identification Number (VIN) he has melted into a liquid at his cousin's iron fence factory, Tran's Iron Works on Washington Ave in Chinatown. The bodies they need to dispose depend on what Long requests, if Long wants the bodies to be found or not. This time they need to cremate the bodies because they are never to be found. For this they use the services of Choi Funeral Home on North 12th Street in Midtown.

Sing Choi opened the funeral home in 1996 because of the business The Flying Dragons were sending his way while he was working at Baker's Funeral Home. He was cremating bodies unbeknownst to the owner. As the number of bodies increased and became extremely hard to hide, he opened his own funeral home, counting on the gang's increasing business. Currently, he takes care of over 200 bodies (murders) a year for them. He is rewarded with $4000 for each body he cremates. After cremation, the ashes are given back to the gang to be mixed into the gardens at The Dragons Den. Choi is an Asian, who is half Korean and half Vietnamese. He is a good friend of Long and Kwan and is highly trusted by the entire gang. He would never leak anything out to anyone, not even his own wife. They live above the funeral home on the second floor, in a three bedroom apartment with twenty-four hour direct access. Choi Funeral Home is the only Asian Funeral home in the Philly area. All the local Asians use their services. Its 11:15 pm when Sing gets a call from Kwan who explains what Long wants him to do, as they arrange to meet at the Choi funeral Home at 1:30 am, in a little over 2 hours from now. While Kwan is talking with

Sing, Duc calls Richard Ng to make him aware that he is bringing over an unmarked patrol car. Ng complains about the hour he is being called. Duc explains the urgency of the matter and that Long would be appreciative if he can oblige. After a brief hesitation, Ng agrees to meet Duc at the shop in less than an hour.

Long changes the Plan:

$\mathcal{K}$wan, Duc and Quang finish cleaning up the murder scene of Inzerillo and Sweeney, while Long has been infuriated, pacing the barroom floor ever since the call from Charlie. Pushing things off tables and yelling in Vietnamese, he's having a temper tantrum, not normal for him. Kwan suspects Charlie is the main reason for his anger, as he has never seen Long quite this rattled; especially since over the years Long is usually calm about everything, a good strong leader for the gang. He's always displayed the characteristics of why he was chosen by Jeong Kim to be the leader of The Flying Dragons in Philadelphia.

His presence to everyone in the gang commands respect, as Long is a motivator with high intelligence. The courage he's displayed many times over in dangerous situations, like during the Asian gang wars in the early eighties between The Flying Dragons, the Triads, and the Bui Doi gangs, throughout the country was the reason for this respect. Because of him, with his physical strength and his willpower, many battles were won. He's always displayed confidence in himself, and with the gang he led into these turf war battles. Long bestows mental toughness, he never showed fear at any one moment during those years. Long's toughness motivated the gang members to respect him and follow even his strangest orders. The Flying Dragons fought for a cause all of the street warriors understood. A plan put together by the greediness of Jeong Kim and Hung Vuong.

The major victories were won in the cities of Chicago, Philadelphia, Los Angeles, and New York against all odds, thus giving The Flying Dragons total control of the drug and prostitution businesses in those cities. The drug and prostitution business is bringing in over one billion dollars a year; those victories in the port cities of LA, NY and Houston made the gang the most powerful Asian crime organization in America.

Long makes a call to Jeong Kim in Chicago, informing him about Charlie and Sherry. They are being blackmailed by an unimportant local man here in Philly.

"He is on his way to Chicago O'Hare Airport." They talk for 15 minutes when Long says, "Ok, we'll be on our way after we care to a few minor loose ends. We should be able to leave early in the morning." Long takes back control of the situation and changes Charlie's plan.

Kwan asks, "Everything OK, boss?" wiping up the blood from the floor.

With a sarcastic laugh Long says, "Better than OK, much better," chuckling aloud. "Our friend Charlie will be greeted at the airport," continuing to laugh, and soon they all joined in.

O'Hare Airport:

Sherry and Charlie arrive at O'Hare International Airport at 12:30AM. *"I'm glad something finally went right today,"* Charlie says to himself. He glances over at Sherry, and she is still fast asleep. He decides to wake her up with one of his kisses, as he thinks, *"She is so beautiful, I simply can't resist."* She awakens like Sleeping Beauty after she is kissed by her prince.

"What?" she asks surprisingly, "did you kiss me? What else did you do while I was asleep?"

Startled Charlie says, "No, nothing, honest, I promise", sounding guilty. "I thought…"

"Sorry Charlie!" Sherry interrupts, "don't think when you are making a decision about me or my body," in an annoyed voice.

"Welcome back to the real world, I am back to being called Charlie", he says to himself, turns to Sherry and says, "I'm sorry, please forgive me. I wanted to let you know we've arrived, and we need to hurry and get a place for the night. I meant no harm, Sherry, I…"

"Stop," she says interrupting him, "You're forgiven."

"Thank you", Charlie replies and continues, "We'll find a place so we can get a few more hours of rest before we make our move."

Soon troubles arose again, as they did the last 17 hours or so. They walk out into the airport terminal and are met by several young Asian men waiting by the exit door where they are heading.

"What now?" Charlie thinks, and taps Sherry on the shoulder. "We have company, let's leave through a different exit."

She asks, "What company?" as Charlie points out the guys at the exit door. They turn around to head for the next gate when one of the guys starts running in the same direction. Three of them go left, three go right, and two stay put. Charlie realizes they were The Flying Dragons waiting for them to arrive. As they walked down the pathway at the airport, Charlie opens the door labeled 'Staff only'. This door led to an employee's elevator which took them out into the front of the terminal, and to safety. Somehow they ended up at the main entrance, where they waited for the next rental car shuttle to arrive. "Lord knows we'll need good reliable transportation to get us around town," Charlie says.

At the Crossroads of Terror

Charlie notices a gang member, as he and Sherry take the first shuttle to arrive, the Budget Rent-a Car Shuttle. Once at the rental car terminal Charlie asks Sherry to talk to the driver and detain him from going back to the terminal for another pickup. She did great, Charlie rented a blue Ford Taurus. When he came out, she was still talking with the shuttle driver.

Charlie walks up to her and says, "Let's get out of here." Once they're in the car he asks, "How were you able to detain him for such a long time?" He glances over at her, she replies without saying a word by giving him that sexy expression of hers and beautiful smile. Charlie replies, "No you didn't?" While flashing Charlie one of *his*.

"Yes", and they both chuckle a bit. Getting back on track, Charlie tells her, "According to this guide I took from the Airport, the Holiday Inn on West Joliet Road is only $134 a night. I'll pay, so let's go."

While Charlie is driving towards Holiday Inn, he is also thinking about Sherry. Sherry is worried about the day ahead, about their safety and her job. Her boss sounded pretty upset when he called her last night. "I'll call him in the morning, as soon as we made our plans, whatever they may be." She turns her head towards Charlie, says to herself, "What is he trying to accomplish. Why doesn't he want any help; is he on a death wish, is he in love with Chelly? If not, why is he doing this?" Now Sherry focuses her thoughts on Charlie, the man, "If only we had met differently. He is an astonishingly handsome man with his tall broad shoulders, his blonde hair and those big beautiful blue eyes. He seems to drive me crazy. He has a charisma about him that makes me want to just squeeze him to death, and yet he is so natural, not afraid to be himself, whether he is scared or trying to be funny. He is down to earth, not afraid to express his true feelings. Could he be tamed? Could he settle down with one woman, or will he always be on the prowl? I wouldn't mind trying like hell to find out the answer. Like I said prior, under different circumstances he'd make a great catch. I'm afraid to get close to him because he might be falling for me for all the wrong reasons."

Finally, they arrive at the Holiday Inn, they check in with the clerk, get two door keys for Room 219 and begin rushing to the room. Charlie opens the door and Sherry gasps and turns to Charlie, "Huh?" The room has only one bed.

"Charles," she says in a stern voice, "Where are you going to sleep?" Charlie begins thinking to himself, *"I guess she doesn't consider me a friend anymore; I've regressed to Charles again.*

"I'm sorry, but I didn't quite hear you," he says. She starts to repeat. Charlie immediately interrupts, "Look lady..." While he begins, Sherry closes the door and says to Charlie as plainly as she can, "Charles, what's happening between us is a sexual thing. Some sort of infatuation and attraction due to the stress we've both been under. Maybe I do feel the same way towards you, but I must be the one to control the situation." She is looking at the devilish face Charlie is making with that sexy look in his eyes. "Okay I do." Pausing for a moment and motioning with her arms, she brushes her hair back through her fingers. "I know for a fact I don't know you well enough to trust you yet, let alone like you in that way." Charlie walks over to the window, trying to think of a way to change the subject.

"This room has a view overlooking the indoor pool." He turns to Sherry, "With the glass roof you can see the rich blue color of the water. Come take a look. Come on now, won't you?"

"Are you trying to change the subject, young man?" Sherry starts walking over.

Charlie says to her, "Do you want to have dinner with me tonight?"

She looks at him and he back at her, they begin to laugh. She asks, "You haven't heard a word I said, did you?"

"I can't . . ." He is giving her a look of compassion, lust and love all in one, "not if it means we aren't together, I can't," A slight pause, moving his hands down her arms, "I won't." They both pause to stare deep into each other's eyes, as if they could read each other's mind. Charlie is hoping everything will work out, and he ends up with the girl, like in the movies. Sherry's thoughts are on Charlie as a person. She thinks, *he is the most attractive and warm hearted guy she has ever met. Usually guys are not as personable. They aren't as caring about my feelings like 'CJ', that's right, 'CJ'. I do consider him a close friend and maybe more.* Aloud she says, "We must get some sleep, we got a big day ahead of us in only a few hours."

At the Crossroads of Terror

Cherry Hill Police Station,

Around 1:15 AM. the next morning:

$\mathcal{A}$t the Cherry Hill NJ Police station, Detective Lieutenant Robert O'Hara is still in his office with several detectives assigned to the Chang murder. A long but promising day, after learning, in the national database the prints on the murder weapon drew a match. The prints belong to a Charles Johnson, 35 years old, who resides at 612 15th Street, Apt. 611, Cherry Hill NJ.

A routine background check on Charles Johnson came back clean, no prior arrests or any trouble with the law, not even a traffic ticket in the last 5 years. *This guy Charlie*, O'Hara thinking to himself, *is a real model citizen. He votes regularly, does volunteer work for the Cherry Hill local town government during the Thanksgiving and Christmas holidays. He worked hard getting The Bully Law passed, in honor of his late friend Helmut Krause. His father is a retired Philadelphia detective.* Knowing whose prints are on the murder weapon raised more questions than it answered. All the detectives on the case are as baffled as Detective Lt. O'Hara about Charlie. The detectives are going over the facts of the case. They are putting together a timeline and review of the statements and labeling each fact, fiction, or still to be Determined (STBD for short). Detective Ray Forster will read the statement to the team.

Fact #1: At 7:33 AM.- Mrs. Chang said while she was in the front of the store bringing her husband a cup of fresh brewed tea, a woman who she says she's never seen before walks in with a claim ticket to pick up a dress she claims she dropped off last week. (All agreed)

Fact # 2: 7:34 AM. So Mrs. Chang goes into the back with the ticket to retrieve the dress. (All agreed)

Fact #3: 7:35 AM - As soon as Mrs. Chang leaves and goes into the back, she realizes the ticket was not from her store. It was from their competition, Dang's Cleaners two blocks away. (All agreed)

STBD #1: 7:35 AM. Mrs. Chang hears a bang but remained unalarmed, thinking it was a car backfiring. She makes her way up to the counter to explain to the woman; she finds her husband lying in a pool of blood on the floor.

When they all agreed, Lieutenant O'Hara tells the team, although Mrs. Chang is an honorable person, this does not have to be a fact. Sounds like an opinion and she could be lying. Therefore, the statement could be false. Let's label this one STBD for now. (All agreed)

Fact #4: 7:36 AM. - She quickly dials 911 and reports the incident. (All agreed)

Fact #5: 7:43 AM. -   The patrol car 4 blocks away gets the call and arrives at the scene within 2½ minutes of receiving the call, on his radio. Actual time is 5 minutes from the time the 911 call came in.

Fact #6: 7:49 AM - Within the next 6 minutes, two more patrol cars with 4 more officers, an ambulance, someone from the coroner's office and detectives collecting evidence at Chang's.

Fact #7: 7:51 AM. – Also arriving at the scene was the WWNJ TV station street reporter Sherry Mann, her cameraman, and a crowd of about 15 outside of Chang's.

Fact #8: 7:52 AM. – We now know Charlie Johnson was out in the crowd too.

Charlie was standing right next to where the murder weapon was found by Patrol officer Jack Andrews. In fact, Jack remembered Charlie Johnson because at that time Jack was pushing Charlie away from the weapon, not to disturb evidence.

Fact #9: 7:55 AM - Ms. Sherry Mann interviews Charlie for her news story. She questions him live at the scene.

Fact #10: 9:30 PM - We found Charlie's prints and no one else's prints anywhere on the gun.

They now begin to discuss the prints. No marks on the trigger, nothing, wiped clean. Another strange fact about the prints on the gun, they were in an odd position. Charlie must have been pointing the gun at himself. As if someone handed him the gun and he took it.

"Maybe his job was to get rid of the evidence, Sir?" Lieutenant O'Hara asks the team, knowing what we learned today, seems unlikely. They all agreed it was quite possible but very unlikely, as the lieutenant is pacing the room.

"One thing I can think of," Lieutenant O'Hara says as he is still pacing back and forth, "what if someone, the girl with the claim ticket, shoots Chang and on her way out bumps into Charlie, hands him the gun. Charlie doesn't know what to make of it and drops it to the pavement. Now this could be a possibility." They all agreed. As the Lieutenant is making his point, his phone starts to ring, "O'Hara, Cherry Hill Homicide," he answers.

"Are you working on the Chang murder?" an unknown woman caller says. Quickly the Lieutenant motions to another Detective to get a trace on this call as the caller ID is a blocked call.

"Yes. Yes I am." Starting to get excited, thinking he might have a lead in this case. "Who's calling?" he replies. He feels this might be the break he needs in order for him and his team to be able to solve this case.

Chang, according to his wife's knowledge, had no enemies, his only friends consisting mostly of relatives, and had little interaction with outside people other than his family. The only outside contact he had was his customers at the counter. However, Chang, according to the authorities, did have contact with a man that goes by the name of "Prince, The Street Prince", but his real name is Hung Vuong and he is a member of the Flying Dragons. He has no physical address listed in any database, criminal or otherwise. This man doesn't vote, drive or have a bank account. He is untraceable. The next thing they found out was Chang tried to get a loan from his bank, Bank of America, in January but was denied due to the current status of his business. His business was starting to decline as the competition increased. Did he get a loan from The Street Prince?

"I can't tell you that", the voice on the other end of the phone says. "What I will say to you is, investigate the Dragon's Den." In a woman's whisper, "That's a good place to begin your investigation, because your main suspect, Charlie Johnson is innocent." Then there was a click and a quick dial tone.

"Did we get that?" The caller's phone was a blocked call so O'Hara had the call traced.

"Yes," he is ready to cheer until he hears, "But you're not going to like this one boss," Replies Detective Ray Forster, "It's a 312 area code, somewhere in Chicago, IL. In fact it's a pay phone on Joliet Road, at the corner of Kensington Ave."

"Way to go, Ray" he excitedly declares. "Get me all the hotels and motels in a three block radius of that corner. Let's contact the Chicago Police and get their registries. I want to know who the lady was that called." As he is shuffling some papers around, "Someone call the Philly PD to get a patrol car over to the Dragon's Den right away." *"Chicago?"* thinking to himself, *"Who could be calling us from Chicago?,"* with a quick response, "Forster, I also want all the flight records out of Philly to Chicago. I think we'll be going on a road trip today." Detective O'Hara grins, "This might be the break we needed."

Inspection of the Dragon's Den:

$\mathcal{I}$t is now 2:15 AM in the morning, patrolmen Allen Kennedy and Doug Burke pull their patrol car through the open gates of The Dragons Den. They were ordered to check out any suspicious activities and findings. They drove slowly, up the long winding driveway, before reaching the parking lot. The closer they got to the building, they noticed a light flickering from inside. They both figure they'd need to look. Allen gets out of the passenger side to investigate. Three cats licking something off the floor are walking past a lighted lamp, laying there on the floor. At first glance, nothing seemed suspicious, so he walked back to the car. While Allen is looking through the window, Doug notices something being reflected by the patrol car's headlights and goes out to inspect. He brings his flashlight and lights the area. He gets to the item and realizes it is a ring of some sort. As Doug delves into it little more, he sees it is a ring, a '25 year of service' award from the City of Philadelphia. Inscribed on the inside are the initials RI and a date of February 12th 2006. Doug is holding the ring when Allen walks up.

"All is clean," Allen says to Doug.

"Then what was the flickering?" Doug asks as he is still looking at the ring.

"It was three cats walking back and forth in front of a lamp that has fallen on the floor. What do you have there?"

"It's a 25 years of Service Ring from the city of Philadelphia," Doug replies while examining the ring. Allen asks to see the ring and says, "Wow! 25 years of service on the Police force."

"How'd you know that?" Doug asks.

"My father got one of those when he was on the force 25 years." As he wipes the mud off the initials and displays the ring in front of Doug's eyes, "Look at the markings, PPD."

"Yeah now I see it. PPD" as Doug continues, "Why would it be here? Do you know anyone who just celebrated their 25th year? This needs to be reported."

"No, I don't know anyone; let's call into the desk to find out if they know," Allen replies as they both head back to the patrol car. Before they had a chance to check in, and radio back to their sergeant, two vehicles pull into the lot, a black Chrysler 300M and a white cargo van. Allen says, "I'll go." As the Chrysler gets closer to Allen, the driver's side window opens and Allen hears the driver ask, "Anything wrong officer?" Before Allen got a chance to speak, the van pulled up beside them, the side door opens and Allen is stabbed numerous times. The van blocked the view of the murder from Doug. Then the van empties and Kwan, Duc and Quang get out and approach the police car. Doug starts to walk over to the van, still holding the ring. He begins to ask a question, but before he is able to let out one word he is shot through the head. No one notices, but as Doug falls down to the ground, the ring rolls from his hand and into the garden along the front of the building.

Long Ngo walks over and says to the gang, "Never to be found," as the boys begin laughing after one of them says, "instant replay." Long says to everyone, "We must hurry with these guys as we need to get to the airport on time for our important meeting tomorrow, with our friend Charlie. Duc and Quang start laughing and talking in Vietnamese.

As Long and the gang members leave the parking lot they notice another patrol car entering the gates through their rear view mirror. Kwan has Duc slow the van down as Quang sped ahead in the patrol car. Kwan wants to say something to Long in the Chrysler 300M. Long pulls alongside and Kwan says, "Looks like the heat is on us boss." As Kwan tries to see Long's demeanor, "It certainly does Kwan, it certainly does." Then Long Ngo drives off in front of the van as he has to pick up Kym & Chelly at Sinh's apartment.

Meanwhile back at the Cherry Hill PD Station, Detective O'Hara wants an update:

"Almost two hours passed since we've called the Philly PD to check out The Dragons Den." Concerned, Forster calls Captain Fennick to get an update since it's out of his jurisdiction.

"Right away Rob" (the informal name he is known as by his co workers). As Forster begins to dial the phone, O'Hara can hear parts of the conversation and trying to figure out his next move. Forster hangs up and calls for the rest of the team to come over for the update. The team gathers around Rob's Desk and Forster gives his update. Forster informs the team they lost contact with the patrolmen they sent over to The Dragon's Den. A second car has been deployed as they have been really busy all night.

"Here is the list of Hotels and Motels in a four block radius, boss. There is only one, a Holiday Inn on Joliet Road, a block and a half from that phone booth, and here is the fax I received of the hotel's registry." As he places the list in front of O'Hara, "Look who is staying there in room 219, Mr. & Mrs. Smith. Look at the hand-written note next to the name, paid with Charles P Johnson's MasterCard."

"Bingo", O'Hara says, "Call the Chicago PD and let them check out our guests." Slight pause, "Is that all?"

"No, that's not all." I got the records from all the airlines of people leaving Philadelphia going to Chicago and found this," as he hands O'Hara the US Airways travel log.

"Holy Crap", O'Hara yells. "You got to be kidding Sherry Mann is on board with him. Did you find out if they were together or is she on an assignment?"

"They're together," Forster answers as they both look at each other and start to smile. "I guess they are Mr. and Mrs. Smith in room 219."

"Get us on the next flight out, Forster. You did a fantastic job on this, Ray; I will let the captain know." They both grab their things and head out to the airport.

The Dragon's Head

Chapter 5

"Someone's at the door, Charlie, please wake up", as Sherry and Charlie were both asleep in the same bed. She is awoken by a sudden knock at the door. Charlie is dressed, on top of the blankets, and Sherry is fully dressed underneath them. That was Sherry's way of keeping control of the situation, or at least in her mind it was. "One minute please", she says attempting to wake Charlie from his deep sleep, as she taps him on the shoulder.

"Who?" Half asleep, Charlie asks.

"I don't know", she says, making her way to the door. Peering through the peep hole she whispers, "Charlie, the hotel clerk from last night."

"Oh okay, let him in", as he wipes the sleep from his eyes.

"CJ", (*Charlie is thinking he's a friend*) "last night you asked me to inform you if anyone happens to inquire of our registry." Charlie nods yes, "Both the Cherry Hill PD, and the Chicago PD called to obtain a copy of it."

Charlie jumps out of bed and hands the kid a fifty dollar bill and says, "I will send in a positive comment to the corporation on your behalf for the good work," as he nudges him out the door. Charlie sees the time is 6:30 am and thinks, *"Do these guys ever sleep?"* "We got to leave right away, Sherry" As he dashes to the bathroom to take a quick shower, he hears Sherry yelling something about calling someone, something-something-something. He couldn't make out what she'd said. He gets out of the shower, and yells, "Jump in, and hurry, we have to leave."

"Did you hear me? I called the Cherry Hill police department to ask them to check out the Dragon's Den."

"What, you did what?" Charlie questions, in an angry tone, "Why did you do that?"

"I called from a pay phone three blocks away and didn't think they'd find us so fast; of course I did tell them that you were innocent."

"Oh my God, I thought she was smarter, I guess not," thinks Charlie. When she comes out of the bathroom wrapped in nothing but a towel, Charlie is stopped in his tracks, he stares in amazement thinking *'wow, what a beautiful woman'*. In noticing some flesh, his manly desires began to take control, as his eyes scan every inch of her body.

Upon catching him she says, "Let's do it, make love to me, I know you want to!"

Charlie, shocked, caught off guard, his mind begins to ponder, *She knows I won't say yes; why's she doing this; is she playing with my head?* Knowing full well they didn't have time for this, Charlie decides to play a quick one of his own: who will break first? So he pulls her body close to his, looking deep into her eyes. Drawing his face closer to hers and with the tip of his tongue, he works her lips apart. Starting at the nape of her neck, as he massages the inside of her mouth with his tongue, he caresses her body, moving downward, reaching her tight derrière. He cups his hands around her plump butt cheeks and squeezes. In a deep sigh, she loses control and lets the towel drop. Without a care in the world, she grabs the back of his head, pushing his tongue into her throat and proceeds to kiss him back in a passionate way. Charlie pulls away and says, "You've won! Let's go."

"I've won?" stunned and frustrated in backing away from him, "That's what you say to me, I've won? What did I win? Tell me Charles, what did I win?" As she stoops down to pick up the towel, she covers her body and with an infuriated pissed off expression about her face, she runs off into the bathroom to put on her clothes.

Guess I've regressed all the way back to when we met, I'm Charles again. He experiences a profound humiliation upon realizing that she wasn't playing with his head. *She actually wants me as much as I want her. Oh my God, how thoughtless of me; I really blew it this time. I'm such a Yom.*

Yom is yet one of many infamous words made up by Charlie. It can be a good word or a bad word. He uses it when he can't remember someone's name; for example, a person comes up to him and says, "Hi CJ, how are you?" He looks at this person, who for the life of him he can't remember, and replies, "Oh, hello yom, how's everything?" Then he will chat with this person, without them ever knowing he doesn't remember who the hell they are. Charlie also uses the word when he wants to call someone out of their name like a fool, a dope or something a little demeaning without them knowing, or hurting their feelings. An example of this is his reaction to the situation he is in now. Instead of calling himself a complete and utter fucking idiot, a stupid SOB, etc., he calls himself a Yom; it gets a less violent reaction. That's what he is right now, a big fat yom, an idiot, a fool. The last thing in the world he wants is to get Sherry mad at him; he can hate himself for being such a yom in this situation. Sherry marches out of the bathroom in a huff.

"I'm sorry", he implores as she ignores him, walking past, giving him the frigid cold shoulder. Charlie grabs the hotel keys and walks out the door right behind her like a silly little puppy dog with his tail between his legs.

As he checks them out at the front desk, Sherry awaits outside. In pulling the car around to pick her up, Charlie sees, to his amazement, not one, not two, but three Chicago patrol cars pull up in front of the hotel. *"Wow we made it, let's get the hell out of here,"* he thought as they drive out onto Joliet Road.

Its killing Charlie as Sherry, gazing out the window, continues to give him the cold shoulder. Sensing her anger, he decides to break the monotonous tension.

"Would you like to eat breakfast with me?" She ignores him, and continues to look away, out the window. He then asks a bit louder, "Do you want to eat or do you want to argue?" as he continues in a softer tone, "although I could use a good argument right now, and it'll probably do me some good to release all the pent up stress that I've acquired from being around you. I prefer to eat, how about you?"

She turns to him and laughs, "Yeah, well I'd rather argue; it'll do us both some good," as she begins laughing aloud.

One glance at Charlie's ice blue eyes and Sherry began to ponder a relationship: *How can I stay mad at him? He is like a child, so lovable and adorable, so huggable like a fluffy teddy bear. I know he didn't want to upset me, he's just being the kid that he is, playing his stupid games, but I wanted a man back there. I need to set the guidelines for him if we're going to have any kind of relationship. He has to know that he cannot play with my emotions. I'm a real person with real feelings and so is he. I won't play with his emotions, and I expect the same. Other than that, I really don't see anything I don't like about him. Oh yes, I do, maybe, is he stubborn or is he just a loyal friend? Is he in love with her, if so, then why is he acting this way? Why in the world does he want to take on 'The Flying Dragons', why? Maybe he is a little crazy. Maybe he's a daredevil. Whatever the reason, he is persistent. I hope he has the means to keep us safe from whatever danger lie ahead.*

"IHOP", Charlie shouts as he rips Sherry from her thoughts. In looking at her pretty face he thinks to himself, *Doesn't she realize I am head over heels for her? When I look at her I see my future. I want to spend my life with her, but she keeps pushing me away. Why? Doesn't she know how I feel? What can I do to make her know?*

"IHOP sounds great," she replies.

"What?" Charlie says as she breaks his train of thought.

"Let's go to IHOP," she replies as she turns to look out the window. She points out, "There it is over there, at the next corner," Charlie slows the car down and turns into the parking lot.

"Do you realize sex has been known to take the place of food? I once heard the more sex you have the less food you need."

"So what are trying to say to me Charlie?" questions Sherry in a sexy, rather playful tone.

"Well, you'll end up with a ton of energy either way?" Charlie says, realizing he's got Sherry's full attention. In turning his head in her direction giving her the opportunity to reply, they make eye contact, only this time she says nothing. Her eyes longingly beckon him, as her body awaits his tender masculine embrace. It was as if he'd singed right through her very soul with those scorching ice blue eyes of his. In a sigh, he reaches out and ever so gently caresses her delicate cheek. He can feel the body heat radiating through the moisture in her breath against his hand, as she softly kisses the inside of his palm. Like an animal tracking its prey, he's captivated by her, and she by him. With inviting sighs of pleasure, she cringes in overwhelming anticipation as Charlie begins kissing her gently on the cheek, moving his tender kisses slowly down to her neck. As he continues up her left cheek, he still maintains focus on those enchanting eyes, as if they were speaking to him in a big way, giving him the courage to persist. At this point, Charlie can barely contain himself as he makes his way to her sexy, luscious lips. Her stunning beauty literally takes his breath away. As they lock into each other in a passionate kiss, Sherry wraps her arms around him, as he melts within her grasp. The heat radiating from their bodies causes the windows to fog, as he gently works his hands down over to her breasts. She doesn't pull away, not this time; rather she pulls him closer. Her tongue is in his mouth, massaging every inch, creating the sexual intimacy he so desires. At this point, Charlie is so uncontrollably aroused, he's ready to explode. As his soft warm hand caresses her inner thigh, a moan escapes her. Suddenly, the loud sound of an approaching vehicle in the IHOP parking lot startles them and rips them apart. In breaking away from one another, Sherry initiates a chuckle and as they both laugh, Charlie notices Sherry quickly look away. In a brief, uncomfortable pause, Charlie breaks away.

"I'm famished, what about you?"

"Yeah let's eat so we can call Long Ngo and tell him where we want him to bring your sexy little girlfriend," as she gives him that look of hers that's been driving him into this passionate frenzy for the last 18 hours. He so desperately wants to tell Sherry, Chelly is not his girlfriend, she is only an acquaintance back from his childhood; instead he says nothing and just nods his head in agreement. He sits there quietly in the car for a little while longer, trying to compose himself after his brief interlude with Sherry.

Upon entering IHOP, they get a table for two, sit down and both order eggs and pancakes, the staple meal. They had not eaten since yesterday afternoon and were starving. As the waitress returns to the kitchen with their order, Charlie notices a large TV in the corner of the room. It was on CBS and the Early Show was airing. Suddenly, a picture of him and Sherry was on. They were airing Charlie's photo from yesterday's mug shot, along with the news report Sherry recorded in

[80]

front of Chang's. Charlie's heart began to palpitate as he motions to Sherry to look behind her. She turns, and upon visualization her demeanor dramatically changes. It was as if her emotions had gotten the best of her, she was speechless. With a defeated look upon her face, she just sat there as if ready to call it quits. Charlie wouldn't blame her one bit if she did; it was as if they were carrying the weight of the world taking on 'The Flying Dragons', at least that's how it seemed. With the adrenalin rush, Charlie's strength seemed to kick in, and he declares, "That's perfect, it's just what we need."

He remained positive as he continued to explain his reasoning, "We only need Long to believe we will pay a visit to his superior Jeong Kim. That way he comes to Chicago with Chelly, alive and well. We are going to use the Chicago PD to help us win, but only after we make sure Long and Chelly are here and we make the trade. Once we've made the trade, the Chicago PD will arrest him for kidnapping, and in detaining him it will buy us some time to collect the evidence needed to put him away indefinitely for the charges of racketeering, drug trafficking, prostitution and murder."

Sherry's phone rings and to her surprise, her boss is on the line. "Yes, I think it's time, I'm going to tell him everything," confides Sherry. Upon answering she proceeds to inform him of the whole account, promising him the story of the year, quite possibly of the decade by the time she's done.

As Charlie watches in awe, he's enlightened with the way she handles herself on the phone. Not a hint of insecurity, her mindset was right back on cracking the case. He was honored to have lent the boost of encouragement she'd needed, as she was making a lot of sense on the phone. She went on to explain how they'd solved the murder and assured him that his station would be the first to air the news. Through Sherry's replies Charlie was reassured, her boss understood the danger they were in and was concerned for their safety. The biggest question of all though was why she hadn't gone to the police for help, as he hears her reply, "...due to the fact that his prints were on the gun, he was afraid." She hands Charlie the phone. As they share the same conversation, she hears Charlie declare:

"Sherry's safety comes first and is of the utmost importance to me sir." As he agrees to keep him updated through constant and rigorous communications, Charlie demands they halt all news reports concerning him. They have Sherry's picture plastered wherever his is. In reassurance Sherry's boss promises to contact the AP services of WWNJ. He also mentions to Charlie his father had contacted the station questioning his whereabouts and his involvement in the Chang's murder case, and most importantly of his safety.

"As chief director here at WWNJ, I'd be honored to assist in any way possible with the news to insure you and Sherry's safe return home." Upon arrival of their food, Charlie realizes one of the patrons staring, so he asks the waitress for two "to-go" boxes. In leaving IHOP, as they make their way to the car, Sherry informs Charlie her boss made mention of two missing detectives that were on assignment in a drug bust involving Thao and Giang, two alleged gang members.

"Do you remember who they were?" Charlie asks.

"Yes, their names are Sweeney and Inzerillo."

"Sweeney and Inzerillo? They were friends of my father from the Philadelphia Narcotics Squad." Charlie decides it's time to contact his dad as he believes his dad's former affiliation with the PD may help them out. The news seemed to shock Sherry, as she hadn't been made aware of his father's involvement with the Philadelphia PD. At first she was upset, thinking Charlie had betrayed her trust by holding back such vital information; she soon realized that's his personality, and really had nothing to do with their friendship. She understands he is quite independent in his way of thinking and he likes to do everything on his own.

"What else have you heard?" Charlie asks her.

She proceeds to tell him of the whole conversation. Charlie felt it was definitely time to call his dad, so he pulls the car over to switch places with Sherry and borrows her phone. The time is 8:15am, and he is quite sure both his parents are awake. Sherry pulls into a parking garage somewhere in Chinatown off of East 22nd Street and So. State Street and Charlie makes the call.

"Hello," he hears his mom say.

"Hi mom, is dad there?"

"CJ is that you!" in a startled voice, "Are you alright?" as she continues, "Where are you? How are you? Where are you calling from? What happened yesterday? I do not recognize the caller ID. Where are you CJ?"

"Mom, I'm fine, I'm in Chicago with street reporter Sherry Mann and I need to talk with dad, it's really important.

"Okay son, here's dad and remember son, I love you."

"Love you too, mom."

"Son, thank God you called, your mother's worried sick about you," as usual Charlie's dad so typically tries not to show his worry, but Charlie knows better; his father was just as worried as his mom.

"I know, dad, I got caught in the middle of the murder at Chang's. The woman who did the shooting walked out of Chang's, handed me the murder weapon. Rather, she placed the gun in my pocket, as I pulled it out it accidentally dropped onto the sidewalk. After the police found and tested it back in the lab, my prints were discovered all over it. In trying to prove my innocence, Chelly was kidnapped, and now she is being held hostage. Sherry Mann, the street reporter is a living doll and has been a big help. I also have a glove that seems to be important to them. That's why I am free and Chelly is held hostage. They want to exchange Chelly for the glove. This glove has Asian writing on the inside, in Vietnamese or Chinese. The situation took us to Chicago, and now we are being followed by The Flying Dragons." As Charlie explains the whole grueling situation to his father, he hopes he hadn't left out any important detail. Knowing his father, he was already trying to solve the problem instead of listening to what Charlie was saying. This must be hereditary from his grandfather; he was funny like that too. Another one of Charlie's sayings, (Funny like that). Charlie was wrong though, as his dad asks,

"What do you need me to do? Do you need me to contact some of the old boys on the force to see what I can find out and input into this case?"

"Yes dad that would be great. I just heard Sweeney and Inzerillo are missing after busting Thao and Giang, The Flying Dragon gang members. I am sure they went to the Dragon's Den because that is their home base. The leader Long Ngo is the principal owner of the club and that's where they are keeping Chelly. Please be careful; they are really dangerous nowadays. They have the latest technology and weapons. I researched all this online. I am trying to get Long Ngo here, to Chicago, to arrange Chelly's release somewhere, by the Chicago PD." As he turns towards Sherry, she glances back

"Slow down, son, is this the phone number you can be reached at?"

"Yes Dad," Charlie replies.

"Give me twenty minutes son and I will get back to you at this number."

Charlie agrees and when he tells Sherry, she not only agrees, she was pleased that he'd asked for help.

O'Hara's meeting with Berkshire:

$\mathcal{D}$etectives O'Hara and Forster arrive at O'Hare airport as they anxiously prepare to meet with the Chicago PD, expecting Sherry and Charlie to be in custody at the Ogden Ave. Station, downtown Chicago. O'Hara truly believes Charlie is innocent and was in the wrong place at the wrong time. He feels Charlie is being set up by the real killer or killers. In his last communications with the Chicago PD, they planned to detain Charlie and Sherry so the detectives can safely transport them back to Cherry Hill, so they can get on with solving the Chang case. O'Hara fears for the safety of Sherry Mann as she has been accused of aiding and abetting a suspected felon. This might cause the killer or killers to do something drastic that'll turn fatal. The detectives were in flight before they had a chance to hear the suspected fate of the Four Philadelphia policemen. Today's Philadelphia Daily News front page headline reads: **'Four of Philly's Finest Gone Missing-Feared Dead'** with snapshots of the missing officers Inzerillo, Sweeney, Kennedy and Burke.

O'Hara and Forster will be met at the airport by two policemen, who would not discuss the failed mission at the Holiday Inn, to apprehend the suspects, Charlie and Sherry. They were instructed to bring the detectives to the Ogden Ave. Station where they are scheduled to meet with Police Captain Clyde Berkshire.

On the same flight, seated in first class, were Long, Kym, Kwan, Duc, Quang and their captive Chelly Robinson, Chicago-bound to meet with Jeong Kim. Duc held a knife at Chelly's side, instructed not to speak to anyone the entire flight. With every little movement Chelly can feel the sharpness of the blade digging in. She so desperately wants to bring this situation to a screeching halt. However, she knew whatever she was capable of doing, would probably be fatal. Not only to her, but to other innocent people onboard, so she decided to behave and stay put.

At the Crossroads of Terror

The sharp plastic knife Duc is holding is as deadly as a steel one. The gang, with their extensive years of experimental knowledge, paired with the latest technology, invented this knife, undetectable by airport security. The knife is housed inside a piece of plastic designed to look like a 12 inch ruler Duc carried on board in a briefcase with other office supplies. This made the case look harmless, so the security guards never examined further. Even if they did they would not be able to find the knife concealed in the plastic housing. Once on the plane, Duc opened the case, gave the ruler the special twist, exposing the knife now held at Chelly's side. Although the detectives were on the same flight, they never noticed the gang, as Long and his entourage flew first class.

The police officers who are going to escort the detectives back to the captain, see Mr. Long Ngo, along with the several other Asian men, un-board the plane and leave the area in somewhat of a rush. Oddly, they also see an attractive Caucasian woman along with them. She didn't seem to fit in, and soon the officers suspected something when O'Hara and Forster walked out and greeted them. One of the officers made a written note, and then they proceeded on with their instructions to take the detectives back to meet the Captain.

Capt. Berkshire, who is scheduled to meet with O'Hara and Forster, had been with the Chicago PD for the last sixteen years; prior to that he worked as a detective for the Elk Grove Village PD for eight years, which is a Chicago suburb, fifteen miles from downtown. He is a decorated officer with a stellar record. He has solved many cold case files, many shown on the A&E television show with the same name. He became the star of the squad by being asked to make special television appearances involving unsolved mysteries. He became a local celebrity in Chicago when he solved a four year-old high profile cold case – The murder of Sarah James, a college student, whose body washed ashore on the North Side Beach in Chicago, fourteen days after she was reported missing.

An autopsy showed Ms. James had been viciously strangled, and the Cook County medical examiner's office ruled the death a homicide. Family members said their understanding of the case, Ms. James had been murdered, and believed her abusive boyfriend was directly involved. Some detectives cautioned it was too early to rule her death a homicide, noting she could have suffered trauma to her neck after voluntarily jumping or accidentally falling into the lake.

Sarah's boyfriend, Joseph Nichols of Naperville, reported her missing March 13th 1999. Her murder sparked the interest of the entire city and they wanted answers to this hideous crime. There was no DNA evidence to further their investigation. Her emaciated body was in Lake Michigan for 2 weeks before being washed up on the beach, and tragically found by local unsuspecting youths as they swam. Due to the family's relentless pressure on the Chicago PD, with the help of added pressure from the media, Captain Berkshire announced he would work on the case personally in 2005. He discovered Sarah was a good person. She won a scholarship and attended the University of Illinois in Chicago, where she studied English in hopes of becoming a journalist or an author.

At the time she disappeared, Ms. James, taking a semester off from school, worked as an office manager for a property development company. She intended to go back to school to finish her degree in 2000. The captain kept a picture of Sarah on his desk as a reminder to himself, she was a real person and mustn't ever be forgotten. Every day, Captain Berkshire worked diligently trying to dig up new leads. Four years after the murder, Captain Berkshire looked over the evidence.

"It's like a fresh set of eyes looking at whatever had been done before, and it gives us new hope," said Gloria James, Sarah's mother, in a television news interview. The Captain, putting pressure on the homicide department, wanted this case and many other old cold cases, solved, where the leads seem to be dead.

"We received two new leads we are trying to confirm," the captain said. He had his department pounding the pavement, tracking down old witnesses; even years later they are able to turn up new leads. "We interviewed them again to make sure their story was still the same, or maybe they have gained additional information regarding the crime, and from there we progressed up the ladder," he added. "The reason almost every cold case gets solved is because someone talks," the captain explains as he says, "You would be surprised by the number of cold cases we solve without DNA, simply because the killer is now talking to someone. The reasons for talking seem to fall into three categories: the killer's guilt, arrogance, or booze, which includes drugs." Captain Berkshire was becoming a local celebrity because of this case and the high media attention. With his daily updates on Fox News and WGN TV, the captain was thought of as a natural born speaker.

"We do have several leads we're following up on, and we have several people of interest we need to follow up on," Berkshire says on one of the daily updates. "Because of you," speaking of the media, "more people are stepping up to the plate to give us new leads," as he continues, "I thank you, the great people of Chicago, for all your support."

In four years of grieving over her daughter's murder, Gloria James has new hope that one burning question will be answered. "I'm hoping the new evidence will make some sense of it all, and ultimately lead to a conviction," as she still gets teary eyed when speaking of her daughter's murder.

Between the media and the heat bearing down on the Chicago streets to solve Sarah's murder, new evidence arises and implicates Sarah's boyfriend, Joseph Nichols. With this new evidence Captain Berkshire was able to get a conviction and put this case to bed, a satisfaction beyond belief. Since this case there has been talk around the city of him running for mayor, after all his name is now a household word and his face is known to almost everyone in the Chicago area, thus making him a favorite if he decides to run in November.

As he awaits his guest's arrival, he receives a call from Philadelphia PD Captain John Fennick with an update for the detectives in the Chang case. Capt. Fennick informs Capt. Berkshire they have new evidence, and believe the Chang murder might be linked with the four missing Philadelphia police officers. They also believe the four officers are deceased and are putting forth all efforts in getting this matter resolved quickly. He continued to inform the captain that they also believed that Sherry Mann and Charles Johnson are in major trouble. New evidence shows the possibility that Mr. Johnson was played patsy by the killer and is an innocent man trying to prove it.

He asks a favor of the captain; he wants to know if the captain can put out an APB (All Points Bulletin) in the Chicago metropolitan and surrounding areas, to help find Sherry Mann and Charles Johnson and get them into custody for their own safety. He will send the photos over to him. The Captain agreed. The car arrives at the station and detectives O'Hara and Forster get introduced to Capt Berkshire as he gives them the update. O'Hara is a little troubled by the fact that Sherry and Charles were able to elude them.

"How'd they do it?" O'Hara asks the captain.

"I just can't believe they could think and react as quickly as they did."

"It looks as though one of the hotel employees alerted our friends for a fifty dollar tip."

The Captain implies, "Your boy Charlie is the son of a retired detective and is knowledgeable to some of our tricks. I found out that he was in contact with his father, whom due to his allegiance to the force and fear for the safety of his son, has contacted the Philly PD. He told them what he knew from his son and, oh boy!" he exclaims, "Charlie is trying to save an old school friend who was kidnapped by 'The Flying Dragons', who are ultimately involved somehow in the Chang's murder case that you are working on."

"The Flying Dragons. Why on earth is this kid doing that? Is he on a death mission?" O'Hara asks. "All I know is we got to find them before the gang does."

All the men agreed as the Captain informs the detectives that "the Chicago sector of The Flying Dragons are feared by the Asian communities; it is hard to generate any leads, let alone a conviction of the leaders. Jeong Kim, who not only runs the sector in Chicago, is their "Nhat-Quo," which means # 1 Soldier, and is the head of 'The Flying Dragons.' He holds his meetings here in Chicago twice a year for a week at a time. That's when we notice a spike in missing persons and murders within the city. In those two weeks the overall crime rate drastically increases. Every once in a while we are able to arrest a street warrior or a thug of The Flying Dragons. But to get a conviction is very rare due to the lack of physical proof which is needed in the court systems. This whole situation is a big reminder of the Italian Mafia and Costa Nostra days in the old Chicago crime files when AL Capone thought he owned this town.

Planning the exchange:

𝓘t seemed longer than twenty minutes, but in actuality only 15 passed, when Sherry's phone rings. She hands the phone to Charlie.

"Your dad."

"Hello," Charlie answers.

"Hi Charlie," his dad answers. "I have contacted a few buddies, and they will look into it for me; in the meantime here is what I need you to do. Does your cell phone have a camera?"

"Yes sir," Charlie replies.

"Turn the glove inside out and take a clear picture of the words. E-mail the picture to me and I will have it translated. I also need you to contact Capt. Clyde Berkshire, Chicago PD and stay put."

Charlie tells his father he will send him the picture, but he wasn't going to contact this captain 'what's his name', at least not yet. He discussed with his father his plans. Charlie's thinking, *"I will only tell my father what I want the Chicago police to know so I stay in control of the situation. I'm planning on my dad letting the word out to the local police, so I'm careful as to what I will tell him."*

They talked for about thirty-five minutes, arguing back and forth, until Frank asks to speak to Sherry. Charlie gives her the phone and walks about 10 feet away. They talk for fifteen minutes, until Charlie interrupts.

"I have to call Long Ngo and I would like you to be next to me for strength." Sherry, totally surprised by what Charlie said, as her eyes locked into his, caresses him. Charlie, standing 8 inches above her head, can sense in her eyes she was elated to know he needed her, for his self confidence. He also needs to get into the right frame of mind, so he ponders the crisis at hand and Long's possible answers. The outcome could be a real killer, he means thriller. Sherry says good bye to his dad and mentions to Charlie what a nice person he is.

"Now you know why I'm so nice, it's hereditary," Charlie says as they both chuckle.

Sherry wants to ask Charlie, in a serious manner, a question she needs answered truthfully. She reaches up with the palm of her hand resting on his chin, her thumb on one side of his face and her four fingers on the other, like Charlie's mom did when only the truth will do. She begins to position his face so their eyes are locked into one another's eyes. She tells him she has only two questions for him, and will take his answers as truth, never to be asked again. Charlie is thinking, *"I doubt it, she will not believe me, unless I answer it the way she is expecting me too."* Her eyes zoom into his eyes deeper as she asks her first question.

"Do you love her?"

Charlie pauses to gather his thoughts, so he can give her a truthful and honest answer. He believes she is asking him about Chelly and would hate to answer her question with a question, but he might have to. Luckily, she repeated it.

"Well do you? Do you love Chelly?" *Wow the big one, the biggest question she could ask me. Why is she asking me that?* He wonders, but as their eyes are locked into each other's eyes, he understands, she needs to know the truth. She does need to know before she will allow her heart to be taken. Charlie experiences her emotions, as if they were his own. As he takes a deep breath and without any more hesitation, he explains:

Charlie begins to tenderly stroke her hair as he continues to look deep into her eyes.

"Yes, I do love Chelly," her eyes begin to water, he continues, "As a friend. I love her as a friend." He continues to tell her, they were best friends from the age of six until they'd both gone off to college at age eighteen. A twelve year friendship he can never forget or let go of. They learned everything together, about life, how to grow from children to teenagers to young adults. They learned how to be a friend and how to treat a friend. Most of all, they learned how never to let a true friendship like theirs die.

"I thought I wanted her as a woman and was in love with her all these years, but now I know otherwise. Love is not infatuation or the thought of having sex with a beautiful woman. I thought I knew what love was, but now after knowing you for a little over a day, I believe love is what I am experiencing with you. I care what you think, say and feel. I do not want to hurt you physically, or mentally. I only want to be at my best and do my best when I am around you, because nothing and I mean nothing less will do."

"What is your next question?" Charlie asks as he continues to stroke her hair ever so gently. Her eyes are talking to Charlie and he understands the man he is supposed to be for her. Sherry is all teary-eyed, with teardrops running down her cheeks, ready to ask her second question.

"Why are you trying to fight Long Ngo and The Flying Dragons?" As she is still holding his chin, Charlie tries to turn away, but she moves his face back, keeping eye contact. In trying to find the right words, Charlie hesitates, knowing this is a two part question, depending on how he answers.

"All my life I let bullies tease and push my friends around in my presence, with no reaction at all except an empty stare. I stood and watched, standing at attention, like a statue. I did absolutely nothing to help my friends. Not because I'm a coward or afraid of being physically hurt, no not good ole Charlie. The reason I didn't react, because I was afraid they'd turn their teasing towards me and I'd become the target of their verbal abuse. I could take any physical harm they could dish out, but I couldn't take the mental abuse. I wasn't strong enough for that. I am too self-conscious with low self esteem and low self confidence." He began telling her of their friend Helmut Krause, the day he exploded and took out years of being bullied on one guy named Arte Bridges.

(Cont'd from pg 32)

..... Chelly looked at Charlie with such anger, anger that in all our years of friendship had never come out. She takes it upon herself to help Helmut. She tried to calm him down, but it was futile, a hopeless but valiant attempt. Between Helmut's strength, and his pent up anger of twelve years, one wave of his arm and Chelly went flying at least a yard away, ending up right at Charlie's feet.

All shaken up, with tear-filled eyes, at the top of her lungs Chelly yells, "Stop Helmut please stop!" She looked up at Charlie, and as their eyes met, she flashed him the most hateful look. At that point, all her anger seemed to be aimed at him. She was so angry, they didn't talk for weeks. That was the longest three weeks of Charlie's life, as she wouldn't return any of his phone calls.

I am not a coward I was telling myself, I just couldn't take all the abuse Helmut could. I wasn't as strong as him.'

"Helmut continued punching and stabbing Arte with the pencil until Mr. James, one of the gym teachers at school grabs a hold of Helmut, pulling him away from Arte, who lay motionless. His blood sprawled around the hallway corridor like a beef slaughterhouse. I stood there frozen, without saying a word. The police arrived and one of the officers said, "Call the morgue, this kid is dead". Helmut gets taken away, never to be a free man again. Helmut had recently turned eighteen and tried as an adult. He was found guilty of murder and was given the death penalty. I remember at the trial Chelly and I begged and pleaded self defense to the jury for Helmut. We explained to everyone all the abuse he endured throughout his school years from being bullied by all the other kids, especially Arte Bridges, who started his verbal abuse of Helmut in the 4th grade. Our plea fell upon deaf ears. Convicted of first degree murder and given the death penalty, and in 1997 he was put to death by lethal injection."

Sherry begins to sob, trying to listen to the end of the story.

"Usually it takes years for the death sentence to be carried out, but not in this case." Helmut being a religious person, refused to fight. His lawyers wanted to motion an appeal, to fight the sentence, but Helmut wanted no part of a long, drawn out appeal. He wanted to die. He believed he deserved the punishment for taking another life."

At the Crossroads of Terror

As Charlie is telling Sherry the story, her tears begin rolling heavier down her cheeks, in a steady stream. He then continues about Helmut's execution.

"At his execution, Helmut is strapped to the Gurney, with three tubes in his left arm. He had three large leather straps tied across his body and two straps on each of his arms and legs. The guards rolled Helmut out in front of the witness window and tilted him almost erect for us to witness him die. It reminded me of the way I imagined Jesus on the cross the day of his crucifixion. Helmut looked around the room trying to see who thought his death was important enough to be there. When he saw me, he nodded and gave me a smile, knowing our friendship was true and telling me, it's OK, he is willing to die.

"The executioner asked if he wanted a mask over his head, Helmut refused. He wanted to give Arte's family what they'd longed for since the killing. I didn't say murder because it wasn't, it was a self defense killing. I blame myself, if only I had spoken up and defended my friend. I let him down every time he was mocked, teased and made a fool of. I let everyone down and I am so remorseful. I should have been the one tied to the Gurney, not Helmut." Charlie gets teary-eyed and his emotions are filled with sadness whenever he thinks of Helmut.

"I began to look around the room to see if any of the kids that used to mock him were present. None of them were, not one, not a teacher, an old friend; in fact, I was the only one from Maple Shade High, and not even Chelly."

"As the time came, he gave his last words to everyone who attended the tragic event."

'Ich bedauere was ich getan habe. Für meine Handlungen and diesem Tag verdiene ich zu sterben. Ich bedauere so zur Arte-Brücke-Familie und für das Schmerz-Leiden, und sie haben diese letzten 6 Jahre erlitten. Ich hoffe, dass mein Tod ihnen Entschlossenheit gibt Ich bin bereit tun es jetzt.'

"He actually said it in German, which upset me extremely since I didn't understand a word. After the execution I was handed, from one of the prison guards, a note written by Helmut and to my surprise, it was

[93]

the translation of his last words. I still have the note today as a reminder of the loss of a true friend." Charlie pauses for a bit and tilts his head up towards the sky.

"I will never forget you, Helmut Krause." His eyes now back down to Sherry as he continues.

"This is what he said,"

'I regret for what I have done. For my actions on that day, I deserve to die. I am so sorry to Arte and to the Bridges family, and for the pain and suffering they have endured these last 6 years. I hope my death gives them closure to resolve.'

Then Helmut said, *'I am ready, so let's do it now.'*

"Immediately the executioner gives the signal to someone out of view. This person pushes the injection's trigger and the poison is released into Helmut's veins. He begins to get drowsy, his eyes start to twitch and blink uncontrollably and roll back as he gasps for air, trying to suck in as much air as he can. He tried to arch his back, but couldn't, because he was tied down tight. His eyes closed for the last time and he went into a coma. His massive body is now paralyzed, and the lethal dose of potassium chloride is administered by the executioner. He is pronounced dead 7 minutes later at 12:07am, September 29, 1997. The lights dim to darkness and the curtain closes, like it closes on the final act of a play when it comes to the end."

"I was uncontrollably distraught, my heart was broken, and my friend lies dead behind the closed curtain. I made a promise that day to honor Helmut somehow, and in some way.

"Till this day, I haven't shared that story with anyone, Chelly; my parents, my sister, no one. You are the only one who knows," Charlie's eyes still lock with Sherry's eyes. "I displayed my coward behavior, over and over, in fact, too many times for me to count. This is my one big chance to prove to the world Charles Peter Johnson is no coward. I'm not afraid of anyone or anything, not even The Flying Dragons."

As he continued he went on to explain, after the trial he was so taken back and upset over the whole incident, he initiated a motion to get a new law passed in Congress. He called it The Bully Law.

At the Crossroads of Terror

"It all started in 1994, while Helmut was still alive and after many years of hard work and perseverance. I had to compose a rough draft, basically to get my idea down on paper. I proofread and edited the draft over and over, until it made sense and didn't violate anyone's rights as a US citizen. With the completed document in hand, I tried to lobby the law and present the idea to any congressman who would listen. After several grueling years, State Senators Barbara Bruno and Deborah Allen endorsed the idea and presented the law to the NJ State Senate. To my surprise, and after a six-year painstakingly hard-fought battle, it passed into law on May 23, 2002. I finally won, unfortunately too late to save Helmut Krause.

"I attended the presentation honoring Helmut; the Bully Law was enacted into NJ State Congress. As of today the Bully Law is active in 32 of our 50 states, and continuing to be presented."

Sherry put her hand over Charlie's mouth, gesturing to stop. The tears flowing harder as she reaches her arms behind him, places her head on his chest and gives him a warm embracing hug and sobs for several minutes. Charlie can feel inside how tender and caring a person Sherry truly is. The questions Sherry asked made him think of all the reasons why he was doing this. It wasn't for Helmut or Chelly, not even for Sherry. He was doing this for himself!

It's now show time. Time to call Long Ngo, time to play a chess game where it's not the strongest who wins, it's the smartest, the one with the better strategy; and now it's time to play this game with Long and The Flying Dragons. Charlie has got to be the smarter one, the strategist!

He appreciated his dad's idea to photograph the inside of the glove. His dad was always a fast thinker. He pondered the concept, thinking once Chelly is set free, the glove will be their ransom to escape. He still has to refine his plan, but first he needs to call Long to tell him where to meet. He only wants Long and Chelly at their meeting place, not Kwan, Duc, Quang or any of his hoodlums.

Charlie decides to make the call to the Dragon's Den, as the phone continues to ring at least fifteen times or so. No one answers, with no voice mail or anything. He thought he might have dialed the number wrong so he redials, getting the same results. He asks Sherry to dial the number, and again, no answer. Sherry begins to surmise trouble.

"Do you think your plan is still working?" Sherry asks, in a fright. Charlie pauses a bit and assures her everything is alright. The time is 11 o'clock in the morning and he is unable to get hold of Long or any of his gang members. That was the precise time Long gave him, and he can still hear his words.

"I'll be waiting for your call." Then he said in an angry tone, *"And if I do not hear from you, you Mother Fucker, by 11:00AM tomorrow, Chelly will be executed."* Then he yelled *"Got it Charlie?"* Charlie keeps hearing those words over and over in his mind, *"Chelly will be executed, Got it Charlie?,"* as it got closer to 11 o'clock.

Sherry's phone rings, she looks to see who's calling and the caller Id reads, J*eong Kim.* She yells to Charlie, "It's Jeong Kim, what'll I do?" Charlie tells her to answer it; it's probably for him. She answers and a female voice on the other end says, "Charlie, I need to speak with Charlie Johnson," as she asks who it was. "Get me Charlie, it's important," Sherry hands Charlie the phone.

The woman on the phone informs him, "Long is already in Chicago and his boys are on the prowl, gunning for you and Sherry, dead or alive, with instructions to the boys *'Kill on sight.'* Then silence. He thinks to himself, *"I have no chance of getting the instructions to Long Ngo unless I contact him first before any of his boys find us."*

Charlie asks, "How can I contact him?" When suddenly he hears in the background, "What are you doing you bitch?" in an angry voice, sounding much like Long Ngo's, then click, the phone is hung up.

"What was that all about, CJ?" Sherry asks with the look of fear on her face. He thanked Sherry first for calling him CJ and then explains what just transpired over the phone. Charlie believes their only chance is to call back to this number and personally request Long Ngo on the phone. So Charlie begins dialing the number, when all of a sudden he hears someone close by in an Asian accent yell, "It's them!" As he looks around, he sees two of what appears to be gang members, running towards them.

He yells to Sherry, "Get in the car and lock it; no matter what happens, do not open the door." As the two guys approach the car, a gunshot goes off and one of them falls to the ground. The second one is a few feet from Charlie, as he sees a knife being swung at him; he instantly ducks as the swing misses. Charlie manages to punch him as hard as he can in the lower abdomen. He makes a grunting noise as he falls over Charlie onto the cement.

Charlie jumps on top of him, but he seems to be unresponsive from his head being pounded on the cement. Charlie takes the knife and the gun he finds on him and puts them into his pocket. Sherry runs over to Charlie screaming, "Are you alright?" As she is running, "Are you?"

Charlie looks around to see who fired the shot or where it came from, then walks over to the other guy, checks his pulse; as there isn't one, he is dead. Then sirens can be heard as they approach, so Charlie yells to Sherry, "We've got to go." He was thinking of taking the one who was unconscious, when Sherry yells, "There is not enough time, let's go." Charlie runs back to the car, they speed off as fast as they can, with squealing tires echoing throughout the parking garage.

Quang Noodle House:

$\mathcal{M}$eanwhile, several blocks away, Long Ngo was invited to eat lunch with Jeong Kim at 11:30am at Quang Noodle House on North State Street in the heart of Chicago's Chinatown, which should be called Asiatown, coinciding with the many different Asian nationalities residing there. Since the early 1970's, the Vietnamese population grew at a tremendous rate, and today the Chinese and Vietnamese making their home here, are almost equal.

The Quang Noodle House is considered a large restaurant and can accommodate 250 guests. Owned and operated by Quang Pham, a Vietnamese immigrant and a close friend of Mr. Jeong Kim. The restaurant is modestly decorated, as the main dining room is basically a backdrop of yellow painted walls with several oil paintings of Oriental landscape. The plain wooden tables and chairs are arranged in rows, cafeteria style, sufficient to seat as many guests as possible for the size of the room. A special dining room, used for noted personalities and seasoned guests to dine, is located towards the back of the restaurant, near the kitchen. The guest list would include the mayor, local professional athletes and television personalities. Unsurprisingly, you might meet someone from the Chicago Bulls, Rich Daily, the current mayor, or Fox News personality Nancy Loo, an Asian American from the Good Day Chicago TV show, along with her husband, and daughter, dining. In the center of the room is a beautifully decorated table, seats twenty guests comfortably. It boasts a set-up similar to a fancy dining room at a millionaire's house. Jeong Kim dines here in this room once a week, and is considered a noted regular.

Long Ngo arrives at the restaurant and is greeted at the door by a young, exotic, Vietnamese woman. He quickly introduces himself and who he will be dining with. She escorts him to the renowned dining area where he will be joining Jeong Kim for lunch. Jeong Kim is seated at the head of the table with two huge bodyguards at his side, when Long enters. Mr. Kim is so very powerful and wealthy, he is never seen without his bodyguards in public. Kim is a small man in stature, stands 5 feet 7 inches tall, with dark black hair, silver highlights around his temples. He wears black framed glasses and dons a walking cane. He doesn't need the cane to walk, mostly a status symbol, but a sword housed within the cane, also a deadly weapon.

Mr. Jeong Kim is an icon throughout The Flying Dragon organization and everyone who knows him is aware he's a perfectionist and will not stand for anything less. This is why he invited Long to Chicago, to upgrade and reprimand him on the crisis in Philly.

"Thua, Nhat-Quo," Long says, as he bows and enters the room. Thua is a Vietnamese custom. Using "Thua" in front of someone's name is a sign of showing respect and acknowledgement of being a subordinate. Kim returns the nod and asks Long to sit. The waitress enters to take the men's order.

"The usual," Jeong Kim says.

"I'll have a cup of pho, a chicken rice bowl, with an iced tea," Long replies.

"Thank you, gentlemen, it will be ready in a few minutes," she exits the room closing the double glass doors behind her.

"Thank you for being my guest today. It's always a pleasure. However, I am quite disturbed by what I am hearing. The problems you have and we face in Philadelphia," Kim says sternly, with a quick tap of his cane on the floor. "You are starting to lose control of the situation. This makes me extremely unhappy." Then he slams the tip of his cane into the floor, as the sound echoes throughout the room to make his stance. He continues, "I would like to listen to your side of the story before I rush to judgment. Start with Thao and Giang being busted, which cost us two million dollars in profit that we lost as a result of the bust."

"Nhat-Quo, I sent Sa'ng and Trung to investigate the details of the bust. Somehow Thao and Giang got into an argument with a white couple. Thao stabbed one of them and police arrested them both. They were given the suicide pills and are now deceased." Kim's face is noticeably upset with each word. With a Killer's expression on his face, Mr. Kim moves in closer, staring at Long.

"Why didn't they come straight back to you with the shipment? What was he doing out of the van abandoning it? Why did he disrespect you? That's a sign of weakness when your warriors," a term the gang uses when talking about their street soldiers, "do not follow orders!" as Kim aggressively stares down Long.

"I understand, I'm sorry Nhat-Quo, I must take back what I lost," Long says as he bows his head down.

"Now tell me what is going on with this Charlie?" Kim says, moving his cane, motioning for Long Ngo to raise his head.

"He witnessed Kym leaving Chang's Cleaners after the murder," Long continues, "and he's got one of our gloves." Then as he pauses for a moment he continues, "The right glove."

"What? You fool! Charlie got the glove, how?" At this point Kim is livid and making it clear he does not want the glove to fall into the wrong hands. The gloves are used to communicate between Mr. Kim and the sectors of The Flying Dragons. With all the latest technology the feds and police use, Kim and Vuong designed a way for the gang to communicate that GPS devices, wire taps, or any other recording devices cannot detect. This type of communication which seems to be quite primitive for this day and age, worked so well Kim decided this will be the only communication link between drug shipments, and any other sensitive information needing to be delivered.

This is how it works:

The Flying Dragons own China Star Clothing located on 2nd Ave. NY, NY. There, at the plant, women's clothing is manufactured and distributed to most of the major department stores across the country. Within the factory, they manufacture the plain white women's dress gloves. All these types of gloves manufactured are shipped to Thuy's cleaners in Chinatown on South Wentworth Street, Chicago, IL. Ms Thuy Dang, who used to work as a prostitute for The Flying Dragons, is now operating the cleaners, which is the front for their communications. She imprints the messages received from one of Kim's bodyguards inside the right hand glove. Only the right glove is used for communications; this is a superstition of Jeong Kim's. The messages in the gloves are the communications Kim needs to get to his associates in other cities, LA, NY or Philly. The information is inked on the inside of the glove with a special dye, and does not bleed through to the outside. These messages get delivered and unnoticed by everyone, including the lady who wears the gloves. The language used for these messages is the ancient language of Annamese which is a combination of Malayo-Polynesian and Cantonese, written in code, known only to the leaders or Sensei's of each sector of The Flying Dragons. No one else understands the language or the code. After the code is imprinted, the gloves are sent back to Mr. Kim. He ultimately has a female prostitute wear them to the city where she will be working and to whom the message is for. Remember, the ladies who work in these massage parlors only stay a week or two in one city before being transported to another. When they arrive, the ladies give the gloves to the *Kieu-Be*, the madam who runs the parlor. The *Kieu-Be* ships the gloves in a sealed envelope to her boss, the local leader of The Flying Dragons, the Sansei. From there an Asian bicycle messenger service delivers the envelope. This form of communication has been going on for the last eight years without a problem, a perfect method and quite effective, at least up to now.

"You are a fool who doesn't deserve your position within my organization," Kim yells at Long. Suddenly, the server arrives with their food and places their lunch down in front of them.

"Is everything alright? Do you need of anything else?" the waitress asks, giving each of them a friendly smile.

"No thank you miss, we need to have a private conversation," Mr. Kim responds. She bows and quickly exits the room. They continue with their talk while they eat lunch. Mr. Jeong Kim gets a call from Danh Duong, his right hand man and second in command in Chicago. Danh informs Mr. Kim of the double murder earlier this morning. Kim is now extremely disturbed when he is told both his warriors are dead.

"How they die?" When he is informed they were shot, he starts suspecting a traitor among the gang. That's when Jeong Kim gives Long Ngo his ultimatum.

"I don't know why I don't kill you right here." Yelling at Long, he pulls the sword out of his cane and places it on his chest.

"You have embarrassed me with the way you are handling operations in Philly. The drug bust that cost us two million dollars, and now the glove situation which might cause us to lose our power within our strategic cities. I do not want to hear one word come out of your mouth. I want you to get rid of this Charlie situation by 6:00 pm tonight. If you don't, I will put someone on it that will. Now get out of my face, you disgust me," as he puts the sword away and the bodyguard escorts Long out of the room. Once Long leaves, Jeong proceeds to place a call to Danh Duong, who is called Danny by everyone, and informs him not to let Long back into the mansion. "Have his men and their hostage evicted from my house. Let him take the step van so they can get around the city."

Meanwhile, back at the Ogden Ave. Station, Capt. Berkshire, O'Hara and Forster are informed of the killings of the two Flying Dragon gang members on North State Street in Chinatown. O'Hara immediately informs the captain he wants to tag along, suspecting this might have something to do with Charlie and Sherry. The three officers leave the station to head for the murder scene.

Face to Face with the Dragon

Chapter 6

*A*s Charlie and Sherry are headed north on North State Street, wandering through Chinatown, trying to decide on their next move, Long Ngo is walking along the sidewalk outside Quang's Noodle House. He appears to be upset and in a hurry.

"Look CJ, Long is here!" Sherry screams. Upon hearing her, Charlie spontaneously slows the car down, catching a glimpse of his hated adversary.

"Holy Crap, you're right!" He pulls the car into a parking spot. Charlie on impulse ponders the opportunity to find out where Chelly is being held captive, he takes one momentary look over at Sherry and quickly back to Long. "You know what I'm going to do, right?" He pauses to listen for Sherry's reaction as he will not allow himself to take his eyes off Long, and replies to his own question, "I'm going to follow this SOB. Let him take us to Chelly. That's what I'm going to do." Charlie was listening for a reaction from her, but he didn't get one. He wants something from her, he needs her approval because he is so borderline on this one, after they were just shot at. He is beginning to realize, as the end of their quest is nearing, the imminent danger they are about to face. At this point, if she asks him to go to the police, he is ready to comply, and if she tells him to follow this SOB, he will. This is the first time since they've met her answer alone will determine what they do as a team. Upon the awful reminiscence of what he'd learned yesterday regarding The Flying Dragons, these guys are natural born killers, with obviously no regard for anyone's life. They hunt him and Sherry like prey. He tensely awaits her knowledgeable response. A stare in Long's direction, who is talking on the phone, as Charlie ponders, *"Who is on the other line?"* Still awaiting Sherry's response, needing her approval, he states, "Might be our only chance to save her." Without being aware, her response will determine their fate and what they decide.

"CJ!" she screams, "Kwan is coming out of a smoke shop, Kwan is also here!" Now Charlie takes his eyes away from watching one despicable person to another. Kwan is heading in Long's direction. Then with a quick glance over at Sherry, their eyes meet.

"I happen to agree with you this time." Exactly what Charlie's been waiting for, her approval. Those words resounded in his ears, giving him the confidence and strength he needed to proceed with what he has to do. The only problem he can foresee is the possible outcome of this precarious mission, an outcome which can be so severe, so harsh and so dangerous for everyone involved. If he loses, he will be responsible not only for his own death but for the deaths of two more innocent people -- his best childhood friend, Chelly, and a precious new person in his life, someone he truly believes is the love of his life and his future, Sherry. Charlie is thinking, "Oh boy can I pick a challenge or what?" He then looks over at Sherry, like a general going into battle.

"Let's do it Stewart!" Charlie yells. Another expression of his that makes no sense but he uses a lot. Sherry shakes her head and rolls her eyes, *"What the hell is he talking about?"* Charlie smiles at her. In anticipation of the sight of additional Dragons' appearance, Charlie is nervous.

"Thank you, I needed that."

"Needed what?" Sherry asks.

"Your approval." He tries to make it clear he does not want to put her in any further danger. When they do find Chelly and are ready to make their move to rescue her, Sherry has to be at a safe distance, away from where the action is, far enough so she can escape to safety with or without him. He could not deal with anything happening to her along with everything else. That's when he spies Long and Kwan get into a cab and head south. Charlie makes an illegal u-turn on a busy street. The cab they're following is from the Cubby Cab Company, designed with the colors of the Chicago Cubs baseball team uniform and their logo. Charlie asks Sherry to write down the cab number and send a text message to his father: "tailing Cubby cabs # 1204 – believes- taking them to Chelly- Long & Kwan on board."

Charlie informs Sherry all cabs have a GPS device on them which police can access to help them resolve crimes. He is hoping they can keep track of them, not realizing rental cars also have them. Kim's Flying Dragons got the vehicle's ID and someone in the gang has been tracking them all morning. As Sherry sends the message she realizes Charlie is using his head, as his decisions are beginning to make sense.

Meanwhile back at the murder scene, Captain Berkshire, along with O'Hara, and Forster pull up into the parking garage in search of Detective Hanks for an update; he is assigned to this case and is gathering evidence from the scene. Detective Hanks walks the detectives around the crime area as he informs them of what he knows up to this point.

"Bì`nh Le and De Pham, two known gang members of The Flying Dragons," as he continues, "they are the so called 'street warriors' who get to do all the dirty work for the gang, while the leaders, Jeong Kim, reap all the profits to keep for themselves. The bullet that killed these boys came from the other end of the garage where the area is taped off."

"Are you saying one bullet killed both men?" O'Hara asks.

"Yes sir," Hank replies. "One bullet got both victims. From what we found, only one spent bullet casing. The murder weapon of choice was a 38 caliber pistol."

"What was Chang's murder weapon?" O'Hara asks Forster.

"A 38 caliber," Forster replies. Then Detective Hanks walks over to the other end of the garage and they all follow.

"The car parked in this spot made a quick getaway. The tire marks go from this point to the exit ramp. I am having forensics make casting of the tire marks. Alongside the car we found a Budget car rental receipt for a 2006 blue Ford Taurus, license plate X71 Z58, and a couple of officers are going to the airport to investigate." O'Hara asks to inspect it.

"Bingo, let's get the GPS Device Tracking number," O'Hara said, in hopes of finding Charlie and Sherry alive.

Charlie and Sherry follow the Cubby Cab, leading them to Windsor Estates, a luxury gated community where only the wealthiest of the people live. People living here have incomes burgeoning somewhere in the millions. Charlie's detective mind kicks in; he's thinking they must be headed to the mansion of Jeong Kim or Hung Vuong; he wondered which one. As the entry gates to the community begin opening, Charlie and Sherry inconspicuously approach the cab entering the gates. Without being too obvious, Charlie speeds up to get through before they close.

"Yeah, we've made it!" he yelps in a low pitch.

"Yeah, either that or we're now caged roosters in an illegal cock fight," Sherry responds.

The street they are on arcs to the right into a cul-de-sac, as they begin to behold a beautiful Oriental designed house set high atop a hill overlooking Lake Michigan. The massive Oriental style roof reminds Sherry of an Asian Tea house.

"What a beautiful mansion," she says. Charlie suspects this is Kim's neighborhood. They approach a bend in the road and Charlie decides to park the car. He finds a perfect place to park, a distance which will conceal them from danger. He believes between the bend in the road and a huge pine evergreen tree, they will be safe. Charlie asks Sherry to get behind the wheel and exits the vehicle. He heads to the bend where he can view the entire estate and its surroundings.

Sherry begins thinking to herself as she witnesses Charlie spying on the gang, "How in the world can CJ think of himself as a coward? He is conquering obstacles the bravest men have trouble dealing with. Although I will admit he is self conscious and from the stories he's told me, seems as though none of his friends ever got to know him like I have otherwise they'd realize, he is no coward. Unbeknownst to Charlie,

At the Crossroads of Terror

Sherry courageously decides to make a call to the Chicago PD with an anonymous tip.

Charlie stays hidden by the evergreen. Kym, the beautiful Asian girl from outside Chang's Cleaners yesterday is standing on the outside of the mansion gates along with the rest of Long's gang, Quang, and Duc, who seem to be restraining Chelly.

The Cubby Cab pulls up next to them in front of the gates as Long and Kwan get out. Kwan pays the cab driver while Long appears to be questioning the gang. A white step van is coming from behind the mansion on a meandering driveway. The Cubby Cab turns and exits.

The step van approaches the gates and as they begin to open, Long Ngo has a strange expression on his face. Long appears frightened, for the first time in the short instance Charlie's known him. He appears quite worried as the van nears. The gates begin to close and six Asian men exit with guns aiming at everyone, including Chelly. Charlie is startled and begins to worry for Chelly's safety. "Oh Crap!" thinking, "What'll I do now?" Another man steps out of the van, holding a set of keys, walks up to Long Ngo. He appears to be giving orders and hands Long Ngo the keys. Charlie takes in Chelly's appearance. She seems exhausted and beaten down. Duc is tugging at her, as if she were a rag doll. Charlie then turns and checks on Sherry; she waves back. He is assured, she is fine. With his attention focused back on the scene, Long Ngo takes the keys and hands them over to Quang. At gunpoint, they get into the van. Duc pushes Chelly into the side cargo door of the van like he was throwing a piece of trash; Kym and Kwan get into the same door. Quang closes the door and walks to the driver's side, gets in and starts the engine.

Charlie is contemplating whether to stay put or rush back to the car. He gestures back at Sherry to hide and nudges his way under the evergreen tree, concealing himself from the gang's view. Quang makes a u-turn as they head toward the exit gates. As the truck passes, Charlie's heart begins to palpitate, he experiences extreme fright. He fears for their safety, thus he prays to God to go unnoticed. His plea was granted, the truck sped right by them and headed for the exit gates. Charlie runs over to the car and signals Sherry to start the engine. He gets in and makes Sherry aware of who is in the truck and to follow close behind without being spotted. His complexion paled after this last event, as he lay his head back on the headrest, panting and breathing heavy. Sherry follows the van out of the gates and heads towards downtown Chicago.

"Crap!" Charlie says to himself, "Holy Crap! Eight patrol cars are entering the gates." In amazement Charlie peers over at Sherry and asks, "See that?"

"See what?" she replies. Charlie realizes Sherry called the police. She was frightened for their safety. "We do make a good team."

Meanwhile in the cargo area of the truck, Duc with ideas in his head begins staring at Chelly in a licentious manner, as both of her hands are cuffed to one of the sideboards of the cargo walls. With her body in a sort of precarious position, somehow her skirt drifts up her thigh almost to her panties, as she is unable to fix herself. Kym notices Duc staring at Chelly and decides to intervene.

"Back off, we have no time for this nonsense!" Kym yells. Kwan, sitting beside her, reaches out and punches her viciously on the side of her face. She slides her across the wooden floor; her mouth catching splinters, begins to bleed. She moans, and finds herself lying on the floor next to Duc. He quickly changes his focus from Chelly to Kym.

"I guess you want me instead," he says, as Kym, knowing what is going to happen, begs him to stop.

"No please no, not now," she pleads. Her words went unheeded and Duc continues on his mission.

Duc grabs a rope lying on the floor and ties Kym's hand together behind her back. He then starts removing Kym's clothes as Kwan starts to cheer him on like a matador in a bullfight.

Chelly stares at Kym in shock; she couldn't believe what was about to happen. How can these scumbags do this? Oh excuse me, they aren't scumbags; scumbags have a purpose in life, these creatures haven't! To them every day is one big party. Chelly gazes into Kym's eyes as she is rolled over by Duc. They seemed to be filled with terror, the look she'd pictured on Phuong's face, the story Kym told her back at The Dragons Den. Tears of sorrow begin to roll down Chelly's cheeks and soon down Kym's face; they both realize this type of abuse will persist, until Kym either dies or escapes.

Kym screams out in pain, she gets slapped in the face by Duc as Kwan instigates the situation, with his loud consistent cheers. Chelly witnesses Kym's body go limp, as her body did when Long raped her and as if Kym's body was gesturing to Duc, 'hurry and get this over.'

[108]

At the Crossroads of Terror

Duc commences to remove his clothes and mount Kym. He viciously rapes her. He pulls out a gun and places it on the floor next to Kym's head. He thrusts his body between her legs. Moving his body up and down and as fast and hard as he could, he forcefully holds her head to the floorboard. That's when Chelly gets the impression he truly believes she enjoys this. Neither one, Kwan nor Duc, contains one ounce of embarrassment or sympathy for her. She is his, to do with what he wants. As Chelly glances over at Kym, her heart is breaking for her. Especially since she started to befriend her after she was raped by another piece of crap, of a human life, without a purpose.

In the front of the truck Long is instructing Quang where to go, to call Charlie. They laugh listening to the commotion in the back.

"I guess the boys are blowing off a little steam, Long says to Quang, as they both chuckle over the sounds of Kym's screams of horror.

Meanwhile, back in the car:

Following the van, Charlie cautions Sherry as she's drives, making her aware if she senses she is going to lose control of the car or herself in any way, either between speeding and weaving through traffic, he wanted to make sure she knew he is ready to take over. Sherry hadn't been talking much since they were shot at this morning, so he tries to make some small talk with her.

"So how's it going?" Charlie asks with a boyish smile on his face. She was so enthralled in the chase, she sat quiet, focusing her driving and the van. So he continues, "What do you want to do tonight after we get Chelly back?" Still nothing, so he asks after a slight pause, "Movies?" He listens and she lets out a slight chuckle. "I am just trying to loosen you up", Charlie explains, "because I need you to be ready for our escape to safety." Then all is silent as he begins asking himself, *Why? I must be a fool to keep pursuing The Flying Dragons.*" His mind begins to ponder how things could have been different.

Suddenly, the truck turns into the parking garage across the street from where Sherry and Charlie were attacked this morning. He cautions Sherry to wait, let them advance well ahead, while he is thinking of their next move. They enter the garage and head up to the second level.

[109]

Charlie tells Sherry to stop the car as the van is slowing down on the third level.

"Wait here while I go up the stairs to check out the scene," Charlie says as he pulls the gun out of his pocket that he'd taken earlier this morning.

"Where'd you get the gun?" Sherry panics, "What are you planning to do?" She begins to fear for their safety. "Don't go I've changed my mind. Let's call the police."

"That's exactly what I want you to do. Call the police, let them know where we are and for them to get here quick. I will take all the necessary precautions. I need to know what is happening, and if I am able to get Chelly. I promise you, I will not put you in any more danger." Then he looks into her eyes and reaches behind her neck. Pulling her closer, he gives her a warm kiss as if he were a soldier being called to duty, letting her know he will be back for her.

With the gun in an upright position, Charlie slowly gets out of the car and walks up the stairwell, keeping a low profile. His heart is pounding and he is shaking with the fear of the unknown. As he reaches the third level, he tries his best to be as inconspicuous as possible. Long steps out of the truck and walks about 20 feet or so away. Then the rest pile out, Kwan, Quang and Duc holding Chelly close. Kym did not get out, and Charlie wondered why. They seem to be making small talk when Chelly calls Duc an animal; she appears quite upset.

"What happened?" Charlie is thinking, "Does this have something to do with why Kym isn't out of the truck yet?" Chelly mentions Kym, but he couldn't comprehend what she said. Duc spontaneously punches Chelly and she lets out a scream that echoes throughout the garage. Duc viciously grabs her and pulls her down to the floor, grasping her face as to smother her sounds. As Chelly lies gasping for air, Charlie is consumed with anger and desperately wants to stand up and start shooting, but he controlled his emotions. Long Ngo now takes a phone out of his jacket and begins to make a call. Wondering who he is calling now, Charlie gets a little closer. Then a loud, clear and distinctive tone is echoing throughout the garage. Everyone recognizes the sound, including Long and his hoodlums. The sound is reverberating throughout the entire parking garage.

"*How could that be?*" An eeriness comes over Charlie. Fear of what he will discover. He turns around and finds Sherry, crying while mouthing the words, "I'm sorry," for not staying put and it is Sherry's phone ringing, creating that sound. Charlie motions to Sherry, "OK, no problem."

"Go back to the car and lock the doors," he says in a stern tone. Long, meanwhile hangs up and redials. Again loud and clear, the sound of Sherry's phone fills the entire garage.

"Hello Charlie, is that you?" Long shouts, as he motions to the boys to circle the area and make sure Charlie does not escape this time, "Or is that you, Sherry? Maybe you're both here," he continues making fun, which irritates Charlie so much. Long says it with a laugh, "Oops," as the gang laughs along and Kwan is getting closer to them. "We found you," laughing some more.

By this time Charlie's brain reacts, not due to fear, but because of his concern for Sherry's safety. He quickly grabs the phone from her and orders her to get back down to the car. He then takes hold of the phone, ringing loud and clear. Sherry goes down the stairs. He quickly lays the phone down in a vacant parking spot and hastily gets as far away as possible. "Maybe they will think we left it behind this morning, this is in the area of the attack." Charlie moves next to the stairs, with Sherry's phone ringing again.

"Hello?" Kwan answers and with a slight pause he yells, "It's for you, Charlie, it's your father," laughing and holding the phone up high. Suddenly Chelly breaks away from Duc's hold. She starts running close to where Charlie is hiding, heading for the stairs. Duc pulls out his gun, points directly at Chelly's back; that's when that familiar sound Charlie has been hearing for the last two days, a sound that yesterday he would think was made by a car, but not today. Today he knows it's a gunshot. Chelly falls forward, lying face down on the garage floor.

"*What a coward Duc is,*" Charlie is thinking, "*She was shot so cowardly in the back.*" The emotions inside him, looking at Chelly lying there, were devastating. Charlie has a pain in his chest and knew now was time for him to act, before anything else happens. He raises himself up to get a better view. Duc is lying on the floor with blood gushing out of his head. Kym is standing at the side cargo door of the truck holding a gun, moving it back and forth between Quang, Kwan and Long. Kym continues as she releases the anger she has had pent up inside, as if an action movie was being filmed here, and Charlie has a front seat to an unbelievable but realistic scene.

"No more, I've had enough of you. That was for Phuong, for killing her. She didn't deserve to die. No more!" she yells again as she is one step from insanity.

It seems to Charlie everyone who is in contact with these bastards builds anger towards them. He has only known these beasts for a mere two days, and he can't stand the sight of any of them.

"We are three, and you my dear are only one," Long replies and they begin that hideous laugh of theirs. "You can't win." They are sounding like laughing Hyenas at a kill. Not one of these bastards even gave one notion or thought to Duc lying on the cement, as if he never existed or had any relationship with him. They do not value anyone's life.

"At least I will get my chance to kill one more of you!" Kym, being the fighter that she is, yells back.

Now everything is in slow motion again. Charlie's heart and mind are traveling too fast for him to comprehend. Long walks closer to Kym with his arms raised. He is telling her to calm down, no more need for violence.

Chelly begins to move. Charlie notices she is still alive. He motions her to come to him. She finally does as she gives him a weary smile.

"Thank you, CJ, you are a lifesaver. I mean that."

"Wow," thinking to himself, "*CJ, you did it.*" Shaking his head in satisfaction, "*I am no longer that coward in Chelly's mind. Even though she didn't say it, I sense it in her eyes, and I'm her hero today.*"

"Go down the stairs." Charlie says. "Sherry Mann is in a blue Ford Taurus and will be waiting for you."

"Thank you, but we've got to save her somehow," pointing towards Kym. Chelly turns and in a low profile heads down the stairs, unseen by the gang who were being distracted by Kym. Quang, who was standing next to the other stairwell holding his gun pointed at Kym, is no longer there. "Where'd he go?" Charlie is thinking, "Now I want to get close enough to get Kym to safety; that's what Chelly asked. This seems like an extremely improbable task to accomplish, but I have to try." In getting closer, Kym screams obscenities at Kwan and at Long but is still wondering, where the hell is Quang? Then Charlie's world starts to unravel once again. Quang appears again, holding a gun at the backs of Sherry and Chelly.

"Oh Noooooo! What the hell happened?" he asks himself and becomes infuriated with the thought of all the bad that has ever happened in his life – to Helmut, to Chelly. His adrenalin was gushing through his veins and the almost unbearable pain in his chest only made it more impossible for him to hold back anything. He has the strength of Helmut and his head is ready to explode with anguish. He is unable to take anymore. Between his heart pounding, the adrenalin, and his mind thinking of all the bad, he does the unthinkable. He stands up and takes a shot at Quang, his body falls to the floor, and within seconds Kym fires a shot at Long; but she misses. Immediately Kwan fires back a shot that hits Kym in her head, and she immediately falls, her blood splatters on the cement. Between her blood and Charlie's anger, they coincide, as the larger the stain is getting the more Charlie's anger grows; and in a rage, Charlie quickly turns to Kwan, looks into his cold and callous eyes, points the gun and starts shooting.

Kwan falls to the cement. His blood now starts spewing out, outlining his lifeless body. It wasn't enough for Charlie, this bastard needed to suffer more. So violently enraged, Charlie keeps shooting and with each gunshot Kwan's body twitches and turns. The sparks fly around from the bullets exiting his body and ricocheting off the cement floor. Charlie was hoping he was feeling every single bullet being fired, so he continues until all that was heard was a clicking sound. Charlie starts yelling and screaming at him, as if he could hear him, "Die Mother Fucker, Die!" He kicked his head as hard as he could. But Kwan couldn't hear or feel anything; he was already dead, and Charlie was out of control, letting his anger get the best of him.

That's when all became silent, as silent as walking out on an early winter's morn, after a fresh new snow. For those of you who never experience this, the only sound allowed is the sound of the snow crackling beneath your feet, and no other sound can be heard. It's like you are the only person alive.

Charlie realizes what just happened. What he did, as he was out of breath, with a rapidly racing heart, tears rolling from his eyes. Now Long Ngo stands up and Charlie turns to face him. Long's gun is aimed directly at him.

"Charlie, it's now your time to die!" Long says in a sadistic and callous way, as he vastly approaches. "It's your turn, Charlie, your turn to die." Over and over he continues with the same line, "It's your turn

Charlie," until he gets 4 feet away from him. Charlie notices his finger twitching, ready to move the trigger. Charlie can sense it's time. Long is ready to take his life away, like many others he has killed in his lifetime. Charlie is trembling with fear, but somehow manages to find the strength to take control of the situation as anger now seems to be taking control of him once again. He looks directly into Long's eyes.

"Not today, you Bastard, not today!" Charlie yells at the top of his lungs and lunges at Long like a rat would when trapped in the corner meeting the face of fear. That's what Charlie did. He looked fear in its eyes and attacked. He attacked for his rights, for the right to stay alive, his right to go on and continue on with his life. *Long does not have the power or the right to decide if I live or die today,*" Charlie thinks as he attacks. As Charlie made body contact with Long Ngo, he realized he is trying to fight a man who is at least 35 pounds of solid muscle more than himself. But it lasts for only a second. Charlie doesn't seem to care. His only concern is to keep swinging as hard as he can, making sure his fists keep pounding Long's face to a pulp. Charlie can sense he has broken several bones in his fist, the pain is excruciating, but keeps swinging, thinking of Helmut and how Chelly called him a coward. They both struggle for control of the gun. They wrestle for control amid voices of women screaming something Charlie couldn't understand. Once again, that sound. This time, it was extremely loud. The sound of a gunshot, and it was so loud it was thunderous. Charlie's body was vibrating from the sound, as it seemed to keep echoing and bellowing from within. Charlie screams, "No, not again!" Suddenly, as fast as it started, it was over. Long's grip was starting to ease, his breath was becoming faint, and he stopped struggling altogether. Charlie loosens his grip and tries to lift himself off Long's lifeless body, but finds it extremely difficult. The blood oozing out of the side of Long's head and chest, the pool of blood on the cement growing larger, by the second. Charlie's body aches all over. He is severely beaten, his arm is throbbing uncontrollably, and the pain in his chest is becoming unbearable. His heart never seemed to beat within normal range for the past two days. On one hand he feels relief, but on the other, sadness. He did the unthinkable. He killed three people, and that is hard to live with, self defense or not. He can now comprehend why Helmut refused to fight his death sentence.

"No!" Charlie is shouting within. Looking upward he says aloud, "Forgive me, please." Sherry tries to console and help Charlie; his senses are starting to come back into reality, finally able to gain some composure. Sherry is sobbing hysterically.

"CJ, are you OK?" tearfully she says, as sirens in the distance start to get louder as they approach.

Charlie grabs hold of Sherry, but the severe pain in his arm and chest pushes him backwards. Sherry is covered in blood. Charlie looks down at his arm only to see a massive blood stain on the side of his chest. He realizes it's his own blood that is all over Sherry and on the cement. He turns around and sees Chelly is lying on the ground, next to Long Ngo's body, with a gun in her hand; there is blood all over her. He grabs Sherry once again, feeling extremely faint, his eyes start blinking out of control and everything gradually becomes dark. He is unable to hold his eyelids open, trying to get what he believes is his last look at the woman he loves. Staring deep into her eyes, everything finally goes black.

Charlie falls backwards to the ground. Sherry is unable to stop him and his head slams against the garage cement floor, making a loud thud that can be heard clear across the garage. He lays there on death's door, hemorrhaging excessively. Sherry is emotionally distraught. She is crying hysterically but quickly realizes she has to help the man she loves if he is to survive. She kneels down next to Charlie and rips open his shirt. Without any hesitation, staring at a massive wound in his chest and seeing a substantial amount of blood spewing out of him, through all her emotions, her tears, and her fears, she knows stopping the bleeding is Charlie's only hope. She places her hands directly on the open wound to slow down the blood from flowing out. She can feel Charlie's warm blood flowing through her fingers, so she presses down harder, keeping her fingers tightly closed until she can no longer feels anymore blood. Screaming, "God, please make it stop. Please help him, he is a good man." Sherry remains there until help arrives, kneeling at Charlie's side, holding his life from leaving his body, weeping uncontrollably and praying for the help of God. "Please help us, God; please help CJ make it through. Please."

Chicago Police arrive:

Within minutes of the first gunshot, the Chicago PD arrived on the gruesome scene. However, with the speed at which everything happened, when they arrived they can see Charlie lying on the garage floor bleeding to death, while a distraught and sobbing Sherry Mann, who is totally covered in Charlie's blood, is keeping pressure on his chest. The scene looked like a small war had just taken place, bodies sprawled in various places on the third level of the parking garage. Everywhere you turn you can see puddles of blood; it just seemed to be everywhere -- Blood, bodies and firearms sprawled across the parking garage floor. At the scene there are five DOA and two injured, as they are quickly taken to Cook County Hospital where they are listed as critical. The dead listed are Kwan Tran, Quang Dang, Duc Pham, Long Ngo, and Kym Nguyen -- all listed as gang members of The Flying Dragons. The two critically wounded are Michelle Kelly Robinson and Charles Peter Johnson. Captain Berkshire, along with Detectives O'Hara and Forster, arrived at the scene. O'Hara sees Sherry Mann and wants her to give a statement. Although they believe she will probably go with Charlie, they decide to ask anyway. Sobbing hysterically, Sherry tells the detectives she is very sorry, but she will be riding in the ambulance with CJ.

"That's where I belong and that is where you can find me, wherever they take him." She also informs them that she is not going to leave his side or Chicago without him. The two detectives, O'Hara and Forster let her go and tell her they will meet up with her at the hospital later for her statement. Sherry hops in the ambulance with Charlie as it leaves for Cook County Hospital.

At the Crossroads of Terror

Jeong Kim hears the news:

Almost simultaneously to the shootings at the parking garage, back at Kim's house the police had 6 patrol cars at the gates of his mansion. They arrived soon after Charlie and Sherry left the estates. They rang the bell, acting on a tip given to them by Sherry Mann while she was watching Charlie spy on Long Ngo at the gate. They were requesting to have the gates opened so they could enter Kim's estate. One of Kim's rules that was to be followed at all times and followed as law, let the police in. Do not give them anything to be suspicious about. First, make sure the place is clean and no evidence of any crime then let them in and give them straight answers. Give them what they want so they will leave quickly and not return to nose around.

Police were let through the gates and arrived at the front door. They were greeted by Danny, who was very respectful and cooperative. The officers found no evidence of any foul play and decided there is nothing going on that they need to investigate. They did learn that Danny had given Long Ngo their step van to get around the city and he was with 5 others. The police left the estate and Danny immediately calls Jeong Kim with the update. When Mr. Kim hears his house was visited by the Chicago PD, he gets very disturbed. He screams aloud and tells Danny, "They all must be killed, and no one must survive, including this Charlie and Sherry!"

The Wounds from the Dragon

Chapter 7

At Cook County Hospital, Sherry anxiously finds herself pacing in the emergency waiting area as Charlie is prepared for surgery. Thirty-two minutes since they'd taken him back to the operating room, and Sherry wants to inform his parents of his condition, but is afraid she will not be able to give them a complete update on his status. She is torn and does not want to ruin any substantial relationship that may be in the horizon. Her reporter skills seem to kick in, she begins writing a script in her mind, preparing herself for the call. Her first call was to her boss Chester A. Wright, the news chief at WWNJ. Distraught, she proceeds to tell him the events from the time she met Charlie. Every grueling detail, from what Charlie told her and her experiences while trying to save Chelly, to the massacre at the parking garage. He becomes excited, knowing his station is sitting on top of the hottest story of the week.

"Can you do a live spot for me?" he asks. "Would you mind? I can get a team to you at the hospital from our affiliate station, WGN TV, in Chicago."

"I shouldn't. I am a mess, my clothes saturated with Charlie's blood, and I'm covered in it from head to toe," sobbing as she speaks.

"People will love seeing all the blood and hearing the incredible story you told me. With the addition, you were an essential part of it all. Its reality TV Sherry, in its rarest form, and you are the diamond. People are going to love you and Charlie after this story is aired." In hearing Charlie's name in unison with the news report, she comes to the realization, this is her one chance to prove once and for all, Charles Peter Johnson was no coward, live and on TV for millions to hear. Listening to his plea, reluctantly she agrees.

"OK, I will be ready when they get here," Sherry agrees.

"Stay the way you are, all messy, with Charlie's blood," Chester says all excited. She decides to call the Johnsons to clue them in on what's happened.

"Hello, Charlie is that you?" A man answered, she assumes its Charlie's dad, Mr. Frank Johnson.

"No Mr. Johnson, Sherry Mann here. I called to tell you, Charlie is in Cook County Hospital. He is being operated on as we speak. He has been shot in the chest." Frank hears Sherry's tearful voice through the phone.

"Is there any prognosis yet? Is he alright?" Then he hears what he fears the most.

"I was told he is in critical condition." After an uncomfortable and brief pause she confers, "My station will pay to fly you and your wife here, to be with your son when he awakens from the anesthesia." She goes on to explain she will give them the complete details when they arrive. Frank thanks her immensely and tells her he can't wait to meet her. Sherry slumps back into the chair, follows her hands to her head and commences to sob. She is the only person in the ER so far tonight, which is unusual as Cook's County ER is one of the busiest in the state.

While waiting for an update on Charlie, her mind begins to recollect the events she experienced over the last two days. Not only the bad ones, but the special moments they've shared together, as she will not allow herself to forget them. Through all the tears, she thinks back to some of the magical moments she's shared with Charlie and seemed to bring a smile to her melancholy face.

With some people, it takes years to get to know them, while with others it seems you knew them your entire life. I can't really put my finger on it, she ponders, *but that was the case with Charlie. He let me in* so I could know and understand him like no one else. He is such a warm and tender being; one look into those breathtaking blue eyes and it was as if I just seemed to know what he was thinking inside. A strong bond was quickly created between the two of us, almost instantly. Like the poem about Jesus' footprints, Charlie's footprints are forever embedded in my heart.

As her eye's fill with heartfelt tears, she is saddened to think after all these years, finding the perfect man, his life hangs in the balance, as he lies there critically wounded on a hospital Gurney, enduring an operation that may or may not save his life.

"How could this be?" Sherry asks herself, "Why? It took me thirty-four years to find him and I am willing to give myself too." She seems to picture his face in her mind as he makes those funny little expressions that drive her wild. Even though she'd tell him to stop, she really didn't want him to, as she so enjoyed every single moment. Then she remembers the story he'd told her of why he so desperately had to do this.

She becomes enraged to think getting the Bully Law passed for Helmut wasn't enough for him. No, he had to go to the brink of death. She continues, I should have been more persistent in my attempts to get him to go to the police. I could have demanded, and he, being the person he is, would have listened. At this point, she begins sobbing and can't help being remorseful for letting it get as far as it has, taking blame entirely.

At the Crossroads of Terror

Sherry waits in the ER, bewildered and upset, recollecting the ever so grueling events of the day; the television news crew from channel 9 WGNTV Chicago, an affiliate of WWNJ in Philadelphia, arrives to film the 'Street Reporter' breaking news update. The cameraman walks up to Sherry.

"Excuse me, miss, are you Sherry Mann?" alarmed by what he sees, the physical condition she was in, ready to film a live report.

"Yes, I'm Sherry Mann. I guess you were sent here on request from Chester Wright, and you are?

"Steven Bailey ma'am, my name is Steven Bailey. Please, by all means, call me Steve, just plain ole Steve. Okay? Are you OK? I mean you look…." Sherry interrupts him --

"Yes Steve, I'm Okay, I've just been through a traumatic experience and I'm ready to let the world in on all the grueling details. So, where do you want me?"

As she is trying to conjure as much strength as her exhausted body will allow, they both decide outside in front of the ER ambulance entrance was best. The crew proceeds to set up the broadcast, and Sherry's reporter skills kick right in; knowing she was doing this for Charlie, she prepares herself for the story of her life.

"Good evening Ladies and gentlemen. I am Sherry Mann, the Street Reporter for WWNJ Philadelphia and WGN TV Chicago."

Sherry stands in front of the camera, clothed in a blood-soaked sweat shirt and jeans, her tattered crimson locks strewn about as they are somewhat tinted with Charlie's blood; she is noticeably shaken up, but the real Sherry Mann is captured and broadcast to millions. For the first time in her career, she is making a profound impression on her viewers, displaying the star qualities she has always dreamed of achieving and unknowingly processes within. Charlie had only told her just yesterday he did not want to make her career at his expense, but unsuspectingly he'd done just that. He has taken an average TV reporter and with his story, propelled her straight into the pinnacle of her career, making her equivalent to the best in the business, all in one very long day.

"We are live and I am standing in front of Cook County Hospital, where two people here are listed in critical condition after both were shot by members of the Asian Organized crime syndicate, The Flying Dragons. As you can see, I am covered in blood from that horrific scene. The blood on me is the blood of a true American hero and one of the bravest. His actions saved my life while putting his in jeopardy and landing him here at Cook County Hospital."

Sherry vocalizes the entire story, detail by shocking detail, of what transpired over the course of one long and grueling day. With tear-filled eyes, it was as if she were making a statement to the police. In adamantly emphasizing Charlie's heroics, she clarifies how he'd solved the Chang murder case in a courageous attempt at saving a precious childhood friend Michelle Kelly Robinson, from the throngs of The Flying Dragons. She exudes an inner strength in her vivid description of details leading to his fingerprints existing on the murder weapon, to the gang's abduction of his friend, and how it landed them in Chicago. She also gave her impression upon uniting with Charlie:

"At first, my actions were selfish, strictly to get an insider's view of the situation and a heck of a story. That is what a good reporter does every day, tries to get the one big story. However, after he opened up to me, I suddenly realized, my story, Charles Johnson, was unquestionably innocent and began to change my focus and a sense of responsibility to him and to my community; to make things right. I am tired of these street gangs and crime syndicates getting off scot-free at the expense of you and me; we are the innocent bystanders."

Suddenly, the live report is interrupted by the thunderous sound of applause that can be heard throughout the hospital and beyond the parking lot.

"As I decided to help this courageous man on a quest to prove his innocence, which by all means should have never fallen upon him in the first place, this is how I ended up soaked in his blood. I am broadcasting this story because we all need to pull together and get involved in every way we can, to stop these heinous crimes from ever happening. We are just as guilty if we don't speak up, because these

crime sprees will continue and more and more innocent people will be killed in the process."

She continues:

"The police in both Philadelphia and Chicago set up a crime stoppers number,
888 Help 888, that's 888- 435-7888*"*

"For anyone with information that can help stop The Flying Dragons heinous crime activities, again that number is **888 help 888**. *We are live at Cook County Hospital in Chicago, where inside a true American hero and his friend lie in critical condition. I'm Sherry Mann, onsite street reporter for Eye Witness News, WWNJ Philadelphia and WGN TV Chicago."*

No sooner than the broadcast had come to an end, hundreds of viewers inundated both stations with calls, boasting positive comments regarding Sherry Mann. For the first time in her entire career, Sherry's true self was captured, which is what the viewers wanted. This was the best broadcast she, or anyone else, has aired in a long time. WGN TV received so many calls, the news director Kevin Scotsman is willing to make Sherry a lucrative offer to stay in Chicago and come to work for him as an anchorwoman. The calls continued with each rebroadcast, giving her instant stardom. Soon hundreds of newspaper reporters were at the hospital trying to get an update to the story, and the ER waiting room was soon packed.

Charlie's prognosis:

$\mathcal{S}$herry returns to the emergency room, waiting for an update on Charlie's condition. Three hours have passed since they'd taken him back to the OR, and she is anxiously running out of patience. In curiosity she walks up to the nurse's station, in search of any information.

"Can someone get me some information on Charlie Johnson? It's been a long time now without any word, please."

"I'm sorry for the long delay. To ease some of your anxiety, the doctor operating on Charlie is one of the best in this hospital," the head nurse on duty tells Sherry and goes to check on Charlie. Several tedious moments pass and the nurse returns with a brief update.

"The doctor removed the bullet and is finishing him up as we speak." It was as if Sherry exhaled for the first time since they'd arrived at the hospital, as she is overcome by a tremendous feeling of relief. Forty minutes or so go by and suddenly the surgeon comes out to the waiting area to find Sherry.

"Are you Ms. Mann?" he inquires.

"Yes doctor, I'm Sherry. How's my Charlie?" News reporters gather round, so the doctor takes Sherry into one of the examining rooms to avoid any possible interruptions. He politely asks Sherry to sit, and begins to explain Charlie's prognosis.

"Charlie owes you his life; if not for you, keeping pressure on his open wound, he would not be alive today. Another couple of ounces, we'd be discussing shipment of his body."

Suddenly, and without warning, Sherry develops a weakness in the knees upon hearing the word 'alive' in the same conversation regarding Charlie's prognosis. Tears sequester amid her moment of elation. She inquires,

"Doctor, tell me how he is doing now?" The physician appears quite apprehensive, his expression speaks in volumes, alerting Sherry's woman's intuition; she prepares herself for what he's about to say next.

"Escaping death from the gunshot wound he sustained, the bullet missing his heart yet lodged into his chest cavity, was extracted. Upon impact, the tip of the bullet slightly punctured the left superior pulmonary vein, creating a rift for oxygenated blood to escape. Due to the massive blood loss, his weakened body succumbed to shock.

"Shock?" Sherry shouts, in distress.

"Yes, and with a reduction of oxygenated blood to the heart and upon the added stress of an operation, Charlie suffered a mild heart attack. Unfortunately there is yet another complication, due to the superficial protrusion amidst his left temporal lobe, which tells us he struck his head quite intensely upon falling, being hit or maybe pushed. Whatever the cause, in the process inevitably thrust him into the comatose state he is in.

"Coma? Oh my God, my CJ's in a coma?" Sherry screams in panic, as her body trembles in fear; she breaks down and sobs again. Her eyes swollen from all the tears she's been crying in the last several hours. The doctor immediately administers a sedative to calm her. He has her lie down in a vacant bed within the emergency ward, for thirty minutes, to observe her reaction to the sedative.

"Sherry, you are one strong woman and the best 'street reporter' I've seen. Charlie needs your strength now more than ever. A person in a coma can still hear tones, voices or other sounds, and sometimes these sounds help the patient recover faster. His brain still functions but only at the lowest level, and the coma Charlie is in typically lasts several days to a week. His prognosis is unstable at this point, but will change, so the best you can do for Charlie is to keep your head up. We'll check on him every hour on the hour, with a heart monitor in place, giving us twenty-four hour access. We will keep you informed of any and every change. You are more than welcome to stay at the hospital, as we promote an open visiting policy for close family and friends.

The Johnson's arrive in Chicago:

$\mathcal{M}$r. and Mrs. Frank and Renee Johnson anxiously arrive at Cook County Hospital in search of their son. They pass through the patient seating area. In making their way to the front desk, Frank boldly requests information regarding Charlie, as Renee nervously awaits with tear filled eyes, holding a picture of him. Upon noticing the state they were in, the receptionist hastily types in the information.

"Are you friends of Charles?"

"No, we're his bloody parents," Mrs. Johnson says in a concerned manner.

"You must be proud of him." The room number comes up on the computer screen. "Oh I believe he is in the Intensive Care Unit up on the third floor, and the elevators are over to your left."

"Thank you," says Frank, "We are extremely proud of our son."

"The reporter announced on the news this morning, your son is a true American hero," she replies with a smile.

The Johnsons take the elevator up to the third floor, as they are offended by what they'd stumbled into, a large crowd of reporters standing outside the Intensive Care Unit. They actually have to fight their way to get to the double doors, as reporters shoot out questions at them.

"Who are you?" one reporter shouts.

"Do you know Charlie?" a second reporter intones. As the questions are upsetting Renee, she begins to cry and drops the picture of Charlie she'd held onto so tightly. The picture lands face down, allowing everyone to see it was signed 'with love from your son Charlie.' Upon noticing the picture, one reporter yells out,

"Mrs. Johnson, will you and Mr. Johnson give a statement on behalf of your son?" Frank having been used to this type of harassment from his years on the force, boldly commands,

"Stand back and let us through, we're not commenting."

The reporters appear to move in closer, as the Johnsons are inundated with questions that seemed to sound more like muffled screams as they reach the door. The Johnsons proceed through the double doors and are greeted by one of the ICU attendants in request of their names. No sooner than they mention Charles Johnson, they're pointed out to his room, which was more like a partition, and all the connecting rooms seemed to form a horseshoe, ten beds in all. The nurse's station was situated dead center, with access to every room all at once. As they make their way to Charlie's room, upon entering Mrs. Renee is startled by all the beeping, and the attendant quickly explains,

"The monitor's alarm notifies members of the care team, like me, when a measurement is detected and out of acceptable range. The constant alarming of these monitors can and will be frightening to visitors and patients alike. Important to remember, this highly sophisticated equipment is designed to provide the best possible care to our patients, such as your son."

"Thank you my dear," says Frank as he grabs hold of his wife's waist, nudging her into the room. The attendant continues,

"Before entering let me give you a quick descriptive tour of what you'll see in your son's room, in the vacant room next store." She begins by pointing each item out, "As you may see, each room comes complete with monitors such as, a heart monitor, pulse ox meter, Swan-Ganz catheter, and arterial lines, the tubes and catheters such as, a central venous catheter, an intravenous (IV), chest tubes, a urinary catheter, endotracheal tubes. There are also life supportive devices such as a ventilator, and an oxygen mask."

"I think we can take it from here, but thank you very much, your kindness is appreciated," says Frank. "I do believe we are ready to see our son." As they approach Charlie's room, they overhear a woman talking; as Frank gestures to his wife to stop, they both listen.

"...and it was aired both in Chicago and at home. So they all know CJ, yes they do. They all know you are a hero, my hero. You'll forever be remembered as the brave and courageous man that took on 'The Flying Dragons'. You've managed to capture and save Chelly and the country from the throngs of Long Ngo. You also saved my life CJ, remember? Because of your bravery I've heard you will be receiving an award from both the cities of Philadelphia and Chicago. I am so very proud of you CJ, and your parents are so proud of you as well, and they are on their way here to see you as I speak. They should be here sometime this afternoon. Now everybody knows, especially all the people you said thought of you as a coward, now they know the truth. As for me, I never thought of you as anything less than the perfect man. That's why I decided to take time off from work, because I will be staying here with you as long as it takes. I will not leave this hospital for one moment unless it's by your side. So when you decide it's time to open your eyes, I'll be right here waiting." Suddenly Sherry hears a sob from behind the curtains and asks, "Is anyone there?" As Mrs. Johnson draws back the curtains in tears, with Mr. Johnson all teary-eyed, standing right behind her, immediately Sherry notices the family resemblance and rushes over. As she reaches Mrs. Johnson first, she gives her a warm hug and they both begin to cry in each other's arms. Then she looks up at Frank, smiles, and proceeds to plant a kiss on his cheek while still hugging Renee. Then she motions for them to go out into the hallway, away from Charlie. Upon entering the hallway, Sherry introduces herself.   "Hello Mr. & Mrs. Johnson, I am Sherry Mann. I am pleased to meet the both of you," as she kisses Mr. Johnson on the cheek again.

"Frank, Ms Mann, you can call me Frank, and this is my wife Renee. The feeling is mutual as we are both not only elated to meet you, but we want to express our sincere gratitude to you and what you did for our Charlie."

"I really didn't do anything, but to stay close by his side." Sherry said as she blushes, "Your son Charlie did it all, he is an amazing man."

"And so is his father," replies Renee.

"I can already tell he is the moment we met."

"Thank you Sherry, but you don't give yourself enough credit, young lady," Frank says as he looks at his wife. "Right dear?" Renee nods. "Captain Fennick told us if it wasn't for you, our son wouldn't be alive. Because of your quick thinking and even quicker reacting, my son is still here, and we both thank you from the bottom of our hearts," implores Frank as he begins to hug Sherry. While Frank's arms are wrapped around Sherry, she senses they've met before. She can't seem to pinpoint when, where or how, but he seems so familiar to her. She quickly dismisses it to Charlie's family resemblance.

"Thank you," Sherry says as she begins to inform them of the whole grueling tale, as her tears follow. Frank and Renee are awed and yet amazed by what they hear, as they cling to every word. She also explains exactly what the doctor has told her and what she has learned about Charlie's comatose state.

"We all need to realize, Charlie hears everything that is being said to and around him. We should include him in our conversations,

[128]

and make him feel alive, because he is able to understand us. His brain is still operating, just in its lowest state; therefore, it is unable to instruct his body muscles to move. Knowing Charlie, and believe me I feel I know Charlie, like I've known him my entire life, right now he feels frustrated and very much alone, so we need to consistently reassure him of the simple fact we know he is able to hear us. The best thing we can do for him is to talk in a positive way. The doctors did all they can do and now it is up to us to stimulate his brain, as they can make sure he's nourished and bathed. All we can do is to wait for him to wake up and keep him company." She informs the Johnsons not to worry, like they overheard earlier, she will remain by his side, holding positive conversations until he awakens from his coma.

"You are a woman in love," Renee says, "I see it all over you, it seems to be radiating throughout this room," as she rubs Sherry's arms.

"Renee, I've only just met Charlie," as she continues, "I know that seems very mind-boggling, and impossible to fall in love with someone I've just met two days ago."

"Mind-boggling yes, impossible no." Renee replies. "Love has no time limits when you find the right person, and you seem to know it the moment your eyes meet. You start being able to communicate with each other without saying a word. I am a woman who has been on this earth a long time and I know when I see a woman in love." Sherry   just smiles back at Mrs. Johnson, realizing she's right. As the three of them enter Charlie's room, with Sherry leading the way, she tells Charlie,

"CJ, it's your mother and father, they came to see you," then she steps back to let the parents have their time with him.

The Dragon's Fire

Chapter 8

Philadelphia Leadership Selected:

𝒯he tragic news of the fatal shootings at the North State Street parking garage ultimately reaches Jeong Kim, as he learns of Long, Kwan, Quang, Duc, and Kim's demise. He is both happy and sad as his long time friend Long Ngô was killed in the crossfire. Although he was upset due to the problems in Philadelphia, his heart goes out to his friend.

"Why didn't he stay strong?" Kim ponders, "Why, my good friend?"

Now a new leader is in order, and the task has fallen upon Kim to decide who will take over in Philadelphia; the city manages all major functions for the communications between Chicago, the east coast operations in NY, Baltimore, and Boston. In realizing he has to select someone who is extremely dedicated, highly intelligent, and well respected by the other gang members, the person he selects has to set expectations right from the beginning, with no margin for error. So he calls a meeting with his leadership council to determine the organization's next move.

At the Crossroads of Terror

Jeong's leadership council consists of six older men, ranging from 65 up to 80 years old, who served in the Vietnamese Military during the Vietnam wars with France, and then the United States. Although they fought for the allies, their loyalty remained faithful to the North Vietnam government. Today their loyalty is given to Jeong Kim and The Flying Dragons. When they came to the US seeking shelter, they quickly found themselves befriending Jeong Kim, and eventually they all joined The Flying Dragons organized crime family. They are in the high council of the organization who help Kim through their vast knowledge, as they have answers to the toughest and yet profound decisions to be made.

The six men in the leadership council are Canh Huynh (65), Hoc Pham (72), Binh Phan (75), Dat Vu (78), Hung Dang (80), and Thinh Ho (69).

The meeting is held at Quang Noodle House, in the back room, where most Leadership council meetings are held. The men are given the utmost privacy by the Noodle House staff. After the meal is finished and dessert is served, the Leadership Council begins to discuss the business requiring their immediate attention. Jeong Kim sits at the head of the table facing the door as he always does. His two bodyguards stand behind him, one on each side. Huynh, Pham, and Phan sit on his right, and Vu, Dang and Ho sit on the left. In the middle of the table sits an Oriental dragon's head made of Bamboo. The mouth is moveable and can be opened and closed. At the base of the dragon's head is the neck, which sits on a swivel and allows the head to be turned in any direction. The Leadership Council uses this for their voting. Before the meeting Kim informs everyone of what they will be discussing, as a list of four men will be considered for the position along with a concise background on each.

The Candidates:

Huc Le is pure Vietnamese who was brought to the US when the war was ending in 1972; he was two years old at the time. The US Army found him with a bomb strapped to his body. He's extremely lucky to be alive as a US bomb squad specialist noticed it and disarmed the bomb before it exploded. He was raised by Mr. and Mrs. Lanh Le of Springfield, Iowa, who fostered him until he was eighteen, the day he left to find himself. He ended up here in Chicago and found himself in trouble with the law for robbery. He served two years in prison and when he was released one of the Street Warriors recruited him with the promise of hot food and shelter.

Khan Min is a Korean, Chinese and Vietnamese mix, with the organization since 2001, when he was recruited as a Street Warrior. He alone managed to save a shipment from being discovered, by his quick thinking. It was then he was promoted to Kim's personal staff, as he lives in the mansion.

Dac Kien, a natural born leader, never once has he failed Kim. He is strong and well respected by his peers. Another pure Vietnamese brought to the US by his natural parents, who raised him until their death. They were murdered by the Triads and when he found out The Flying Dragons were at war with the Triads, he joined the fight. Kim gave him the opportunity and he has proven himself many times over; he magnifies the intelligence needed to lead one of the sectors.

Danh Duong (Danny) is Kim's personal favorite, second in command, he trusts with his life; they built a strong relationship together, since day one. Never once has he refused or questioned any of Kim's orders. He followed them as requested and earned the opportunity for this promotion the day he saved Kim's life, back in, 2005. It was because of Danny's actions that Kim is alive today. He stopped Kim's assassination while putting his own life on the line.

As they finish their meals, Kim speaks to the Leadership Council in an attempt to inform the congregation of the consequences to the entire organization if the wrong man is selected. What it will cost the organization in regard to profits, communications, and in their strategy amidst their continuous battle with The Triads, and the Bui Doi, to keep control of the East Coast.

"Gentlemen we all know what's at stake," Kim explains. "Our communications to the east coast cities of Baltimore, Boston, and New York City." Kim stands, his cane at his side, and occasionally taps the floor to stress a point and begins walking around the room. "Philadelphia is the hub for our East Coast drug business. It's also the central point between Boston, Baltimore and Chicago." Slamming the cane on the table, "We need someone in there we can trust, who is highly respected by the rest of the gang." He looks around the room in disgust, "Lately several street warriors began disrespecting Long Ngo, which led to the arrest of Thao and Giang and also the loss of the shipment they were delivering. We must make sure the murders of the four Philadelphia police officers get traced back to Long and the other four warriors who were lost today." Kim pauses and is silent, then in a loud tone,

"Otherwise the PPD will start digging into our operations. We worked hard to get where we are, and I would hate to have it destroyed by a leader's weakness. Our latest communications have been intercepted, so we will need to change our plans."

"We've been bitten by an outsider." He now taps the floor again with his cane. "He is lying in Cook County Hospital in a coma, while his partner sits by his side." As he raises his voice, "We need to wait out his situation before making a commitment. Our freed hostage is in critical condition, at the same hospital." A little louder, "She must be eliminated," as he slams his cane hard onto the floor. "She has seen the inside of the Dragon."

"So you now realize the leader we choose will be tested from his first day. He will have to jump into the fire and put it out before it spreads. Does the council understand?" Kim implores, peering around the table at each of them.

"We all understand, Nhat-Quo," Canh Huynh replies, looking around the room at the others in the council.

"It's time to vote," Kim says as he gazes out the glass doors, into the main dining area at the Noodle House. Each member of the Leadership Council grabs a pen and voting pad as the voting commences. They write down their selection on the pad, rip off the page, and place it into the dragon's mouth. The member who is facing the dragon's mouth goes first. After his vote, he turns the dragon to the next council member. The first ballad took several minutes and one of Kim's body guards brings the Dragon's head to Kim, seated at the head of the table.

"Nhat-Quo we are ready," the guard says.

Kim walks back to his seat and peers around the room at his council as to say, 'You guys will be responsible for the outcome of this decision.' He opens the Dragon's mouth slowly and begins to tally the votes. Both Dac Kien and Danh Duong get three votes each.

"Gentlemen," Jeong Kim says, "It looks like we have a tie between Dac and Danny." Kim, eyes squinted thinking, *"Perfect, we will assign both to Philly and one will keep an eye on the other."* Kim asks his Leadership Council for their opinion.

"What if we make Dac Kien the Sensei of Philly and send Danny along to be his second, similar to Long Ngo and Kwan. Danny could report back his discoveries and the progress Dac Kien is making, or quite possibly, not making."

The council discusses the positives and negatives of the plan and comes to a decision.

"The positives outweigh the negatives, Nhat-Quo, and the plan will enable The Flying Dragons to survive the worst. We all agree to move forward with your plan," Thinh Ho says.

Kim decides the two other men, Huc Le and Khan Min, will be reassigned to positions in Philadelphia, to make up the leadership team lost at the North State Street Parking Garage.

The meeting continues on into the evening as they discuss the remaining items to be decided at this time. The agenda included changing the May 15th drug shipment and whether they need to change their method of communications, since Long Ngo had a glove intercepted. They needed to make one important decision after another, which meant a long night for all at the Noodle House.

At the Crossroads of Terror

A Dragon's Meeting House:

$\mathcal{T}$he Chicago chapter of The Flying Dragons does not have an establishment like the Dragon's Den in Philadelphia. Their meetings are held in a warehouse near the Chicago Shores. The warehouse is owned and operated by Jeong Kim for his trucking business presently, Far East Trucking. Their main business is delivering imports from Asia to businesses throughout the United States. The trucking business was established in 1986 after The Flying Dragons took control of most of the country by winning the Asian gang wars in the early eighties. The plan was a front for the drug trafficking business The Flying Dragons now find themselves in complete control of. The drugs will never enter the Chicago warehouse in any way, shape or form. Jeong Kim and his Leadership Council are way too smart, and the fact it would be too easy for the government to find. The distribution center in Kansas City, Mo. is where these trucks pick up the drugs to be delivered throughout the United States. Kansas City was chosen because of its central location. The drugs enter the US from two port cities, Boston and Miami and the US and Mexican borders between Texas and California. Once the drugs enter the country, they get shipped to Kansas City, Mo. by railway. The route the drug shipment travels is carefully chosen, as the train engineers of these routes are all members of The Flying Dragons. There they're distributed by The Far East Trucking Company throughout the rest of the country. The Far East Trucking Company has terminals in all the major cities the gang has control of: Boston, Baltimore, New York City, Atlanta, Philadelphia, Kansas City, Chicago, Dallas, Houston, Los Angeles, San Francisco, and Portland, Oregon. These are the cities that control the drug business for Kim's Flying Dragons. The shipment, originally scheduled for May 15th needs to be rescheduled in case the message was deciphered on the glove that Charlie had in his possession.

Nhat-Quo has scheduled a meeting at the meeting house aka The Far East Trucking Company warehouse, in an attempt to communicate to the Chicago street warriors the news of the deaths of Long and his leadership team, along with the new plans for Philadelphia. Kim's Leadership Council was also expected to attend, as they are listed as corporate management for The Far East Trucking Company. It is apparent The Flying Dragons are operating as a very high level organized crime syndicate.

As Jeong Kim and his Leadership Council enter the meeting room, the two hundred plus gang members begin to shout 'Nhat-Quo Long Lac Quan, Nhat-Quo Long Lac Quan' (Number One Soldier Dragon Lord) continuously. As the meeting begins, Kim takes center stage at a podium in front of the congregation. As he makes his speech, he announces the new Philly plans. The congregation cheers the new leaders on, to wish them well and show their agreement with the decision.

The meeting gives Kim a real sense of power. To command and keep this size of a congregation in control is an achievement, and astonishes his Leadership Council. The crowd chants as Jeong Kim steps down from the podium and makes his exit:

"Nhat-Quo Long Lac Quan, Nhat-Quo Long Lac Quan"

A Dragon's Trail

Chapter 9

WGN TV offer to Sherry:

$\mathscr{T}$wo days have passed since the 'North Street Massacre', as it was beginning to be referred to by all the news media in Chicago and Philadelphia. Sherry hasn't left Charlie's side except to shower and freshen up. She talks to him as much as she can and even began reading him romance novels, thinking maybe he can will himself awake from the throngs of this comatose state he dwells in. Furthermore, for the simple fact she enjoys a good romance every now and then, and after all, he does have a strong sex drive. His parents Frank and Renee come in every day and spend two to four hours, ultimately affording Sherry a well deserved break. It's about 2:30 in the afternoon and Sherry, Frank and Renee are sitting in the room with Charlie, when suddenly the ICU attendant enters the room requesting Sherry's attention. As they step just outside the door for privacy, the attendant promptly makes Sherry aware she has a visitor.

"There is a Kevin Scotsman in the waiting area, claiming to be the Chief News Editor of WGN TV, requesting to speak with you."

"Ah yes, thank you, I've been expecting him. He left me a message on my cell regarding a job offer."

Sherry makes her way out to the waiting area. She is hastily greeted at the door, due to all the reporters.

"Hello Sherry, my name is Kevin Scotsman, I am the Chief News Editor for WGN TV Chicago," reaches for her hand.

"Hello?" Sherry responds, in a curious tone.

"Sherry, after you finished your live broadcast, covered in the blood of a '*True American Hero*', as you stated, the viewers of WGN TV inundated us with phone calls inquiring about you."

"I'm sorry Kevin," Sherry apologizes.

"No, I'm not here for your apology, I am here with a lucrative job offering." He continues on excitedly, "The phone calls were all positive. Your charisma that night drove the television viewers into frenzy, they absolutely loved you, and they want more of you." Sherry begins to cry and Renee walks up and gives her a consoling hug.

"Why are you crying sweetie? What we heard was good news about your broadcast. You should be proud of yourself." Sherry looks up at Renee and turns to Kevin.

"The reason it was so real and I was so genuine is because I was talking about CJ." She turns back to Renee, "Because it was my heart that was talking. Whenever I talk about Charlie it comes from the bottom of my heart."

"No it has nothing to do with that," Kevin interrupts.

"Yes it does, and I do not think I'm capable of doing another broadcast like that on a routine basis."

"Yes you can, I can spot talent, and you Sherry Mann definitely possess it. That is why I am offering the night news anchor spot to you." Kevin continues, "Whatever you are making at WWNJ will be doubled and it comes with added incentives."

As far back as Sherry can remember she wanted to be a star anchor, especially one in a major market. Chicago is the third largest television market in the US behind New York and Los Angeles. This was her dream and it was finally coming true, a dream that is so unbelievable. Only those who ever had a dream of something as big as this would understand how incredible this offer is. Under any other circumstance Sherry would be jumping with joy and grinning from ear to ear, however she doesn't.

"Although this offer is probably the best offer I could ever imagine, and I realize in television you must strike while the iron is hot, I have to decline, until I have a chance to discuss this with CJ. So if you can't hold this offer, which I know is unrealistic for you to do, I will have to decline. I won't be able to give you a definite answer until CJ wakes up and that may take a week, a month, or even a year." Kevin looks around at Frank, Renee and Sherry with disappointment and amazement on his face.

"Ms. Mann, I understand your decision and what it is based upon. What I want from you is an understanding of your natural potential, what I see in you is very real. So my offer will stand, and it will be waiting for you whenever you are ready to become a star. That talent is one the television news hasn't seen in years, and you have it. You have it all -- intelligence, looks, voice, and a wonderful smile." Kevin hands Sherry his business card, turns to Renee and says, "Your son is a very lucky man. I wish him well and hope he awakens so he can see what we all saw. This beautiful woman is not only his guardian, she is deeply in love with him. Again, I wish him well." He then thanks Frank and Renee, reluctantly he says good bye and he apologizes for any trouble or inconvenience he has caused them by his appearance. Renee hastily turns towards Sherry.

"That was an exceptional offer, Sherry. I need to tell you something to prevent you from making a mistake. If you are waiting for Charlie, you may be disappointed." Sherry is shaking her head and mouthing the words 'no.' "My son is afraid to make any commitment. Over the years I have seen many girls who felt like you, only to get disappointed. Please understand, I never would interfere with the relationship between you and my son; it's just I would hate for you to lose an opportunity like this while waiting for Charlie to wake up."

"Renee," Sherry says, "I know all about CJ and his avoidance to commitment when it comes to women. I am a mature adult and I realize when I made my commitment to stay by CJ's side nothing would be guaranteed between us. In fact, he may wake up and not even recognize me. That is a chance I am willing to take. I don't want any problems with our relationship, so I hope you do not get upset with me for wanting to try." As Sherry's eyes fill up with tears, Renee hugs Sherry and says, "Neither do I, Sherry, neither do I."

New Bloodshed in Philadelphia:

$\mathcal{I}$t is now Tuesday May 2nd 2006, two weeks after the North Street Massacre in Chicago, and it didn't take long for Dac Kien to get the message out to the Asian Communities that there was a new leader in town, to be careful not to cross The Flying Dragons. The bodies of Long's loyalists were starting to be found in strategic areas throughout the city as Dac Kien weeded them out and had them executed. Police found Trung Duong inside a dumpster outside Choi Funeral home as Kien wanted to make a point to Sing Choi. Sa'ng Phan's body was dismembered and placed around Ng Auto body, another tactic, frighten Robert Ng. Another one of Long's loyalist, Sinh Tran, was kept alive from a severe beating and left for dead, in front of Chang's Cleaners. Sinh later died at Kennedy Memorial Hospital in Cherry Hill, New Jersey. Needless to say, fear quickly consumed the Asian community in Philadelphia. Dac Kien's new regime of The Flying Dragons began with total control of the city and the gang members. What he does with this control and power is yet to be seen.

The Philadelphia and Cherry Hill Police were mind-boggled with the thought of a sporadic, gang-related war and twenty dead bodies resurfacing in a two-week time.

Now Dac Kien and his leadership team of Danny, Huc, and Khan start to plan their future. The Dragons Den's business is booming and their Asian massage parlor business was strong. Dac Kien felt he inherited a goldmine. All he and his team had to do was obey the boss' orders and keep everyone in line and their future will be secure. Dac took a liking to Ly Linh and made her a part of his leadership team. The next order of business was to make sure the police charge Mr. Long Ngo and his boys for the murders of Sweeney and Inzerillo. Kim made it clear he didn't want these murders to get traced back to The Dragons Den, and The Flying Dragons. They heard all the facts from Rudy, who is still bartending at the club, getting the police to focus on Long Ngo and stop any further investigations of the club and The Flying Dragons. Dac calls a meeting with his team to go over the details to plan their approach.

"Boys," Dac initiates, "we need to get the heat off of us and make sure Long Ngo and his team are the ones to be accused of the murders of all four police officers." As he looks around at his staff,

"This case has got be closed for us to move on, otherwise we will be fighting an uphill battle to keep the organization profitable."

'Yes Doi-Moi', they replied, a nickname they gave Dac meaning renewal, referring to the renewal of leadership and The Flying Dragons themselves. Danny, Huc and Khan started to bond and respect Dac as his decisions made a lot of sense to them; it appears the feeling is outstandingly mutual among the street warriors. Once he gained everyone's trust, he had it for good.

"We need to make Rudy own up to the police as to what he knows of the murders that night. He waited this long because he was fearful for his life. Once he found out Long Ngo and the rest were killed that's when he decided to step forward and make a statement to the police," Danny, who is second in command said. Dac was simply impressed with the thinking of Danny.

"Let's make sure Rudy only tells the police what we want them to know."

"Yes Doi-Moi, Yes," they all replied in unison.

Agitation Building in Chicago:

$\mathcal{I}$n the meantime, Jeong Kim dials a friend of his, Dr. Melanie Lu, located several blocks away from Cook County Hospital, and he wants Melanie to pay Michelle Kelly Robinson a visit. "Melanie my dear, it's been a long time since we've talked. I am calling to see how you are," Kim says on the other end of the phone. "I'm fine Mr. Kim, and you?" she says, knowing he is going to ask for a favor or something of her. "Things couldn't be better. The reason for my call, I need you to see a patient at Cook County Hospital for me. Her name is Michelle Kelly Robinson and everybody there knows her as Chelly. She's in ICU on the third floor. I heard she is going to be moved into the general population at the hospital tomorrow because of her improvement."

"And you want her to have a setback, I presume?" Dr. Lu shoots back.

"Ah, you've always been so smart and perceptive my dear" Kim says with a smile. "There will be a little something extra in the mail for you this month."

"OK, I will go see her tonight when I make my rounds," Dr. Lu says. "Peace my friend."

"Peace to you my dear," as they both hang up the phone.

Dr. Melanie Lu has a residency at the Cook County Hospital. She is an internist who also performs minor surgeries like removals of cysts, moles, birth marks, and ovarian cysts. She also performs appendectomies, tonsillectomies and other minor surgeries. She is a graduate of The University of Washington Medical School in Portland, Oregon where she graduated at the top of her class. Mr. Jeong Kim met Melanie Lu as a 15 year old runaway, downtown Chicago. He took her into his home thinking she would work in one of his massage parlors. But soon after having several conversations with her, Kim realized she was a very smart and intelligent girl. He had her IQ tested and realized she could be of better use to him and the gang. So with the help of his Leadership team the decision was made to get her a Medical degree from the best medical school in the country. She graduated with honors and is now working as an internist in Chicago and for the Flying Dragons. Dr. Melanie Lu considers Jeong Kim as her father and respects him dearly for what he has done for her.

Chelly Dies:

$\mathcal{S}$uzanne Davis, a registered nurse of Cook County Hospitals Intensive Care Unit, had just clocked in for her morning shift. As she is pouring her usual cup of coffee, preparing for the shift change report, she suddenly spies two guys from transport headed for Michelle Robinson's room. At that moment, she hastily makes her way to the nurse's station on inquiry of Michelle's file. As she looks over the night shift's report, she notices that Michelle had died after a brief and sudden bout of symptoms, and the time of death was listed as 7:30 pm. Suzanne was shocked by what she'd read, as Michelle was responding quite well to the medications prescribed; in fact, so well she was to be transferred to a private room. In curiosity, she anxiously reads on, as she is determined to find any symptoms that inevitably piloted Michelle to her tragic demise.

The report read as follows:
5:34 pm- complains of nausea, administered Promethazine 25mg

5:36 pm pt. proceeds to vomit uncontrollably. Temp 101* slightly elevated BP undetectable administered another Promethazine 25mg and Acetaminophen 500mg

5:37 pm upon observation pt. skin appeared yellow and blotchy, respirations were shallow and labored, complained of dizziness, pt states- I feel like I'm going to pass out, I can't breathe!   pt appeared frantic

5:41 pm pt administered oxygen, temp. 104* pulse irregular BP-undetectable pt seems not to respond to meds as identified by a rise in temp complains of weakness and numbness in lower extremities

5:50 pm put in call to Dr.

6:10 pm pt suffers complete pulmonary arrest pt intubated with pulmonary edema as identified with pink froth rising up tube upon insertion

6:15 pm pts Dr. arrives Pt administered EKG

6:30 pm pt suffers complete cardio-pulmonary arrest medical staff administer CPR

[143]

6:40 pm pt administered epinephrine temp 104*

6:50 pm pt undergoes defibrillation-

7:30 pm Time of death

Suzanne hastily gestures to Sherry to come over, as she'd come out to the nurses' station attempting to find out who was on duty and to get her morning cup of coffee, as she alerts Sherry of her findings and the fact that Michelle 'Chelly' Robinson was in route to the hospital morgue. "Oh my God, I thought she was doing so well," Sherry says, thinking about Charlie's reaction when he hears the news. "Why do you think they're performing an autopsy? Do you think she was murdered?"

"At this point I just don't know what to make of it, but there is one thing for certain, you must keep a watchful eye on Charlie. You are his only protection now." Suzanne is stunned. "I will go down to find out more information, and as it becomes available I'll be sure to update you."

"Thank you, Suzanne for everything, you are a blessing."

Sherry ponders last night's conversation with Chelly, *how ironic, what could have possibly happened to Chelly during the wee hours of the night? Yesterday, I paid her a visit and she was doing well, so we shared a long conversation; in fact, it lasted about an hour and a half. She first told me how Charlie's parents stopped by to say good bye to her, before they'd set off for their trip home. She also mentioned they were a sweet and dear couple and considered them her second parents. She even spoke about Charlie, how he'd given her the name Chelly and became childhood friends; she even mentioned how she'd ultimately begun having a crush on him in high school. Charlie liked her back then, and she never let on she knew. She wanted to see how far he'd go before he'd finally break out of his shell and tell her, unfortunately he never did. She also told me about several childhood events, some funny, some sad, but the story that stood out the most for her was the one concerning their dear friend Helmut Krause. Even though I'd heard it all already from Charlie, interestingly enough I figured I'd give Chelly a chance to get it off her chest.*

At the Crossroads of Terror

Chelly explained how she'd become so distraught with CJ, to the point that she'd begun cursing him out, calling him a coward over and over, but he never reacted. That was the side of Charlie she claimed to despise the most. She could never understand why he was like that. CJ was strong and a good fighter as well, she continued, as she'd seen him sparring at the gym, and one of their teachers told her that he should try out for the Golden Gloves; that's how good he was. By the time the police came, Arte was dead, lying in a pool of blood that seemed to go on forever. They'd arrested and charged Helmut with first degree murder. She was devastated and wanted CJ to know just how she'd felt about him not standing up for Helmut. So she'd gone over to his house a few days later, and when she saw him, she told him how mad she was and how much she'd hated him for being such a coward. That's when I asked her if she still thought him to be a coward; her reply was 'no way'. I felt happy for Charlie, because even though he doesn't know it yet, he did exactly what he set out to do, he accomplished his goal, and you just can't get any better than that. Chelly then continued with her experience while being held captive. What they did to her and how she was befriended by Kim, who in the end helped save her life along with CJ. She mentions some of the worst things I have ever heard when she explained to me the details of her rape. How Long Ngo had his way with her and made a beautiful act of love making into something as trashy as he did. I'll never forget that story for as long as I live. The horrid details of that day will haunt me and I felt her pain as if I'd gone through it myself.

In her words,

My heart started to pump extra hard and my vision was starting to blur from the tears and the alcohol. I began to be tense, when I felt my clothes beginning to be ripped off my body. Then I felt the weight of his huge muscular body on me as he pushed his way between my legs. I tried to struggle with all my strength, but I was no match for him. I told him to stop many times over and over; I also tried to push him away. However, he just kept hushing me, kept holding me down and kept taking my clothes off while touching and kissing me everywhere. I did all I could do with the power that I had at that point in time. I did not think about screaming, nor did I think about scratching or hitting him.

He seemed extremely strong, and it didn't seem to make any sense to keep trying. I was worn out and tired. I was on my period and also had a few drinks. I had a tampon in, and I told him all these things trying to make him stop, but he would not listen! He first penetrated me, being on top, and later flipped me over to penetrate me from behind. My tampon was never removed, it was in during the whole incident. By the time he started penetrating me from behind, I had completely given up.

My body stopped, I stopped. I felt like I was having an outer-body experience. It seemed as if I stepped out of my body and was watching what was happening, from a different part of the room, not being able to do anything about it. All I was thinking was that he could take my body, but I would not let him take my soul!

I did not feel anything, I didn't feel pleasure, nor did I feel any pain. When he first started penetrating me, I could feel him, but the longer he was inside of me the less I felt him. I just shut down. When he was done, he got dressed, turned and looked at me, as if I was supposed to enjoy what just happened. He snickered as he opened the door and just disappeared.

Chelly's eyes were watery, but she refused to cry. The first step she must take, to become a survivor.

She also went on to tell me the grueling story of Phuong, who was raped, tortured, and killed. How Kwan and his friends enjoyed the whole experience with Kim watching the entire rape. Again, her eyes watery, but refused to cry, holding back her tears from falling down her face.

Chelly continued with the events she experienced in the van. How Kim was raped trying to stop her from being raped, for the second time. That rape became Kim's breaking point. Chelly saw in Kim's eyes how infuriated she was and knew it wouldn't be long for her to turn and attack the men.

My mom used to say, in regard to situations like this, may she rest in peace. God acts in mysterious ways and things happen for a reason. I guess that is the case with Chelly's death, it happened for a reason."

Autopsy Findings:

Dr. Herman Fink one of six pathologists for Cook County Hospital performs the Autopsy. Here is his report for Chicago PD Captain Berkshire:

I, Herman Fink, MD declare as follows;

I am the pathologist at Cook County Hospital who conducted the forensic medical investigation into the death of Ms. Michelle Kelly Robinson. After intensive inquiry and analysis, I have determined the death of Ms. Robinson was due to acute selenium toxicity.

It is my opinion that Law enforcement investigation is now necessary to determine how Ms. Robinson was exposed to selenium.

I have discussed this with the County's Chief Forensic Pathologist and he is in agreement with my conclusions and the need to further investigate.

The foregoing is true and correct and if called as a witness, I could competently testify thereto.

Executed May 2nd 2006

The report gets sent to Captain Berkshire for him to start a full investigation. The captain knows this has everything to do with the Flying Dragons, he just has to prove it. He does not want another unsolved murder case sitting in his files because of the lack of evidence implicating the gang.

WGN TV Nightly Report:

&very night Sherry puts the television on to watch 'News at 9' on WGN TV 9. She contemplates the idea, accepting the job offer from Kevin Scotsman, realizing her lifelong dream can become a reality with a 'yes' answer. Extreme emotions are clashing deep from within her, between her passion for her career and Charlie, for his well being and desire for him. She struggles with these sentiments each waking moment.

The station broadcasts a nightly update on the survivors of the North Street Massacre, Charlie and Chelly's condition. Its WGN TV street reporter, Jason Cornwell's responsibility to satisfy the curiosity and need of their Chicago viewers, by discovering new juicy information, along with updated facts of this case with a five minute time slot during the show. The hundreds of viewers that called in on Sherry's behalf, demand it.

This is WGN TV News 9 at 9 –

From the TV:
    "Hello everyone, I'm Gloria Stewart, and I'm Jason Cornwell with your Nightly news at 9".
    "Tonight we have a tragic update for you on one of the North Street Massacre victims, Michelle Robinson. This morning she was pronounced dead, just three days from upgrading her status from critical to stable. Police Captain Clyde Berkshire had an autopsy performed as her death seemed suspicious. Here is Jonathan Baker with the latest on this story."
    "Thank you Gloria, and good evening folks." **Jonathan begins**, *"I am standing outside Charlie Johnson's room at Cook County Hospital, where this morning Michelle Robinson passed away. According to reports, she died 7:30 am, prior to her being moved out of ICU to the general population of the hospital. Her body was sent down for an autopsy when earlier I was fortunate to get a statement from Dr. Herman Fink, the doctor who performed the autopsy. Let's go to the tape.*

Dr. Fink: *"I determined the death of Ms. Robinson was due to acute selenium toxicity. And in my opinion, a full investigation is necessary to find out how Ms Robinson was exposed to selenium."*

Back live to Jonathan: *"You just heard it, it has now turned into a murder investigation."*

Gloria Stewart asks: *"Do you have any new information on Charlie's condition you can tell us?"*

Jonathan: *"Yes I can, his parents left yesterday morning, after staying two weeks here in downtown Chicago to visit their son daily. Sherry Mann, who hasn't left his side for any amount of time since the incident, is still at his bedside tonight and continues to sleep in the same hospital room, in an adjacent bed. Charlie is still in a comatose state but remains stable. Meanwhile, the doctors still believe there is a chance with rehabilitation that Charlie may return to a normal life."*

"Thank you Jonathan, we'll catch up with you a little later on in the broadcast," **Gloria** addresses the TV viewers.

Sherry immediately turns off the television. Stress builds and her body trembles, in fear and the anticipation of the unknown. Worry for their safety is the major concern; wondering how Charlie's unconscious reactions, with the news of Chelly's murder, is her second. Believing The Flying Dragons are not going to let up, until they are all dead, she decides to call Frank Johnson to see what he knows back home, and if he can call to have a patrolman guard Charlie's room.

"Hello, this is Frank," Mr. Johnson says.

"Frank it's me, Sherry, I need your help," Sherry says anxiously trying to get the words out. "Have you heard about Chelly?" she waits.

"Yes, I was about to call you after I heard the disturbing news, it saddened us; she is a second daughter to us and Renee is grieving hysterically. Do you know what happened?" Frank asks.

"She was poisoned. I've just found out she was poisoned. Oh my God, she died from acute selenium toxicity. That's why I need your help," almost in a scream she exclaims, "I fear for Charlie and my safety, I believe we need protection at our door, or to be moved."

She can sense Frank is extremely worried and is very distraught after hearing about Chelly being poisoned, but at the same time trying to stay calm for her sake.

At the Crossroads of Terror

"I agree," Frank replies, "I will call to have that arranged. In the meantime, call 911, and get some people to stay in the room. You cannot stay there alone, you've got it? Stay safe. I'll call you back as soon as I can. I will call you on your cell." As soon as she hangs up the phone with Frank, Charlie's arm starts to rise.

"Oh my God," Sherry says to herself. "He must have heard what I've said to his father. Crap! It looks like Charlie might be on the verge of waking up." Sherry walks up next to him, takes a good look into his eyes and ponders:

"He is unable to move his eyes, they're opened but they are locked in a vacant stare. His look is going right through me. This might be the 'slow awakening' I heard the doctors talk about. He is talking to me through his eyes. What are you trying to tell me, CJ? What are you saying? I wish I knew. Those beautiful eyes of his are starting to come alive. I hope so. I need him now, and we've got to get out of here.

Sherry picks up the phone to dial 911, the lights in the room start to flicker and everything goes dark. She hears a noise coming from the hall, she begins to panic and becomes troubled. She starts to sweat, fearing the worst and learning of Chelly's murder.

"I got to get Charlie out of that bed and fast. What is happening?" Panic is setting in rapidly, yelling inside her mind. She begins to move Charlie and realizes this may be impossible for her. He is much too heavy for her to lift; she prays she can. The fear of failure is controlling her every thought. She must be courageous and find the strength, for their safety and future. She refuses to give up, lifting Charlie's upper torso in a sit up position, wrapping his arms over her shoulders and dangling his legs over the side of the bed. Panting out of exhaustion, Charlie's head resting on her shoulders, she begins to stand, and lifting his body off the bed, she grunts from the strain of raising his lifeless body, as the sweat, pours down her face and her heart pounds. A sigh of relief comes over her, comprehending she now has Charlie standing. Needing a place to hide, Sherry immediately rushes over to the ventilators. With each step, lumbering like an eternal journey, fear controlling her quivering body, she digs deep from within to find a mysterious physical strength and willpower, to move them closer to safety. She is feeling intense agony, but the closer they get to their hiding place, sense sanctuary. They reach the ventilators and fall to the floor. Charlie lets out a moan.

[151]

"I'm sorry darling," she says as they lie on the floor. Noticing Charlie's not completely hidden, his leg is exposed to whatever danger they are about to face, she profusely struggles to pull Charlie behind those massive machines. Out of the darkness, accented voices, and someone enters the room.

"Oh my God," she screams inside her mind, panting harder, knowing Charlie's feet are still exposed. *"No,"* she cries, *"This is not the way it will end."* She takes in a deep breath, *"I will not let it!"* Out of breath, one more pull, using every force she can muster in her body, with determination and her physical strength, she digs the soles of her shoes into the tile floor; she pulls on Charlie, a little screeching sound is made, but somehow she manages to get him behind the ventilators for cover.

The lights come back on, her heart yet pounding, her eyes affixed to the action in the room. She wipes the beads of sweat rolling down into her eyes to get a better look. Two men and what appears to be a woman doctor or nurse, all Asian descent, walk towards the bed. In curiosity, they start looking around the room. The two men are holding knives and the woman has a syringe. Sherry assumes it must be the same poison injected into Chelly. "Now they want to inject CJ, and possibly me with the poison." Sherry's body is emotionally overtaken by fright, like the night at the parking garage. Her mouth is dry and she sweats with fear of being savagely murdered. Her heart is pumping at a rapid pace, feeling the pulsation in her forehead. She fears the unknown and that they will be discovered, pondering what will happen to them if they are. The terror is making her heart pound so hard, her arms now tremble and her eyes begin to twitch. The thought Charlie and her are in the same room, with people trying to kill them, is disturbing. Perceptive to the fact, the gang members are born killers and kill without a second thought. *"God,"* she screams in silence. *"Please help us, please."* That's when she notices one of them start walking over to the ventilators. She is almost ready to scream out for help as she is in pure panic mode; he is getting closer. Sherry is preparing herself for the worst, her eyes twitching so drastically, everything becomes a blur. He is about three feet away, getting ready to look behind the machines. *"God!"* Sherry is repeating in her mind, *"Please, please, please, please."* Suddenly Dr. Melanie Liu yells aloud.

"Let's get out of here, something is up, they must have moved him!"

He turns around and follows Dr. Liu and the other man, as they exit the room. Little relief to Sherry, she knows this will be a reoccurring scene if they stay here in Chicago. Finding it hard to get up, feeling physically exhausted, she somehow because of her fear of being found, musters up the strength to get to her knees. Once again, Charlie's arm begins to move and Sherry manages to push Charlie off to one side so she can stand and call for the nurse, and calm herself down. She walks over to the door and opens it a crack to look out to the nurse's station. The Asian woman is in an animated conversation with the nurse on duty. Sherry assumes she is inquiring about Charlie, trying to find out where they'd moved him.

"We've got to get out of here right now," she whispers, closes the door, and searches the room for a weapon for their defense, when she suddenly spots a wheel chair in the far corner. Reacting quickly and without any hesitation, she runs over to the wheelchair and brings it over to Charlie and somehow gets him into it. Realizing the door behind the ventilators leads to the next ICU room, she sped out the door, as the woman returns with the nurse.

"Sherry, where are you?" the nurse yells. She turns to Dr. Liu, "I have to report this. We have a missing patient."

Charlie and Sherry scoot into the next room to hide. When she hears the nurse, she decides to take their chances and runs into the hallway to find a safe haven. In panic mode, thinking of the possible tragic outcomes, Sherry pushes the wheelchair at a rapid pace down the hall. Her eyes begin to widen as fear controls her senses. Her brows are drawn together and her blood pressure is rising quickly, she is short of breath and starts to get a headache. She opens several doors to find the safest place to hide. Finally she discovers a vacant room and decides to hide there. She begins praying for their safety, hoping they will make it through this dreadful night. Panting heavily and out of breath, her body trembling with fear, she is unsure, wondering how long it will take The Flying Dragons to start checking the other rooms. Charlie moves his arm again, only this time he grabs hold of Sherry's hand as if he understands the stress she is under, and wants to calm her down. Sherry begins to sob with the relief of escaping the danger they avoided.

While Sherry is contemplating their next move, she begins to reflect on her relationship with Charlie.

Is this love? Is this true love I am experiencing with Charlie? Even through all this danger, we had some unforgettable moments. These experiences are etched in my mind and will stay with me forever. I just wish we met in some other way, so I know for sure.

Thinking about some of the experiences Charlie's mentioned to her, she believes his past benefited him. No matter how tragic, it made him the person he is today, a person who is down to earth, warm, friendly and personable. Especially with all his silly sayings, he is someone I feel I can truly get close to. Sherry then starts to reflect on her past and how she always had to work a little extra harder than most to get the things she has. She starts to feel a little self pity as her emotional state has taken over her thoughts.

Thinking to herself:

When I was growing up, I wasn't liked by any of the boys or girls. I wasn't a pretty girl, so the boys had no interest in me. In fact, I was rather homely and out of shape. I preferred reading books instead of mingling with the neighborhood kids. I was considered a loner, a hermit, staying safe, keeping my feelings to myself, in my own little world. The girls didn't want me because I wasn't interested in going out with boys and making out like the rest of them. They made fun of me just like they made fun of CJ's friend Helmut, calling me out of my name. Only difference between me and Helmut, he let it bother him while I didn't care. It didn't disturb me in the least. I escaped through my books, Nancy Drew Mysteries and novels like Gone with the Wind and Salem's Lot. I escaped to a fantasy world by reading. All the reading seemed to spark my interest in becoming a news journalist. As a little girl I would pretend I was Rosanne Darienzo, the news reporter in Trenton, N.J., using the stories from Nancy Drew as my news. It was hard, but I escaped all the pain of that childhood teasing. Everything in life, for me, was extremely hard to accomplish, as if I was being tested by someone or something. I had to earn everything I got, tougher than most, and a roadblock at every turn.

Like the time when I was trying to get accepted into the University of Southern California. Because of their excellent journalism classes, I felt that a degree from them would be the ticket to jump-start my career and would be worth the tuition. Knowing my parents could not afford to pay for a USC education, I applied for 150 scholarships. I felt I would get the majority of the tuition paid since I was valedictorian of Trenton Central High class of 1989. I quickly learned how wrong I was and how hard it was to deal with one disappointment after another. Soon I lost all scholarship opportunities to the minorities that applied. I did get accepted to USC, but I needed a way to help my parents afford it. I subscribed to LA Times and applied for numerous jobs around the college. I ended up not going to USC and settled for Rutgers University in New Brunswick, NJ where I received my degree. When I applied to CBS Channel 2 New York, ironically, I lost out to a USC Graduate. Then she uses one of CJ's phrases and smiles, *"How Rare?"*

Roadblocks were all she knew or came up against, trying to achieve her goals in life.

The stress changes Sherry's disposition to an uncommon trait for her. She begins to sulk in self pity and reflects on her love life. Unpopular in high school, she became a loner, she never was asked to any school festivities, the prom or homecoming by a boy throughout her teens. She was considered a book nerd and the other children used to ridicule her. With the help of her college roommate, she finally learned current fashions and to make herself up to look attractive. She began to work out and eat right, while a sophomore in Rutgers. She started to get noticed by the opposite sex. She recalls the night she met a clean cut, handsome boy at the first and only party she attended while in college. He paid attention to her, like she'd never experienced before, and she began to enjoy it. She hung out with him all night, and later he talked her into drinking her first alcoholic beverage; it was a White Russian, a drink he told her was mild. After she had a couple of sips, she started to feel groggy. The boy offered to take her to her dorm. Feeling as sick as she did, she allowed him to take her back. Along the way, he tried to rape her, he ripped off her top and bra. She did manage to escape, but the experience will have a lasting effect on her. He spiked her drink with Rohypnol, known as the date rape drug, used by predators and perverts to attack their prey sexually. From that day forward, she stayed away from the guys at college. They were partying boys, wanting to prey on the female students in an unrespectable manner, and she wanted no part. Again, as she was in high school, she became a loner getting educated and didn't attend any festivities at Rutgers. In other words, Sherry went back to be a book nerd who studies day and reading books at night. She ended up graduating in the top 5 percent of the class.   She   still hasn't become close to any man physically or mentally, that is until she met CJ.

Speaking of CJ, saying to herself, *ironically it looks like we both achieved our goals in life. Charlie proved his courageousness and I am that journalist I hoped to be.*

While she was a junior in college, there was yet another big roadblock to overcome. Her parents were found murdered in Philadelphia at the construction site of what is now known as The Dragon's Den. The case was never solved and is now in the cold case files at the Philadelphia Police Department. Her father was a train engineer for Philadelphia, Bethlehem and New England Freight Company. His route was from Philadelphia to Kansas City and back again, and her mom was considered a housewife. Both were model citizens and had no known enemies. The police could not find enough evidence to generate any leads in the case. The case has been cold since 1992, fourteen years now. Sherry spends every vacation trying to generate interest and new leads to get some closure. She has made a promise to herself, and has set a goal in her life to get this case solved before she dies. It was hard, but somehow Sherry, who is a survivor, has set a goal in life just like Charlie did, in order to overcome a tragedy from her past. Sherry is somewhat amazed how CJ's and her life was almost parallel. She sits on the floor next to Charlie, holding his hand, kissing it ever so gently as she falls asleep.

At the Crossroads of Terror

Aye Lam is called in to Help:

 $\mathcal{W}$ hile Sherry and Charlie sit in an empty room at the hospital, Nhat-Quo Jeong Kim hears more upsetting news from Dr. Lu that Charlie and Sherry managed to escape their deaths. This simply irritates him to the point that it is all he begins to think about. He cannot believe Charlie can be this elusive, especially lying in a comatose state! This starts consuming him to the point of being a distraction from his daily business. After a meeting with his leadership team to decide Charlie and Sherry's fate, the decision was made to call Kim's trusted friend Aye Lam in New York City.

Aye Lam, once a formidable foe, now a trusted and respected friend, has a reputation of being the eliminator. He has been a member of The Flying Dragons since 1997, ever since his return flight from a trip visiting his family in Vietnam. On the plane, he met Jeong Kim and they both realized they had a lot in common especially when it came to politics. Kim invited him to Chicago and it was there Aye learned of the organization and was offered the position of running The Flying Dragons in New York. He took the position and started building a reputation as being the eliminator for Kim whenever asked. Although his position in New York required a lot of his time, he loves working on special assignments for Kim. He uses a posse of ten, including himself.

His Quan-De-Kha'n, means Loyal Royal soldiers, a team of highly skilled killers, experts in Thanh Long or White Flying Dragon, a deadly, Vietnamese martial art. Thanh Long or White Flying Dragon, as some call it, is the deadliest martial art of all. They can kill a man with one strike to the neck, head or face. The fighters prefer to attack from the side instead of from the front. The style is very quick and unlike other martial arts, their best defense is being on the offense. The techniques used in Thanh Long or White Flying Dragon are based on the assumption that the opponent is not Vietnamese and therefore likely taller and heavier. Hence the fighter constantly moves, changes positions, changes the directions of movement, uses counter-strikes to attacking arms or legs. The men in his Quan-De-Kha'n are experts. Jeong Kim makes the call to Aye Lam to ask for a favor. It is custom within the organization for Kim to ask instead of instructing. This method has been very effective getting things accomplished.

"Hello," Aye answers his phone.

"Thoa Kwonjongnim," Kim replies' on the other end. As soon as Aye hears those words he knows its Nhat-Quo Kim. 'Thoa' is a Vietnamese word used to show respect to the one who is being addressed. 'Kwonjongnim' is a word used meaning master. Kim usually uses those two words in his opening with Aye Lam. "Nhat-Quo,   what gives me this pleasure?" Aye says to Kim.

"My friend, I need a very big favor from you," Kim says.

"Anything," Aye replies.

"I have a little trouble with a project manager from Cherry Hill, NJ and a woman reporter that I need you to take care of for me. This man, Charlie Johnson, has eluded us three times. Once in Philly, twice in Chicago, and I need someone who I can trust to get the job done." As Kim pauses to take a drink, he continues, "The woman is a reporter from WWNJ, same town. Both threaten the fate of The Flying Dragons by exposure to the law and feds."

"No Problem Nhat-Quo, where are they now?" Aye asks.

"Somewhere in Cook County Hospital Chicago, and the longer they live the more threatening they become," Kim says, sounding very upset.

"I'll get on it at once Nhat-Quo. I will get much enjoyment from this one," he says as both men chuckle a bit. They stay on the phone discussing their next meeting, as Kim is scheduled to be in New York on July 7, 2006.

Charlie awakes from his coma:

 $\mathcal{T}$ he next morning, May 3rd, 9:30AM, Sherry is asleep, in a sitting position on the floor, with her head resting on the armrest of the wheelchair next to Charlie, who is stroking her hair. Awakened by his touch, she excitedly stands up and reaches for him. Charlie is not fully alert, sporting an empty stare. However, he is coming out of his coma. She suddenly remembers what the doctor told her about the day Charlie awakens.

"When Charlie awakens, he may not remember anything. The events he experienced recently, he may never remember. He probably won't talk or even move like the Charlie you knew prior, but in time and with therapy, I believe he will recover."

"When Charlie regains consciousness, reactivity and perceptivity must both be present for him to appear normal. These two elements are necessary for a state of awareness. Often, many elements of perceptivity such as speech, self-care, must be relevant for a normal life as we know it."

"Some common difficulties Charlie will face are memory, mood, and concentration. He may also experience significant difficulties in organizational and reasoning skills. For example, learning, cognitive and daily functions may frustrate him into anger. Then again, Charlie may awaken and in a few hours regain all his normal functions. I believe the latter will be the case, because Charlie's brain injury is considered minor."

Sherry's positive attitude prepares her for whatever waits ahead, no matter how long it takes. The need for communication with Charlie is essential for their safety. She looks deep into his eyes, puts her hand into his and asks him to squeeze. She can feel him struggle, but he squeezes her hand.

"I want you to squeeze my hand, once for yes and twice for no. Do you understand?" While keeping her hand in his, she waits for his answer. The road to safety will be extremely hard. Somehow, Sherry has learned from passed experiences, the roadblock in front of her can be overcome with patience and a positive attitude. Charlie squeezes once, bringing a smile to her distraught face and astonishingly, Charlie smiles back.

"Do you remember what happened to us and why you are here?" She asks.

Charlie squeezes once for yes, much quicker this time.

"Do you think you are able to walk?" He squeezes twice for no, which means they aren't quite ready to face the trouble ahead.

While looking into his eyes, she reaches behind his head and pulls him closer and gives him a warm but gentle kiss on his lips. She can feel the movement, in Charlie's arm muscles trying to hug her, but he is incapable. With that kiss, she realizes Charlie is starting to respond, hoping the doctor was right when he told her he believed it will only take a few hours for him to get his normal functions back.

Looking for her purse, Sherry remembers she left it behind fanatically escaping the room last night. Without a phone to call for help and ensure a safe trip back, Sherry starts to shudder. Now morning, the hospital should have a full staff on duty, making it easier for their safe return. Still frightened for their safety, she remains cautious. Suddenly, she hears voices outside the door.

"I'll check this room, you go onto the next." Sherry begins to panic, her heart begins to beat harder, the sweat beads start to form, rolling from her forehead down her face. She has nothing to protect them from this danger. Her body trembles with horror as fear once again, takes control of her body and senses. Thinking only a matter of time before The Flying Dragons discover where they hid and quickly eliminate their existence, Sherry pushes Charlie into the bathroom with terror in her mind. She closes the bathroom door and positions Charlie sideways against it. She sits on the floor with her back against it, preparing to stop any intruder from entering. With her back against the door, she digs her feet into the ceramic tiles for leverage. She can feel the door being pushed open, and lets out a loud scream.

"GET AWAY! HELP US! SOMEBODY PLEASE HELP!"

The fear in her is now in full control of her emotions and actions. Realizing she doesn't have the strength to stop the intruder, panic overpowers her. She screams louder and pushes against the door with all her strength. The harder she pushes, the more she can feel the intruder push. With the feeling of defeat, her heart pulsating, the sweat now a steady flow, she looks over at Charlie and he is in the chair at a 35 degree angle, ready to tip over. Sherry screams hysterically. Charlie has a frightened look, seeing Sherry in tears, seemingly out of control of her senses, releases the pressure on the door. She grabs Charlie to prevent him from another fall. The door swiftly opens and Charlie falls on top of Sherry, the wheelchair falls on both their legs. Emotionally frightened to death and crying frantically out of control, Sherry looks up only to see a face in the opening of the door as it opens slowly. "**HELP!!**" Sherry is screaming at the top of her lungs, hysterically and in a panic. She has lost total control of herself, all she is capable of doing is screaming and crying. The face emerges and it is a policeman. He pushes the door to enter the room. Even with the relief of knowing they are safe, Sherry can't seem to take control of her emotions; she continues to scream hysterically in a panic and can't seem to stop.

"Calm down lady, I am here to help you. Please," the officer says in a consoling manner. "Are you alright?"

As he tries to help Charlie and Sherry off the floor, she remains hysterical, kicking and punching the officer, who so desperately wants to help.

"I need help," the officer yells out. Several other officers and one nurse come to the aid of the officer. They finally get Sherry off the bathroom floor and escort her to the bed.

Several minutes passed and Sherry is still gasping for air, holding on to her chest and shivering with fear from the events. She is on the verge of passing out and the nurse calls a doctor in to evaluate her.

"This woman is frantic." The doctor says, "Nurse, bring me a syringe with 2 cc's of midazolam."

"Right away, Dr. Miller." The nurse runs to get the sedative.

"How long has she been like this?" Dr. Mille asks the officer.

"I don't know. She has been like this the ten minutes I've been here," one officer replies.

The nurse returns and Dr. Miller injects the sedative.

"Wait five minutes before you move her. She will be a bit groggy but this should calm her down." Dr. Miller tells the nurse, "Call me if she remains in a panic state."

"I will doctor," the nurse replies.

In a mental fog from the sedative, Sherry can hear the officer call someone on his radio.

"Found them sir, in room 310, and I will have them escorted back once we get the okay from the nurse to move Sherry."

"What happened?" Captain Clyde Berkshire asks.

"She had a panic attack and was given a sedative."

It takes a little longer than five minutes, but finally the officers are given the ok to move Sherry.

During the events of the morning, Charlie was making strange noises, he wanted to get over to Sherry and comfort her, but this is an impossible maneuver for him at this stage of his consciousness. Still unable to command his body, the nurse notices tears running down his cheeks.

"Are you able to talk?" she asks Charlie, as he is making inaudible sounds. The nurse tries some TLC but quickly realizes he needs to get closer to Sherry. She wheels Charlie over to the bed and he moves his arm to touch Sherry's hand, his tears subside and a smile brightens his face.

The two are escorted back to room 352, with a nurse's aide pushing Charlie and several officers at their side. She also sees detectives O'Hara and Forster with that decorated Chicago Captain, she forgot his name, wondering why they are back in Chicago. As they get closer the detectives walk over to Sherry and tell her they have been looking for them, fearing for their safety. They have been worried since Charlie's dad Frank called in a frenzy. "He is worried about the both of you. He insisted we come up to Chicago and bring the two of you back to Jersey where you belong." With all the excitement, it took a while to notice, but Charlie was awake and as the detectives raise his arm to give him a handshake in congratulating him for his heroics, unnoticed, he shakes back.

"Are you alright? You look like you've been through hell?" Detective O'Hara asks Sherry as her eyes were swelled from tears and her hair soaked from her sweat.

"I'm ready to go, let's get back to Jersey," she says despairingly and enters the room.

At the Crossroads of Terror

Captain Berkshire's News Conference:

Captain Clyde Berkshire was a natural at these news conferences, as he's had many appearances on A&E's Cold Case television shows. He opens with the facts and what they have learned about Chelly's murder. He went on to state the events of last night's murder attempts on Charlie and Sherry. He has stated that the Chicago Police Department is giving this case a high priority because this is a continuation of events that spilled over from Philadelphia. He mentioned they will put a lot of pressure on Chicago's Asian community and feels that somehow this is gang related. Although he has no evidence, he wants to get The Flying Dragons' attention on this one. He also added the fact that he feels a local Asian doctor is connected somehow. He announces Charlie is awake but still incoherent. He and Sherry are scheduled to be moved to a safer location. The reporters and television crews at the scene want to see Charlie and Sherry for a statement, as the Captain thanks everyone and walks away from the podium. The crowd can be heard calling for Sherry through the Hospital room window where they are. Sherry's phone rings.

"Hello Sherry, it's me Kevin Scotsman WGN TV Chicago," he says anxiously. "Can you do another live spot for me with Charlie?" he asks, as he desperately wants her approval.

"Why, is this necessary?" Sherry answers back.

"Yes, and you will be paid handsomely for this one spot," Kevin pleads with her. Sherry agrees to do a short spot as long as it doesn't put her or CJ in any more danger. She wants it aired right from his hospital room 352, where the two of them have been staying since the North Street Garage incident. She asks for Suzanne Davis, a registered nurse here at the hospital, with police security all around, and only one cameraman. Sherry requests Steven Bailey. Kevin agrees and with the help of Detectives O'Hara and Forster and Captain Berkshire, Sherry Mann the street reporter again goes live in Chicago and Philly.

Sherry Man, Street Reporter, Live Broadcast:

𝒯he broadcast was set up within 25 minutes. Although Sherry is unhappy doing a live broadcast without any glamorous makeup she usually wears, once again she will present her true self to television viewers, wearing her street clothes. In the meantime, back at the estate of Jeong Kim, Mr. Kim has been informed of the upcoming broadcast and orders all televisions be tuned in to Sherry's broadcast. He wants his warriors to know what Charlie and Sherry look like. Sherry's broadcast that captured the hearts of the people in Chicago, and in Philadelphia a couple of weeks ago, during her live report at the hospital soon after the North Street Massacre, is still fresh in the viewer's minds. Her persona continues to charm the television viewers who watch now.

Her hair is combed straight back and not her usual perm. The reddish color of her hair seems to brighten the room with her elegance. Wearing everyday street clothes, a lightweight sweatshirt and a pair of stylish blue jeans, she begins the broadcast. Holding the microphone up to her face, she begins with the story of her escapade last night with Charlie, as he was healing from the wounds he suffered defeating The Flying Dragons at the North Street Garage.

"Good Afternoon, my name is Sherry Mann, the street reporter for WWNJ Philadelphia, and WGN TV Chicago. We are reporting to you live from inside the room, where Charlie Johnson and I have spent the last 16 nights. With me today is Charlie 'our true American hero'. To his right, Cook County's registered nurse, Suzanne Davis, who befriended me at my time of grief and my favorite working here at the Intensive Care Unit."

Sherry continues to explain the events that took place overnight from the time she learned the cause of Chelly's death until she was found by Officer Joe Collins from the county's Sheriff's office. She told of the startling details that terrified her so, while making it interesting for television viewers to hold onto her every word. This is something hard to accomplish, and only a few, very experienced, developed and talented reporters can do. However, Sherry manages to shine, as her natural talent seems to overcome everything she has been under these last few weeks. She was back there in her childhood, pretending to be Rosanne Darienzo as she explained the attempted murder, like a well-

[164]

polished and veteran reporter. She explains the extreme fear she felt and how the panic attack she experienced took over all her senses while she was lying on the bathroom floor with her back against the door trying so desperately to protect herself and Charlie from the intruder. The heightened fright that overcame her when the door opened and she saw a face peering in at the two of them. She lost all self control and went uncontrollably berserk and needed to be given a sedative by the hospital staff doctor in order to calm down. She was simply fantastic doing this live spot that even Steven Bailey, the cameraman, was impressed with the outcome. He can already tell he'll have very little editing to do for tonight's rebroadcast. He believes, just like everyone else that is watching Sherry's broadcast, that she is a natural at this, and soon she is going to be a big star.

"Charlie can communicate to us by using a simple hand language we came up with. With his hand in ours he squeezes once, replying yes answer and twice for no. RN Suzanne Davis will hold Charlie's hand and relay Charlie's answer to your questions. WGN TV has set up a toll free telephone number known to all of you via API services. The calls will come directly into this room and will be answered by our cameraman, Steven Bailey."

The first call is a question for Charlie, sitting in from of the camera, with a blank stare, trying to remain focused.

"Were you aware of Sherry by your bedside while you were lying there in a coma?"

Nurse Suzanne answers, *"He squeezed once, so that is a yes."*'
The next question is directed at Sherry.

"How does it feel to be loved by almost everyone in Chicago? All the people who have seen your broadcasts do."

"I don't understand, what do you mean?" Sherry asks the caller.

"You have been the topic of all the radio talk shows here in Chicago, as people are trying to find out everything they can about you. Where did you come from, are you married, how old are you? I work for the Chicago Sun-Times and we have received thousands of letters from people asking the same. You are the most popular person in Chicago right now. So I ask you, how does it feel to be loved by almost everyone in Chicago who has seen or heard you?"

Sherry blushes with embarrassment and shock, as she knew nothing about what this caller has mentioned.

"I am honored to be loved by the people of Chicago. I was oblivious to everything but Charlie's well-being." slight pause. *"My whole life I have dreamt of a moment like this, but today my thoughts are not on me or my career, but only on Charlie's rehab."*

Everyone watching can see the sparkling of her eyes through the camera's lens as she becomes a bit teary-eyed.

"Next question," she says.

That question seemed to change focus of the callers, from Charlie to Sherry. The questions were addressed to her, and after the third straight question she makes the following statement.

"I am honored to be asked all these questions but I would prefer for the questioning to be asked to Charlie, after all he is the real hero in all of this."

The broadcast continues for another 5 minutes. She uses the final minutes to remind the viewers of the phone number the police have set up.

"Let us not forget the hotline set up by the Philadelphia and Chicago police departments".

"For anyone with information that can help stop some of The Flying Dragons crimes, that number is **888 help 888***"*

"Once again we are live at Cook County Hospital in Chicago. So from all of us here: Charlie Johnson, Suzanne Davis, Steven Bailey and myself, Sherry Mann street reporter for Eye Witness News, WWNJ Philadelphia and WGN TV Chicago, be safe and have a fabulous evening."

As soon as the broadcast ends, television viewers start to flood the phone lines of WGN TV and WWNJ, raving about Sherry's report. Something like this never goes unnoticed by the television station executives. Everything has to do with ratings and Sherry had the highest rating of all the local reporters in Chicago, Philadelphia, and northern New Jersey, year to date.

At the end of the broadcast Jeong Kim slams his cane on his desk and says, "This has got to end."

At the Crossroads of Terror

Continued violence in Philadelphia:

$\mathcal{T}$he whole area was glowing in orange, as the flames from Chang's Cleaners engulfed the entire street. The smell of ash was everywhere as people started to gather around outside to see this astonishing light show. The sirens were deafening and seemed to take over the sounds of flames flapping high into the night air. The smoked filled the surrounding neighborhoods as the fire department had a van traveling around the streets with sound speakers, asking people to evacuate their homes. The feeling was eerie and people were gasping for air as the streets were being taken over with the scent of burning chemicals, causing their eyes to burn. The fumes from the burning cleaning chemicals are deadly if inhaled for a long period of time. The mayor ordered an evacuation for the surrounding 2 block radius. It was Wednesday evening, 7:30 pm on May 10th 2006, when neighboring business owners of Chang's Cleaners began calling into 911 reporting the fire. The fire spread rapidly throughout the store as it consumed the dry laundry in its path. The cleaning chemicals added to its intensity and the blaze was so intense the sprinkler system failed to slow down the fire's fury.

The Fire Department was on the scene within 12 minutes after the first call, and according to Cherry Hill Fire Chief Jeff Andrews, that was 12 minutes too late to save Chang's. The fire was eventually taken under control and stopped from spreading to neighboring stores, but the intensity of the fire caused Mr. Andrews to become suspicious. Fire Marshals David Farley and Corby Ryan were sent in to investigate the fire. Over the past several weeks, these guys have been scrutinized in the local papers for conducting a bogus investigation using junk science in 'the state vs. Smith.' This case is getting national attention and Court TV is broadcasting the case daily. Everything seemed to be smoldering after the fire was out. Gas masks were worn to protect against the deadly chemical fumes. In the corner of the stockroom, they found the charcoal remains of two bodies. These bodies were so badly burned that they became fused to the floor boards and some of the body parts had to be amputated in order to free the remains, for forensics to obtain a positive identification.

The news spread quickly throughout the Asian community about the bodies found in the Chang's fire. Hearing there was an arson investigation and finding the two bodies inside the store, Cherry Hill Police Captain Steve Laper assigned two detectives to help in this investigation. It appeared to be a clear-cut case of an accidental fire, until the dry cleaning chemicals were tested. The chemical label read Tetrachloroethylene, but forensics tested the residue in the containers and found ethanol, an accelerant which fueled the blaze. This was now considered a homicide by arson. Through forensics, the bodies were identified as Mrs. Chang and her daughter Linh, who turned 21 last week. Soon Asian bodies were turning up again and on May 13th, three days after he made a statement to the Philadelphia PD, the body of Rudy Van, the bartender at the Dragons Den, turned up dead in his home in Camden NJ. He testified former gang members, Long Ngo, Kwan Tran, and Duc Pham were responsible for the murders of the four missing police officers. His death was listed as a homicide by stabbing. Since Dac Kien took over in Philadelphia, all possible threats to the organization were taken care of except for two, Charlie and Sherry.

Nhat-Quo, Jeong Kim, wanted Charlie and Sherry dead so bad that he offered anyone who brought their dead, lifeless bodies to him a $100,000.00 reward. The gang never heard of such a thing but everyone was in and on the lookout. The reward was even made to the external people who did business with the gang. Needless to say when Sherry goes back to her street reporter's job, she will be an easy open target for the gang.

The Dragon Goes Hunting

Chapter 10

Two months later:

$\mathcal{J}$uly 4th, two months since Charlie had awoken from his coma and astonishingly, made a full recovery. In Sherry's mind, she thought it would take much longer, as she had to work harder than most to get what she wants, and she wants Charlie more than anything. For the last two months a physical therapist has come to see Charlie daily. The therapist has been working with him so he can get back to his normal activities.

Sherry and Charlie have been staying at the Johnson's summer house, on the Jersey shore in Point Pleasant. Summer is now in full swing as the local homes in the area are rented; vacationing families, blankets and umbrellas fill the white sandy beach. The days were so beautiful, Sherry began to see why so many families owned beach houses. The air is fresh and clean, a pleasant smelling scent with the salt from the Atlantic Ocean.

Children are building sandcastles on the beach along the breaking waves, feeding Sherry's desire to join in the fun. She desperately wants to bask in the sunshine with the cool salt-air breeze blowing on her face, hoping Charlie is soon up to it. She sees couples holding hands, walking along the boardwalk where there are plenty of activities to enjoy. Restaurants, coffee shops and cafes create the aromas for a great evening with your lover. At night the place pulsates with the lights, the rides from the amusement park and the local taverns, where music is heard into the night. The place is amazing, and she wishes her parents vacationed here when she was a little girl.

Today is the Fourth of July and tonight is the big fireworks display. Out in the Atlantic, Sherry can see 3 large cargo boats beginning to line up about a half mile from shore. Meanwhile Charlie is in the den doing the last of his exercises with his therapist.

"All done for today, great job, CJ," the therapist says as she walks out to say goodbye to Sherry.

"How is he doing?" Sherry asks. The nurse looks at Sherry with a smile.

"He won't need me anymore after today, he is as good as new." As she heads for the door, "Have a great fourth everyone," then she exits.

"Good as new," Sherry thinks, *"Maybe we can finally do something to enjoy ourselves today."* Sherry is stir-crazy, not being allowed to go and do as she pleases, being held captive for their safety, from the dangers of the Flying Dragons. She sleeps in one of the smaller bedrooms and Charlie sleeps in the master. This is the sleeping arrangement since they arrived.

Charlie is still working out when Sherry walks in.

"I think you've had enough, there, big boy," she says and walks up to him and rubs his shoulders. "Let's stroll the boardwalk today and have a little fun to take our minds off everything. What do you say?"

"Sounds great, but I need to work out another fifteen minutes more. I haven't been in this shape my entire life, and I am beginning to like it." Sherry's eyes widen as she watches him lift.

"Wow, he sure does look fantastic, but I've liked his physique from the beginning," thinking to herself as a smile brightens her face. Sherry doesn't know it, but the reason Charlie has been vigorously working out, he is trying to build muscles to avenge Chelly's murder.

Charlie has kept the secret, knowing Chelly was murdered, because he knew Sherry wanted to be the one to tell him when she thought he could accept it without a setback. Internally, Charlie is fuming and ready to take action. All his life, never being afraid of a physical fight was something his friends never saw, because most of the kids feared Charlie. His physical strength and his boxing ability was enough to scare them away.

"Don't forget your parents are coming today to spend the fourth with you," Sherry says as she throws one of those beautiful smiles at Charlie.

"I'm sorry, they phoned yesterday while you were getting some sun. They had to change their plans and are spending the fourth with my sister and her family."

The last several days Sherry noticed Charlie starting to get forgetful. "I hope it isn't permanent." The phone rings.

"Hello."

"Sherry, can I speak with Charlie?" the man on the phone asks.

"CJ, it's for you." She puts the phone down on the table and walks back into the kitchen.

"Hello, this is CJ," holding the phone to his ear.

"Gotcha," then click, to a dial tone. Charlie starts to worry.

"Oh my God, they found us." He wasn't quite ready for this yet, and he must have looked shocked when Sherry walked back into the room and begins questioning him.

"What's the matter? Who was that on the phone? CJ, talk to me, please," with the resounding feeling of panic inside of her. He looks back at what he perceives to be the most precious person he knows.

"We've got to pack and leave here right away. They know we're here."

"Who, CJ? Who knows we're here, The Flying Dragons?" Sherry says as she looks into his eyes. At that moment, a loud bang, sounding like a gunshot, they dive to the floor simultaneously to take cover. Charlie lifts his head and realizes it's the fireworks, so he gets up.

"Let's go, it's probably kids shooting off fireworks, it is the fourth you know."

They get up, pack a few items and head for the garage. As Charlie is loading the car, he notices two Asian youths on the boardwalk, one looking down and pointing at them while talking to

[171]

someone on the phone. Without telling Sherry anything, Charlie motions for her to hurry and get into the car. He pulls the car out of the driveway and turns on Beach Street heading towards Ocean Ave., the exit out. He really doesn't have a plan of action. He knows they need to hurry for safety reasons. Glancing over at Sherry, who is extremely worried, beginning to shiver with fear, Charlie feels sadness for getting her involved in this situation because of a stupid hang-up. He knows Sherry has emotional feelings for him, maybe it's love; to stay around this long, it has to be. She has been here by his side the entire journey, caring for his every need, consoling him and when he was unconscious, through the danger. She even saved his life several times during this mess. He feels he has to say something to loosen her up.

"I'm sorry," keeping his eyes straight ahead. "Did I ever tell you I was sorry for getting you involved in all this?" Sherry looks at him and replies a little differently.

"No, but did I tell you about my woman's intuition?" sensing something is terribly wrong.

"More than once," as he looks into his rear view and can see that they are gaining, so he decides to speed up.

"Well I will say it differently this time. What's wrong? Why are we speeding?" Sherry asks as she is trying to look at all the cars around them, "Who's following us?" Charlie sees that she is staring into his eyes. He knows she wants the truth but he also does not want to frighten her any more than she already is, and thinking, *I got to be strong."*

"If I tell you, will you be okay with it?" She nods as he continues, "I think it is only two this time," as he persistently looks into the rear view mirror. "Yep, there are only two." Then in the corner of his eyes he spots Goudy Ave., and turns off Ocean parkway. He remembers the treehouse Chelly, Helmut and he built on Ridgefield Drive. If it is anything like he knew it as a kid, he thinks he can protect Sherry and fight back as well.

"Where are you going?" Sherry asks, as she is starting to get a little more nervous seeing only a few houses and mostly woods. Charlie's adrenalin begins to flow through his veins.

"To fight these bastards, I want to stop them. I am tired of looking behind my back every day." Then he pulls into the wooded lot on Ridgefield Drive and shuts off the car. He motions to Sherry to hurry and says, "Stay close, if you can't, let me know."

At the Crossroads of Terror

"*Wow CJ is feeling like a soldier and not like the laid back guy he was a few months ago.*"

"There it is," he says sort of stunned, "It's still here." He looks at Sherry and tries to show her that this tree is one of the easiest to climb, even for a girl. "Follow what I do, put your feet where I put my feet and let's climb up." He looks into her eyes and says, "Please let me know if you have difficulties," as he starts up the tree.

"Get moving slowpoke, you're slowing me down," Sherry says as Charlie looks back and sees a smile on that pretty little face of hers.

"At the top of this tree is a treehouse, small but adequate for us to fit in." Charlie says as he enters, "Climb on in, now we sit and wait." Charlie looks at Sherry, deep into her eyes and thinks, "*Even with all we have gone through, I am extremely lucky to have her sitting in the old treehouse with me.*" Aloud, "I built this house," he says as he gives Sherry one of those faces. She gives him a strange look, like he is insane but he continues, "That's right, with the help of Helmut and Chelly we had the best treehouse of anyone." Then the car enters the lot, parks behind their car to prevent them from leaving.

"Hush," Charlie says to Sherry as the two guys get out, each holding a knife. They look like hunters in search of their prey, Charlie and Sherry. One walks to the right while the other to the left towards the tree they are hiding in. Sherry begins to sweat, letting her fear get the best of her, like the fear she experienced in the hospital. When she looks at Charlie, she begins to calm herself down, seeing a man who is not going to let anything bad happen to her. No not this time; she has extreme confidence in him. Charlie looks over at Sherry and thinks, "*Man, I am lucky,*" then looks down and notices the guy that made a right is out of view. The time is perfect for Charlie to make his move once the guy coming towards them passes the tree. Charlie decides to go down and take care of him with a baseball bat that was always kept in the treehouse for protection against wild animals. He grabs the bat and starts down the tree. Sherry reaches behind his neck, pulls him closer and gives him a kiss.

"Be careful, I need you," she says with watery eyes. Charlie carefully climbs down the tree without making any sound. The knife welding guy is crouching down, trying to see through the brush. Charlie slowly walks up behind.

"Looking for me?" In a clever tone, and as the kid turns around, Charlie whacks him with the bat and he falls unconscious to the ground.

Charlie reaches over to check his pulse, see if he is alive; he was, but he will be out for hours. Charlie takes his knife and checks for a gun and right in the belt in the back of his pants, he finds a loaded gun. He takes the gun and heads back where the second guy is in a heated discussion on the phone, still managing to search for Charlie and Sherry. Hiding behind the brush, waiting for this creep to get closer, Charlie impatiently waits to make his move. Charlie notices this guy is moving very slowly and Charlie is getting the urge to urinate from being so nervous. He is trying to hold it in, when this guy finally passes. He sneaks up behind him, when the sound of a snapping twig breaks the silence, a twig Charlie just stepped on. The kid turns around looking at Charlie, displaying an angry and intimidating look. Charlie is too far away for the bat to do any damage; this guy rushes toward Charlie like a wild animal would and leapt into the air feet first. Charlie's heart is pounding, anticipating the impact; his feet hit Charlie in the center of his chest causing Charlie to fly backwards. The impact was harder than Charlie expected and winded him. Like the time Long Ngo punched him back at the Dragon's Den, several months ago. Charlie feels a sharp pain, in his chest like a rib was cracked, but knowing he has to protect Sherry, he manages to raise himself, thinking of her and avenging Chelly's death. Charlie is ready and so is this guy, to attack again. He is rushing towards Charlie, whose only choice is to use the gun. As he gets closer Charlie yells, "Stop, I have a gun." He yells again, "Please stop or I'll shoot." This guy didn't and left Charlie no choice but to use the gun. Charlie sees him make his leap and is heading straight towards him again feet first. Charlie puts pressure on the trigger and hears that sound once again, bringing to mind the memories of why he has to continue. Avoiding the impact of his second kick, Charlie manages to shoot this guy, who lands on his back and blood starts to stain the green grass and weeds that surround him. Charlie realizes he didn't miss, he shot him and he is dead. Charlie goes over to check, noticing that he is a child, he looks like he is only about 18 years old. Charlie asks himself, *"Why didn't he stop? Why? He is awfully young."* Soon Sherry's panicking voice is heard as she runs over to see if he is okay.

"CJ, are you alright? CJ, where are you?" Charlie hears through the bushes and yells back, "Over here, and yeah I am okay, I'm over here." They stand there for several minutes, devastated with the happenings of these past few months, when suddenly the youth's phone starts to ring. Startled, they look at each other and Charlie bends down to answer it.

"Hello." Charlie answers.

"Quang, mission accomplished? Did it come to an end?" the voice on the other end of the phone inquires.

"No, it isn't accomplished and it's only the beginning."

"Ah, you must be this elusive Charlie I've been hearing so much about," the mystery man says.

"Now you know who I am; who are you?"

"The man who is going to kill you, mother fucker. Now you know who I am!" the mystery man yells and hangs up while chuckling.

"I am going to search this punk to see what I can find, and I'll keep this phone to stay in touch with our friend, Mr. Mystery."

Charlie searches the kid and finds in his wallet a business card of a Mr. Aye Lam in New York City. Charlie looks at the card and checks the phone and "Bingo, the last call's phone number matches Mr. Aye Lam." He also finds a handwritten note:

8 PM - 07/7/06
Saigon Republic LLC
58 West Palisades Parkway
Englewood, NJ
201 210 7777

Charlie doesn't know what it to make of this, decides to take it from his lifeless body, along with his gun, knife and phone.   "It's time. It's time for me to put an end to it all. Put a period at the end of this sentence, so we can live our lives without constantly looking over our shoulders. I am done, stick a fork in me, I have had all I can stand. How about you, are you?" With the note in his hand, he reaches over and finally sees the look he desires, the look she had when they first started this mess. Charlie moves closer and gives her a kiss. When they break Charlie says, "Let's get out of here." Without any hesitation he notices she is just as ready as he is to end this mess. Now he is forced to take immediate action, avenge Chelly's death and protect the woman he loves.

Knowing where they're headed, and with three days to get there, Charlie thinks this is a good time to do some detective work.

"Let's head for NYC and see what we can find out. We'll spy on our friend Mr. Aye Lam." As they head for New York City, Charlie looks over at Sherry. She has her seat in a reclining position with her head resting on the back of the chair, looking out into the starry night, with flashes of colors from the fireworks that seem to be coming out of everywhere. He sees her beautiful legs stretched out as she is wearing white shorts. Her silhouette against the colors of the fireworks is the reason for his existence. She looks simply spectacular in every shape and form. Now the most frightening thing to him is being rejected by her. She is always so focused on what they need to do. That's when he sees her head turn towards him and her silhouette with the New York skyline behind her is even more spectacular than the one he was amazed with before. He is so mesmerized by her, it is simply astonishing. Charlie has never felt like this before, ever. He can't seem to get enough. He hates to take his eyes off her, but he needs to drive and get them safely over the George Washington Bridge into Manhattan, a borough of New York City.

They enter the city and check in at the Comfort Inn on West 35th street, in the garment center, close to Mr. Aye Lam's office building. As they walk up to the front desk, Charlie notices the desk clerk Robbie Jones eyeballing Sherry up and down, as if he has never seen a woman as perfect. So Charlie turns and also looks at her and sees a wholesome, beautiful woman with an absolutely gorgeous face, reddish blonde hair tied back in a pony tail, wearing a red, white and blue halter top with that Silver Star in between those perfectly shaped breasts holding the halter together, along with white form fitting shorts that display her outrageous athletic shape and beautiful legs. She is perfect.

"Beautiful, isn't she Robbie?" Charlie says to Robbie. He said it loud enough for Sherry to hear and catches a little blushing action on her face. Without saying a word, she shoots him one of those 'you're crazy' looks of hers.

"Stunning," slight pause, still engrossed with Sherry's appearance, "You, my man, are a very lucky person."

"Yes, I certainly am, Robbie, a very lucky man," Charlie chuckles. He tells Robbie the same thing he said in Chicago, "If anyone starts asking questions, please let me know immediately; there'll be a big tip if you do." He hands Robbie a hundred dollar bill for a tip.

Charlie turns towards Sherry and asks, "Separate rooms?" giving her that stupid look of his he thought Sherry loved so much. She doesn't reply verbally, just returns one of hers. "I guess we'll need only one room tonight Robbie," Charlie says with a chuckle, and then he requests room 219 if it's available. Charlie always asks for room 219 as that was the hospital room his grandfather had when he passed away. Charlie is a very superstitious person. He feels that his grandfather will be looking down on them, keeping them safe and bringing them luck. It was available, so Sherry and Charlie grab their two small suitcases and head for their room. Knowing they have three full days to spy on Mr. Aye Lam and check out the Saigon Republic, Charlie asks Sherry what she wants to do tonight. There is so much to do in NYC, he gives her some choices. She mentioned she would love to go to Little Italy for dinner, then walk around a bit and come back and get some rest for their journey ahead. Charlie agrees with her as it was a great choice. Since he has never been here before, he needs to find a good place to eat. He is a modest person and hates to waste money by eating in a strange city, at a strange restaurant and paying a lot more than he needs to for a bad meal. He decides to call down to Robbie at the desk for a recommendation, but soon realizes Robbie doesn't know what he is talking about. "How rare," Charlie says aloud. So he pulls out the phone book to get a referral to a good Italian Restaurant in Little Italy, as Sherry looks at him like he is insane. He looks through the Manhattan white pages and randomly looks for any Italian names like Di Maria, Davino, Esposito, Nicoletti, Maresco, or Puglia. The book opens at the letter P and he spots Pellegrino, Anthony. He figures you can't get any more Italian than that, Tony Pellegrino. So he calls and gets him on the phone.

"Hi Tony, my name is Charlie Johnson, first time in New York, and I am looking for a good Italian restaurant in Little Italy. Do you have a recommendation for me?" At first Tony starts laughing, thinking this is a practical joke or a television stunt.

"Hey yo, am I on TV, radio or what?" he replies laughing.

"No, Tony, I can guaranty, you are not on radio or T.V. I really need to find a great Italian Restaurant to take a very special woman. Like I said earlier, I am new to the area." Tony finally understands but still thinks it is strange.

"Yes, Fratelli's Restaurant on Mulberry Street is my favorite and their chicken picatta over penne is to die for."

"Thank you Tony, I will have Ms Sherry Mann, a reporter from WWNJ, mention what a Good Samaritan you are. Have a great evening."

"Hey yo, no problem," Tony replies, laughing.

Sherry is staring at Charlie, with a crazy look, so he asks, "Penny for your thoughts?"

"Is there anything you can't do?" Sherry says through a smile. Charlie looks at her standing there in her halter top and shorts, a perfect specimen of a human female body. He pulls her close and with a serious look, gazing deep down into her eyes so she understands how he feels about her, "Yes, I can't seem to get you out of my mind. Every day and every night I see your beautiful face looking at me, I begin to hear your laughter, that sound I never want to end, knowing you are happy. I see the way you walk, walking towards me with those sensual, passionate lips of yours, making a big beautiful smile and everything you do. I can't, I won't, and I don't ever want to, get you or anything about you out of my mind." Charlie moves closer to her so he can wrap his arms around her, to feel the warmth of her body. She seemed to be melting in his arms the way he was melting in hers. She doesn't pull away, seems to pull him closer, like the time they were at IHOP in Chicago. Only this time they are not in a car. They begin to kiss passionately as their tongues were doing that lovers' dance in each other's mouth. At the end of their kiss Charlie realizes they were meant to be together, when her lips touched his, the sensation she created within him went throughout his entire body. Her lips are the most sensual he has ever tasted. He has never felt this way before with just one kiss. As they pull away from that warm embrace, he felt everything was just right.

"Is this the right time for you?" Charlie says while his eyes are fixed in a sensual stare, but afraid of what she might answer. He doesn't take rejection very well, not because he can't take no for an answer; it's because if he hears the word no, especially at this point in their relationship, he will start to think negative things about himself. Negative things like, he is not good enough, not sexy enough or not man enough, and that she doesn't want any part of him. So his body is tense while waiting for her reply, which seems to be taking too long for her to give him a positive response.

"CJ," Sherry says in a very sensual tone, "What I am about to tell you is for your ears only, and I want you to promise me you will never mention this to anyone, promise?" she asks as she is holding his face, like the time in the parking garage, between her thumb and her four fingers, holding them face to face.

"I promise with all my heart," Charlie replies as he feels a little frightened by what he might hear.

"I hope you know I want you as much as you want me. I know I told you that in Chicago, but figured you might have forgotten since the incident. I do want you. You are the only man I have ever wanted in that way. However, I need a little more time to take the next step, as I have never been with any man before, ever. I am embarrassed to tell anyone that because of my age. Nowadays, the average girl loses their virginity at the age of sixteen. I never had the opportunity because I was homely at that age. So homely and unpopular I became a recluse, a loner and found enjoyment and happiness in books." She pauses to get a good look at Charlie to make sure she has his complete attention, and to see if there is any reaction. She didn't know it, but the words leaving her mouth made him desire her even more, not because she is a virgin, because she is a true person. So true, he knows she is the woman he wants, and he is willing to marry her on the spot. Sherry continues to talk as her eyes start to glisten, "I went through high school and my teenage years without ever being asked out by a boy. I never went to a movie, a dance, a lunch or a ballgame with a person of the opposite sex, unless it was my father, or one of my cousins or uncles."

Charlie finds that so hard to believe by looking at the woman who is standing in front of him.

"When I entered college, my roommate turned me on to the world of makeup, designer clothing and the world of exercising and eating right. I enjoyed it so much I kept at it, and soon I made a complete turnaround from that insecure nerd to what I am now. I am still not a beauty queen, but I realize I am attractive to the opposite sex. I began realizing that fact back in my old college days at Rutgers University. One night my roommate talked me into going to a party with her at one of the frat houses on campus. There I met what I thought was a nice clean cut and rather handsome young man. He started giving me the attention I never got from men, and I started to enjoy it. We hung out all night, and he finally talked me into trying a White Russian drink that he told me was mild. Even though I was 20 years old, I never tried alcohol nor had any desire to. I was talked into it not only by his words, but by looking around the room and seeing how everyone seemed to be enjoying it. He came back with the drink, and I had a couple of sips and within minutes I felt groggy, thinking it was because I had never had alcohol before. He notices this, and asks if I want to get driven back to my dorm. Feeling the way I did I said yes. We got about a mile away when he pulls off the side of the road, and stops the car. It wasn't long after he stopped the car, I felt his hands all over me like I was being attacked by an octopus. I felt arms and hands everywhere. Soon I felt my blouse and bra being ripped off my body as he is sucking, biting and licking every inch of my upper body. I can feel he was excited as he starts humping my leg like a dog in heat. He is sweaty, awfully sweaty, and I can feel the heat being generated from his body onto mine, I couldn't breathe or move, but I had to find the strength to get away from this beast. He is now taking off his pants, and I realized he will soon be taking off mine. So he positions me a little to the driver's side as he lifts himself up off me to remove his pants. That's when I start to realize if I do not do anything now I'll never get the opportunity again. I look at the dash and push in the cigarette lighter. Waiting what felt like an hour, still feeling woozy from the drink, my arms shaking like a leaf, I hear the sound of it popping out. I grab the lighter and push it into his face as he screams like I never heard a man scream. It was still very hot when I pushed the lighter into his groin, catching one of his berries. He lifts up his body entirely as I punch his face as hard as I could. He then rolls back over to the driver's seat, I open the car door escaping, and screaming for help. I hear him screaming at me, "*Bitch, you Fucking Bitch*." Again Sherry pauses to concentrate on Charlie's reaction. She sees his eyes are watery holding back his tears as she continues, "I am outside the car screaming at the top of my lungs. I was topless when a Campus police car arrives. I felt humiliated standing there in front of three men, all of them enjoying the view of me being topless like I was going to put on a show for them. I calmed down enough to find my blouse and bra that was thrown out of the car window. I put them on, and walked the rest of the way back to my dorm."

"That's when I felt it. I started hating every man I met, especially the male students at Rutgers University. They weren't there for a college education; they were there to get as much action as they could. Although in the court of law I was assaulted, I felt lucky no penetration was made. With my luck I would have a fifteen year old child, leading a different life right now." She turns away for a moment then back again looking at

Charlie standing there. "You asked me if this is the right time. I am not sure if it is, but what I do know for sure is that you're definitely the one. The only man I have ever desired in that way, the only man I feel I can trust, and the man I fell in love with."

By now Charlie is speechless. He doesn't know what to say. How could he not grab her and squeeze her with all his might? However, he just stands there like the old Charlie, afraid of everything. He sees Sherry walk closer to him and wraps her arms around him.

"It's okay CJ, I know you care and are probably afraid to say the wrong thing." As her warm embrace is comforting him, Charlie says to himself, *"Damn, she does have a strong woman's intuition."* He pushes away from her embrace in order to look directly into her eyes thinking, *"She just told me she loves me, wow."* A big smile grows on Charlie's face.

Fratelli's Restaurant at 8:35 PM:

𝒮he two catch a city cab and go over to Little Italy to have dinner. During the cab ride Charlie glances over at Sherry thinking about how sumptuous she looks tonight. Her hair is down, emphasizing her facial features that make him stare in awe, amazed at her beautiful perfection. She has on makeup, but it is not overly done and it emphasizes her natural beauty. He enjoys the complexion of her skin and the beauty of those gorgeous hazel green eyes. She has on an opened laced, white teal blouse, which enhances the color of those eyes even more, and a gold chain hanging around her neck with a heart-shaped locket that almost reaches her cleavage. She has on black pants, not extremely tight but tight enough to make her body look sleeker than normal and even more athletic. She is wearing her white sneakers as she plans on walking around Little Italy tonight after dinner for a romantic stroll.

Sherry looks over at Charlie and gives him a warm smile, as if she is saying thank you for being so empathetic back at the motel. She never told anyone that story about the attempted rape, not even her mother who was very close with Sherry. Only because she knew her mother would have made her press charges against that boy, and she would have to relive that horrible experience again, in court. With all the horror stories she has heard over the years, she felt it was easier to try and forget about it.

Chinatown, New York City:

Several blocks away in Chinatown, Aye Lam and a few of his Quan-De-Kha'n are having dinner at Wong Phatz on Mott Street, where mostly Asians eat authentic Asian meals. The utensils at the restaurant are chopsticks and small wooden shaped spoons for the soup. Aye Lam says to his group, "Its perfect weather for the fireworks that will start at about 9:00 pm; after we watch, we'll need to prepare ourselves for our leader Nhat-Quo Kim's arrival. He will be here the day after tomorrow, so we have to have the shipment ready to be loaded onto the express rail to Kansas City.

"Are all your boys ready?" he says, looking at his men sitting at the table. They all answer, yes they are ready. Aye Lam informs the men about Charlie and Sherry; it's the first time he mentioned them. The last two months, street warriors were on a mission to find them, and today they did. Unfortunately, Charlie and Sherry managed to escape once again. He tells them they're in New Jersey and probably heading this way. "I will make sure when they do arrive they wished they hadn't." He goes on to tell them how they have been causing trouble and have been a headache for Nhat-Quo Kim. They are more than ready for Charlie; they are specialized killing machines that neither Charlie nor Sherry has ever seen the likes of. When they attack, they usually need only one attempt to make the kill. The men continue, until the fireworks start.

Back at Fratelli's Restaurant:

Sherry and Charlie have finished their dinner and decide to take a stroll through Little Italy. The sites are amazing to the both of them as they've never seen a place quite like this before. Hand in hand they were looking more and more like lovers; the two are overtaken by the scents, sights and sounds of Little Italy. While walking down these narrow streets, it felt like they were walking around in Italy, although they never left the streets of New York. They are becoming an extremely close couple and love chatting with one another so much they haven't noticed they entered what is known as Chinatown. Little Italy and Chinatown are right next to each other, both touching at Canal Street, in lower Manhattan, New York City. Charlie looks up and notices all the signs written in Chinese.

"We should start turning around," Charlie says to Sherry, when suddenly, out of nowhere, they are approached by three Asian gang members.

"What are you doing here mister? Are you looking for some trouble?" They begin to encircle them.

"No, we are tourists, sightseeing," in a concerned tone, scanning the area, assessing his defensive strategy.

Now several more Asian men appear out of the dark alley and stand alongside them. The nervousness, realizing his chances of protecting Sherry is near impossible, as Charlie stands in front of her.

"Look guys, I really don't want any trouble," reaching into his pocket for his wallet. "I don't have much, but you can have it all." Surprisingly, one of the men orders the thugs to leave.

"Thank you sir," with a sigh of relief, Charlie shakes his hand.
"No problem, they're punk kids looking for excitement," the stranger says and hands Charlie his business card. As fast as they all appeared, everyone was gone. The men walk towards the East River where the fireworks are about to begin.

"That's him, Sherry" Charlie says, excitedly. "That was Aye Lam." Charlie and Sherry look at each other then back at the men walking away and realize, without a word, they need to be more careful. Anything can happen at any time and without any warning. With nerves shaken, they begin to walk back to Little Italy and grab a cab back to the motel.

At the Crossroads of Terror

𝔗oday is July 5th; it marks the day Sherry and Charlie start their investigation. They decide to inspect Aye Lam's office, not far from where they are staying in the Garment District. Upon arrival, Charlie notices the name on the building China Star Clothing and realizes this is a major clothes manufacturer in the US. Aye Lam's office is inside, he is listed as the CEO of the company. Sherry and Charlie decide to inspect the grounds that surround the building. Charlie walks over to a dumpster in the back of the building to inspect some of the garbage. He sees several gloves that look like the same glove Kym wore when he first saw her, the day of Chang's murder, the glove that he still has in his procession back at the hotel. He doesn't know why, but he reaches down into the dumpster to take one of the gloves. He also discovers several discarded bills of lading and sees these gloves get shipped to Thuy's cleaners, S. Wentworth Street, Chicago. He decides to take several of them. Sherry says, "It looks like they make the gloves here and maybe imprint them at Thuy's cleaners." Charlie replies, "I guess that could be one clue; let's take the gloves and see what else we can find out at Saigon Republic." They then catch a cab to Englewood, New Jersey. As they are nearing the Saigon Republic, Charlie asks the driver to drop them off about a block past the club.

"This looks exactly like the Dragon's Den in Philly," a surprised Sherry says; Charlie agrees. However, after they walk through the front doors, they realize it is an exact replica. The two are greeted by an exotic Oriental waterfall decorated with bonsai trees along the waterfront. Charlie looks around and sees the three different pathways leading to the 3 different dining areas: the red room, the green room and the white room, thinking, "The Saigon Republic is identical to the Dragon's Den and Sherry is very perceptive." They get to the red room and see a few street warriors hanging around.

"Sherry, let's leave. I have a great Idea. We'll come back later for lunch or something." They get outside and he explains to Sherry his plan. Charlie starts, "What if I told you that you have an excellent opportunity to get a new story like no other, the story of the century?

Would you like that?" Sherry sits without saying a word. "Well would you be interested?" Charlie asks.

She nods yes and says, "Tell me more."

"I am going to buy some electronic equipment, a digital video camera, wireless microphones and wireless audio recorders. We enter Saigon Republic and pretend to be a couple getting married and want to book the place for an Oriental wedding reception. As we check out the place we strategically place these wireless microphones under tables, stools, or wherever we can find a good spot that will remain hidden until after their big meeting. We record the meeting they have on the 7th. Then you do a video on everything we find out, and email it to your station for them to air. In the meantime, we stay far enough away from the action to stay safe until it's right for me to make a move." Charlie looks at Sherry to gauge her thoughts.

"Everything sounds great except the end. When it's the right time to make a move, we call in the police and hand over all the evidence in building a case against them," Sherry says as she stands, getting closer to Charlie. She puts her arms around him, looking at him in a very sensual way. "I don't want anything to happen to you like in Chicago." Charlie smiles and remembers the way Jackie Gleason on the honeymooners felt in certain situations and says, *"Huminah huminah."* *Then says,* "I just got these lips and haven't broken them in yet," another expression he uses randomly. Then after a slight pause, "Okay, let's do it Stewart."

"I'll call my boss to see if he can supply the equipment." Sherry calls her boss Chester A. Wright. Not only is he interested, he wants to send one of his spy teams for their protection, and to have consistent communication between them. He tells Sherry to pick up the equipment at WPIX in New York. He will make sure it is ready in an hour. It looks like Sherry is now back at work and not on a leave of absence anymore. Mr. Chester Wright gave instructions on making contact nightly with him or the spy team no matter what happens. They all agreed and start to put the plan in action.

The two disguise themselves in case someone recognizes them. They get back to the hotel where Sherry has been in the bathroom for an hour and a half. Charlie knocks on the door.

"Is everything alright in there? Do you need a scissors? Are you still counting hairs?" trying to make light of the situation. At that moment Sherry comes out of the bathroom looking like a young Cher,

her hair dyed black and she has color contacts to make her eyes brown, and wearing a woman's ebony tee shirt with dungarees and black boots. As she comes out of the bathroom Charlie has to take a second look.

"Wow," Charlie says as he gives her that ole Charlie look of his. "No matter what you have on, you are the prettiest woman I have ever laid my eyes on." She smiles at him and gets close.

"Thank you, big boy." She tries to make him laugh, walking provocatively, then begins to rub his leg with the palm of her hand. "Is that a banana in your pocket or are you just happy to see me." Charlie just couldn't resist, so he looks at her very romantically, moving closer to her lips, then quickly backs up and says, "No it's Quang's cell phone," as he pulls it out of his pocket. They both look at each other, trying to hold back a laugh, and then begin laughing nervously.

Charlie has a graying mustache and beard glued to his clean-shaven face. He dyed his hair with gray streaks to match the new facial hair.

"You look rather distinguishing, young man," Sherry says as she can't believe how he looks with a mustache and beard.

"Do you like it?" Charlie anxiously asks.

"You look old enough to be my father." She couldn't get the words out fast enough and through a laugh says, "Not really, dad."

Sherry and Charlie enter the Saigon Republic at 2:30pm, looking for help with pricing and touring the club for their wedding reception. They make contact with Chi Vu, sales rep for the Saigon. "Hello, my name is Chi Vu. Welcome to our Oriental garden house. What brings you in today?" she says as she seems very sweet and polite.

"We need to get pricing for a wedding reception for about 125 people next May sometime," Sherry says, and Charlie believes she is enjoying this even more than the time she got him out of jail in Moorestown. Meantime, they get a tour of the red room, the green room, and the white room. Charlie manages to plant microphones in each of the rooms. He even planted one on the podium where Ms. Chi Vu told them there is a guest speaker here on the 7th, and on that day the club will be closed to the public. Charlie tries to get more out of her without being too suspicious. The only thing he managed to get was a name "Nhat-Quo", which neither he nor Sherry heard of, but at least they know it was recorded.

Ms Chi Vu gives them pricing and the menu options before they mention they need to leave. They give her a big thank you for her hospitality. When trying to leave, they see Aye Lam with several gang members.

"Want a drink?" Charlie asks.

"No CJ, let's not," a nervous reply, but she sees in his eyes that's what he needs to do. They walk over to the bar and each order a Mai Tai as they are holding the paperwork Chi Vu gave them. Sherry and Charlie look as if they are going over the Saigon brochures, discussing their wedding options, when Mr. Lam walks over to them and introduces himself.

"Good afternoon and welcome to the Saigon Republic, my name is Aye Lam. So when's your big day?" he asks. Charlie notices Sherry is beginning to get startled.

"May 2007," Charlie answers, as Mr. Aye Lam kisses Sherry on her hand.

"What did you think of the place?"

"It's fantastic, especially the outside gardens for our wedding album photos," Sherry replies.

"Great. What other places are you considering?" he asks, trying to gauge his competition. Knowing that neither one of them know any other place, Charlie answers for her.

"You are the first place we've checked. We really haven't considered any other place yet. You can say it's still a work in progress." Lam seems satisfied.

"I hope we will meet again," he says thinking they will have their wedding here.

"I am almost positive you will," Charlie says and they smile at each other as Mr. Aye Lam walks away. They exit the club quickly without any hesitation. Charlie wants to build her confidence by telling her she was wonderful.

"Great job Mrs. Johnson," he says smiling at her; she looks at him funny then grabs his arm and walks to safety.

About a block away Charlie tests the microphones he planted. He turns the receiver on. Each microphone has its own frequency, so he can change it to catch the action in each room. He clearly marked the room and frequency numbers, so he can follow conversations as they move throughout the club. They catch Aye Lam talking to one of his guys in the white room near the podium. "Quoc, are your men ready for Kim when he arrives?" Quoc Bao Gia Xuong is second in command in New York. He handles much of the day to day while Aye controls the communications with Chicago. Quoc replies, "Just waiting on the train Aye." As Aye Lam answers, "Great, all we have to do is wait for Jeong Kim to arrive. Who is scheduled to ride?" Lam asks. "Bao Dai is going to ride the train to KC, and manage the distribution," someone answered as we hear cheers in the background: "Long Lac Quan, Long Lac Quan, Long Lac Quan." Sherry later found out its translation, "Dragon Lord."

Now they know, Jeong Kim will be the special guest speaker Ms. Chi Vu told them about. Charlie looks at Sherry and they both sense they are talking about a drug shipment, and it will be taking place in Kansas City or right here in New York, to be distributed across the U.S.

"I think it's time for your first news video, what do you think?" Charlie asks. Tears are starting to build in her eyes, but she refuses to cry. "What's the matter, do you want to give up?" Charlie asks as he wipes the tears with his fingertips.

"No, I think I am going to discover something I've been searching for, for the last fourteen years, and you are the reason I will finally find it and get it resolved," as she lays her head on his chest.

"What have you been searching for? You never mentioned anything to me?" Charlie asks, as he is very concerned. She begins to tell him the story, another sad story about her past.

Sherry begins:

"While I was a junior in college I received a phone call from then Rutgers University President Edward Bernstein, informing me that something came up at home and I needed to get there right away. He said he had arranged transportation to be ready in an hour. At that moment, I didn't know what could have happened. So I called home, what seemed like 100 different times in that hour, but I got no answer. I decided to call my aunt and again no answer; I couldn't imagine what happened, but I knew it had to be serious. Maybe my father had a heart attack and was in the hospital. My mind wondered at every possibility without ever thinking what I was about to learn. I wasn't taken home. I was taken to a Philadelphia Police Station, and that's when I started to get real worried about what I was going to be told. There I was met by two detectives. I only remember the name of one, John Fennick, who was recently promoted from patrolman to homicide detective, working on his first case."

Charlie interrupts, "John Fennick, the Police Captain?"

"Yes, same guy," Sherry says as she continues. "He tells me my parents were found murdered. Their bodies were found at a Philadelphia construction site which I know now is the Dragon's Den." The tears begin to flow harder down her face. "My father was found with his throat slashed from ear to ear, so deep it severed the nerves in his spinal cord in the back of his neck. His tongue was cut out of his mouth and was found near my mom. They also found he was shot in the head, back and chest execution style. The cause of death however was murder by stabbing. So he was alive when they slit his throat; then to make sure he was dead, someone shot him four times."

"Sherry do you need a break?" as he is holding her for a minute.

"No, I want to continue." She says, "My mom's body was found several yards away and must have been held there to watch my father's murder; that's what Detective John Fennick believes. Her autopsy found she was raped by as many as 4 different men. She was then stabbed seven times in the chest area just missing her vital organs, so she would die a slow and painful death. This crime was so horrific, at that time it was considered the worst murder in Philadelphia's history. I can't imagine how terrifying that must have been for my mom." Sherry begins to sob uncontrollably as Charlie holds her tightly to comfort her and ease the pain she is feeling. His heart is breaking for her as he begins to cry along with her. Charlie tries to get her to change the subject, but when something is that deep inside of you like this is with Sherry, you constantly think about it every moment of your life. She lifts her head and wants to finish as Charlie kisses some of the tears away from her cheeks.

"The case has never been solved, and it is now one of the cases in the cold case files at the Philadelphia Police Department. My father was a train engineer for Philadelphia, Bethlehem and New England Freight Company; his route was from Philadelphia to Kansas City and back again, and now my women's intuition is telling me this will be the train company that is going to Kansas City. Not only that, I believe this will be my father's route. My mom was a housewife and both my parents were model citizens and very active in the community. They had no enemies that I knew of. Soon it became clear to detective John Fennick and the rest of the Philly Police Department this case will never get solved. They could not find enough evidence to generate any leads in my parent's murder. The case has been cold since 1992, fourteen years now. I spend all of my vacation time trying to generate a renewed interest in this case to get the Philly PD to reopen it, without much success. I have made a promise to myself that before I die someone will be held responsible. Someone will get convicted of this horrible crime that has consumed my life." Charlie sees her tears are gone and she is now angry. Like the anger he has inside for Helmut's and Chelly's deaths. They wrap their arms around each other in a warm consoling embrace.

While he is holding her, Charlie starts to remember his dad working on a murder case similar to what she'd described, only the last name wasn't Mann. "No, I think it was Manley, yes that was it, Manley, Dennis and Marie Manley." He'd told Charlie some horrible stories that went on behind the scenes about that one.

Saigon Republic LLC:

𝒯he day is finally here, July 7th 2006, the day the big man Nhat-Quo, Jeong Kim is in New York City holding a very important meeting in front of the entire 700-plus members of The NY Flying Dragons. He is extremely excited today as his scientists have figured out how to make cocaine, heroin, Crystal Meth and methamphetamines undetectable with the current methods used by the Feds and local police. The scent is undetectable to specially trained dogs that are trained to sniff out the smallest amount of drugs. Kim feels this new invention made by the Asian Scientists employed in South America and Vietnam, will skyrocket their already profitable drug business into new, amazing heights. The Flying Dragons will be able to cut down on the expenses made just trying to cover up the distribution of the drugs. Today is the day they are going to test this new invention of theirs with the largest shipment of cocaine, heroin, Crystal Meth and methamphetamines they've ever distributed!

The invention is an additive that virtually eliminates all odors from their product. It is a liquid that is mixed into the drugs before they are shipped to the US. These drugs currently come in from the Texas Mexico border and the California Mexico border. With this new invention, the drugs can come into major airports and all US ports in box shipments of Oriental wax candles, and other common items that get imported daily. Sherry and Charlie are outside the club, sitting on a bench about a block away so that they can hear and record his entire speech. With the recordings they make, they plan on giving them to the police as evidence against Kim and all his highly trained criminals. They want all The Flying Dragons to pay for the crimes they've so adamantly committed, especially Chelly's murder, and possibly Sherry's parents. Sherry's appearance is driving Charlie wild, her hair still has the black die from the day before, making her gorgeous hazel eyes stand out even more. As she sits there looking sexier than ever, Charlie grabs hold of her arm.

"Are you ready for this? Will you be able to deal with the worst possible ending?" Charlie always believes that when you are indecisive about a decision to be made, if you can deal with the worst possible result then go with it. If you can't, then the decision should be no. "Well, can you?"

"No, but I need to do this."

Kim walks into the room and the crowd starts chanting – *"Nhat-Quo, Long Lac Quan, Nhat-Quo, Long Lac Quan, Nhat-Quo, Long Lac Quan."* The crowd repeatedly chants, as Charlie pictures Kim walking up to the podium, waving his arms in the air holding his cane, with his bodyguards Aye Lam and Quoc Bao Gia Xuong escorting him to center stage. "Kim seems to me to be a real insane and egotistic person, like the sorts of Ramses of Egypt, Hitler of Germany, Lenin and Stalin of Russia, and Saddam Hussein of Iraq. A person the world would all be better off if they were never born."

"Is the recorder on?" Charlie inquires. Sherry nods yes. With their headsets on, they portray typical New Yorkers listening to their favorite music. Ordinary people, but in reality they were hearing a monster at work.

"Thank You. Thank You. Thank you everyone," as the gang is still chanting he then begins, *'Today will go down as our greatest achievement ever."* As the crowd roars with approval, *"Our family back home in Vietnam along with our family in South America has made a remarkable discovery together as one team. Their discovery will not only make our lives easier but make our organization much more powerful,"* as the roars get louder,

"They have given us a way to distribute our goods without the fear of getting caught," again a loud and boisterous roar comes from the crowd. *"Today we get to test its power, so we can create the life all of you deserve."* Now the crowd starts back with, *"Nhat-Quo, Long Lac Quan"*

"Everybody was given instructions by your Sabamnim (teacher) as to your role in our test today, and what is expected of you. Is everybody ready?" The crowd roars back.

Nobody knew it, except for a few high ranking members, Aye Lam, Quoc Bao Gia Xuong and a few others, but Kim was conducting an experiment using some of his street warriors as guinea pigs.

Many of the street warriors were given plane tickets to different parts of the country, and instructions to bring a suitcase they are about to receive from New York to the local Sensei of The Flying Dragons meeting house at their destination. They are instructed to give the suitcase only to the Sensei (leader) at that location. All the suitcases were lined with a quarter pound of cocaine and Crystal Meth. In some of the suitcases the drugs were treated, and in others the drugs were not. Each suitcase was numbered and logged if the suitcase contained drugs that were treated or not. Only Kim and his high ranking leaders knew which suitcase contained what. Kim needed to know for sure if the new invention worked. The Senseis of The Flying Dragons received their instructions from Kim as well. They were instructed to open the case, and report the number back to Kim's secretary. Once all the cases are tallied, Kim will know for sure if this new invention worked and if all the treated drugs made it to their location undetected. The street warriors were given plane tickets and instructed to randomly pick up a suitcase on their way out, and head straight for Kennedy, LaGuardia or Newark airports.

"I wish you all the best, now let's get the job done." As Kim wishes everyone well and gives a big cheer for The Flying Dragons Success, the crowd roars then begins to chant as they exit the club, *"Nhat-Quo, Long Lac Quan, Nhat-Quo, Long Lac Quan, Nhat-Quo, Long Lac Quan!"*

Charlie motions to Sherry that it's time to leave.

"Let's catch a cab to the China Star Clothing factory and snoop around a bit. Let's give this tape to Chester's Spy team. Did he tell us who they are and where they will be?"

"No, he only told me how to contact them." She looks for her phone, "I will send them a text message to 1 866 spy team."

"Let's do it Stewart," Charlie says aloud as Sherry gives him her 'you are crazy' look, and Charlie just smiles back.

"I already received a reply from the spy team. I am instructed to leave the tape under the newspaper that is lying in the wastebasket next to us." Charlie now knows there is a spy team nearby and they are being protected. He looks around but does not notice anyone.

Unbeknownst to Sherry and Charlie, the spy team nearby were federal agents, tracking their every movement and waiting to close in on Jeong Kim and the high ranking leaders of The Flying Dragons. The digital video camera has a built-in transmitter, signaling the FBI. The FBI will be tracking their every move the entire way. The tape recorder is also transmitting. However, it is always on, to catch all the actions and conversations between Charlie and Sherry.

The Dragons Fire

Chapter 11

$\mathcal{M}$eanwhile, en route to the China Star Clothing Factory, Charlie and Sherry begin a debate on whose plan will prevail, as Sherry is quite headstrong in involving the authorities when it comes to their safety. Charlie looks over to Sherry in a concerned manner.

"After careful consideration, I've decided the best course of action would be to follow the drug shipment, so first we must find out which boxcars they'll commandeer. Then we'll need to locate a safe and inconspicuous place to jump aboard."

"Whoa there, now slow down just a bit CJ. I think it would be much safer if we record them loading the drugs onto the boxcars, then notify the proper authorities," explains Sherry while looking at Charlie like he's crazy.

"Although you make a lot of sense with what you say, and I am almost positive your plan will work, however, if we follow your plan, we may never find out if 'The Flying Dragons' are indeed responsible for the deaths of your parents."

"Oh I see," Sherry replies sarcastically, with her hands on her hips. "Only how will we get past the warrior's they'll entrust to guard the boxcars, because indeed CJ they will be on full guard of their property?"

"Don't you worry your pretty little head about that; leave it to me. I'll make sure we get on the train safely." Charlie ponders, *I'm just not too sure yet on the specifics, but somehow we will get on that train.*

The cab turns and stops directly in front of China Star Clothing factory. Charlie anxiously directs the driver to continue ahead another block.

"Looks like we made it here in just thirty minutes from Englewood," Charlie observantly informs Sherry as he pays the driver.

Upon exiting the cab Charlie discovers train tracks running behind the China Star factory. In curiosity, he hastily takes Sherry by the hand and heads towards them. There are six trailers being loaded in the back of the factory. None of the trailers have wheels and Charlie has an inquisitive look on his face, knowing this is the shipment to Kansas City. How will they get loaded on the train, he wonders? Sherry gives Charlie a poke to get his attention.

"I'll tell you how it's done," and with a wink and a smirk says, "It's my woman's intuition."

"Okay, you're right," Charlie replies shaking his head. "Now will you tell me how this will end for us with that woman's intuition of yours?"

"Yes, after this is all over, I'm going to beat the heck out of you," she interjects quite angrily, just aching to elicit a reaction from him. A concerned expression comes over his face and she still decides to wait a bit longer, just to prolong it enough and says, "Gotcha," and immediately starts to laugh.

Charlie was seriously contemplating an apology, possibly on bended knees, begging for her forgiveness. "Whew," he replies as he is experiencing an immense amount of relief. "I'm sure I can use a good beating from you, and I might actually enjoy it, tremendously," slight pause, "but, we should save all of our hostility for the bad guys," as he points over towards the building. "You're going to tell me now, right?"

"Okay, those types of trailers get moved by a tractor with a side loader. Once moved into position, the side loader lifts the trailer onto the

railcar. After it's loaded it will be secured with heavy chains and straps."
She smiles.

"I do not know what the heck you are talking about. I hate to ask you, but what is a side loader?" Charlie timidly asks.

"I see one over there," as she points to what Charlie considers a tractor.

Thinking to himself, *"But what the heck do I know anyway. I am just a project manager for Barley Systems."*

"Great, great, can you drive one?" Charlie asks with a smile, as Sherry just looks at him, shaking her head and rolling her eyes. "The train will be coming from that direction," as she points east. "Our best point of entry is down the street as the train begins to slow down. Then we'll jump aboard." Charlie quickly grabs her by the arm and says, "I told you, I'll get you onboard safely." She chuckles as they head east on the north side of the tracks. Inconspicuously they spy two limos pull into the back of China Star.

"Quick, pass me the video camera!" Charlie hastily instructs, and begins to video everything in sight: the trailers, the employees greeting Kim, the rail, and then he zooms in on Jeong Kim talking with Aye Lam, making sure to get clear and precise images of their faces. Again Sherry pokes him as the train is coming down the tracks. Charlie is in the midst of recording a video of the train when he suddenly hears someone right behind them in a heavy Asian accent.

"Hey whatcha guys doing here man?" He immediately looks over his shoulder, only to see a youth swiftly approaching, as he flaunts his Flying Dragon Street Warrior tattoo like an advertisement or a warning sign. He proceeds to pull out his blade and hastily begins swinging it towards Charlie.

"We're only tourists, taking photos of New York," Charlie anxiously states as he positions his body in anticipation for the attack. The street warrior lunges and swings the blade across Charlie's stomach, cutting through his cotton shirt, slicing into his skin. As blood splatters out from the incision, Sherry being the nurturing person that she is, immediately rushes over to Charlie's rescue. In doing so she leaves herself wide open as the thug takes full advantage and proceeds to plunge his blade in her direction. In witnessing this, Charlie takes out one of the switchblades in his pocket from the tree house incident and instantly pushes the button to release the blade. As he hears the thug laughing and making crude sexual gestures, while simultaneously lunging at her with his blade, just inches away from her face and neck, Charlie realizes the next swing of the blade may be fatal. Acting on an impulse, his boxing skills seem to kick in like a natural reflex. Suddenly, it's as if he sees everything again in slow motion, catching every detail of the action. As he follows every move the thug makes, with his forearm he blocks the next swing, causing him to lose his grip on the knife which goes flying over towards the tracks. Charlie simultaneously pushes the blade into the warrior's stomach like the one two punch he's used many times in the boxing ring.

With his eyes focused on Charlie, the warrior reaches for his stomach and stumbles backwards a bit; the sarcastic smile on his face quickly turns to a grimace as he begins to experience the agonizing pain. With an expression of disbelief, realizing he has been stabbed, he hunches over, looks back to Charlie and says, "You'll be sorry." With a quick look up to the sky Charlie pleads, "God please forgive me," as he glances over at Sherry and then proceeds to punch the thug with all his might in the face. Upon impact his body is thrust around and falls face down. They both hear a terrifying moan come out of him as he hits the pavement. He landed on the knife, plunging it deeper into his body. In a moment of silence, Charlie looks over to Sherry again, only this time with his head hung low, obviously feeling a sense of sadness for what he had done. Sherry stares on with a similar look, as they both begin to realize that in order for them to end this violence, a lot of blood will be shed.

The train approaches rapidly and Charlie and Sherry need to make their move. As they get close, simultaneously they look up to see in big letters painted on the side of the locomotive, 'Philadelphia, Bethlehem and New England Freight Company.' Charlie remembering Sherry's story about her mom and dad's murder, instantly, they look to each other; again no words were exchanged as they knew that this was the company Sherry's father worked for. Charlie grabs hold of Sherry's hand and rushes over to the train.

"We'll wait until the three empty rail cars pass before we jump aboard there," pointing at the boxcar with its sliding doors open. "Jump on my back, and wrap your legs around me, tightly." She wraps her legs around his abdomen and Charlie feels like he has the strength of ten men from her body touching his. As the train approaches, Charlie grabs hold of the large handle next to the door, he leaps on the step bar and pulls them into the car safely.

"Whew!" Charlie moans aloud, "We made it." The boxcar is half full with several crates of garage door openers and the metal tracking, heading to Link Controls in Kansas City, Mo. Charlie presumes they're safe, knowing the boxcar will not be unloaded in Philadelphia.

Sherry appears quite distraught, sitting alone in the corner with her head leaning on the wall, looking upward. Her eyes have been teary throughout the mission. However, she is being strong, not to let her emotions interfere with their mission. Charlie seems upset, to see her suffer as she is. He realizes her intuition will be correct, knowing this is the company her father worked for when he was murdered. Charlie believes this will be his route and they will find out that 'The Flying Dragons' were involved somehow, and she will finally get the answers she has continuously sought after these past fourteen years. Suddenly, the train comes to a complete stop, as they can hear voices and commotion all around them. Charlie reaches for Sherry and they take cover behind a wall of boxes lined up in the back of the boxcar. Nervously, they look around, then to each other for comfort. They do not have to say a word as they can feel each other's emotions, whether it's pain, joy, anguish, sadness or excitement.

Charlie looks at Sherry and wishes, *"only the best for her cause anything less just won't do."* Then a silly expression enters his mind, *"Good enough is not good enough,"* especially for her.

Two street warriors begin checking out the cars for hobos; they open the door of the boxcar. Charlie starts preparing himself for a fight as one warrior walks over to where they are. As he nears with each step and is virtually a few feet away, Charlie can feel the sweat beads on his forehead, as panic sets in. He slowly pulls out the second switchblade from his pocket. Sherry appears quite terrified as it is displayed all over her face. Suddenly, a third warrior comes by and calls for them. Sherry and Charlie look at each other, wondering if it is okay to relax. Charlie whispers to Sherry, "Just hold your position until the train starts back up."

They sit there for two hours, nothing happening; then, several boxes start getting loaded into their boxcar. The China Star workers unknowingly are loading illegal drugs for delivery.

A young lady discovers their presence; she nods, as if she is letting him know it's OK and she will not tell anyone about him. Her name tag "Anh Nguyen" was hanging from a neck strap. Charlie returns the nod and smiles, letting her know he understood. Another close call, but somehow with the help of sheer luck they are getting through it all. They have no choice but to sit quietly behind the boxes, waiting for the next step of their journey. Then as the workers load the last box onto the car, Charlie hears a faint click and Kim, along with Lam, walk up to another Street Warrior and give him orders to ride in the car to keep an eye on their shipment. He replies, 'Yes Nhat-Quo' and hops on. He sits on one of the boxes when Aye Lam yells at him, 'CHA RYUT' and he jumps to attention without saying a word. Aye Lam then says in a lower tone this time, "Kamsahamnida."

Suddenly, the door is closed, and soon the train starts moving. All the while Charlie keeps his eyes glued on the warrior, watching his every move. Then he hears another faint click and wonders, *"What the hell it that?"* Charlie looks around and discovers a few screws lying on the floor next to him, he picks them up and whispers to Sherry, "I need you to make some noise when I give you the signal." She nods back and mouths the word, "Okay." He slides over to the opposite side of the boxcar, keeping far away from Sherry. The warrior is just standing there, as if looking into space, unaware of his surroundings. However, Charlie doesn't realize the power of martial arts; he isn't looking into space, he is in a meditating state and all his senses are acute and on the alert. Charlie is holding the switchblade in one hand and the screws in the other. He tosses one of the screws down onto the floor, behind the warrior, and signals to Sherry to make a noise, thinking any normal person will turn towards the noise and then back to the second noise, giving Charlie the opportunity to attack from behind. No such luck, he was anything but normal. Charlie should have realized, these warriors aren't normal and automatically his martial arts' mentality kicks in and he immediately took his fighting stance. one that Charlie had never seen before, and as he is holding an open switchblade, he is yelling something in Chinese, Japanese or Vietnamese. Since the members of 'The Flying Dragons' are very mixed, they use a mixture of all the Asian languages to communicate, so it is not uncommon. It sounds like he is yelling "June Bee, June Bee," over and over. "Joon Bi" was the word the warrior was saying as he was hopping on one foot and spinning his body with the other. While contemplating his next move, Sherry stands up.

[200]

"Oh Shit," he thinks, *"Why? I guess she leaves me no choice."* Charlie stands up and runs after the warrior, tackling him from behind as he was heading towards Sherry, like Quang was headed toward him at the treehouse, moving like a wild animal. They both land on the wooden floor and instinctively Charlie slams the warrior's head into the floor repeatedly, knocking him unconscious.

"Thank you for being so kind", Charlie says. This time he was thanking God for keeping them safe, especially Sherry, who was the target of the attack. As Charlie begins to stand, he feels Sherry helping him up and realizes she is always there for him, whenever he needs her. As he looks deeply into her eyes he says softly, "Thank you." Then he turns back to the warrior and immediately strips him of all his weapons, ties him up with his belt and a shipping strap lying on the floor of the boxcar.

"By the way," Charlie asks Sherry, "did you hear a faint clicking noise earlier?" She looks at him and takes the recorder out of her purse and just clicks it on and off. With a smile Charlie utters yet another one of his silly expressions,   "I guess I'm not the sharpest tool in the shed." Shooting back at him, "Nor the brightest star in the sky," and they release some tension with laughter.

Sherry proceeds to videotape the shipment Kim and his warriors loaded at the China Star Clothing Factory. Charlie helps her open one of the boxes addressed to Thuy's Cleaners in Chicago. They find 50 dozen pair of white gloves, several fine silk fabrics over some bags filled with what looks like white sand, like the sand, you would find at Miami Beach, the Bahamas or even Point Pleasant, NJ. However they know otherwise; this is the treated cocaine, and Sherry videotapes it all.

"Do you think we should remove all the drugs and put them into the door operators, just to break his balls some, giving Kim a little more aggravation?" she questions Charlie.

"Serves no point, we don't want to disturb too much evidence on Kim; he can claim we have tampered with it and get the charges dismissed. Especially since you're taping it, he might say we set him up," Charlie explains, sounding more like his father during an investigation. He then takes a good look at Sherry, after recollecting her story about her parents, proceeds to pull her close as he holds her face, like the times she held his, between his four fingers and his thumb; he looks deep into her eyes.

"Your birth surname is not Mann, correct?" Charlie can see that she is taken aback by his question. The pupils of her eyes become larger as she seems to be hesitating, so he asks again, only this time a little differently, "Your real name is Manley, isn't that true?"

"Why do you need to know, CJ? Do you know something? Are you hiding something from me? Please tell me," and with a pause as her watery eyes start releasing those tears they have been holding for all these years, "Yes it is."

"My father worked on the Manley murder case while I was living at home, in my early twenties. The police were thinking the Italian Mob was involved because of your father's line of work. They knew from the beginning it had to do with the illegal drug trade within Philadelphia, but like I said, they were thinking Italians not Asians. Back then the Asians were just starting to become organized from what I've learned. They flew under the radar for years until now. We are going to expose them, and not stop until we get to what they refer to as Nhat-Quo, our hated friend, Jeong Kim." While they are still in conversation, the cell phone, taken from Quang at the tree house, rings. "The only one I know who will call this phone number is another hated friend of ours, Aye Lam." Charlie answers, "Hello."

"Hello Charlie. I hope Sherry and yourself are enjoying one another, because by tomorrow night you will both be executed. Your bodies will be left where you will be found. I should say you and Sherry posed in an awfully embarrassing position for all to see," and begins to laugh. Suddenly, he stops. "What's that noise, Charlie? Is that the sound of a train? Are you riding a train?"

"Don't worry, and don't bother to call me. I will call you. I will call to break your balls. That's right, you, Kim and this other guy, what's his name? Oh yeah, Quoc Bao Gia Xuong. You guys won't know what hit you." Charlie hangs up the phone and starts to worry.

"What did he say?" Sherry asks as he pulls her close enough to give her a kiss, but she pulls away from him as fast as she can. "CJ this is serious, and I'm so scared of what will happen next." Then she sits on the floor and puts her head down.

"Sorry, but I just can't right now", but he worries if Aye Lam can figure they are with the shipment. Sherry will make her first news videotape.

"I guess I will be your cameraman, right?" looking at her with his head tilted down and his eyes up at her. "How much will I be paid?"

"If you are good enough maybe you'll get the guy at the end of the movie." They both chuckle a bit.

The First Video Evidence:

"Good Afternoon ladies and gentlemen, I am Sherry Mann, on the street reporter for WWNJ Philadelphia and WGN TV Chicago. I am here with my acting cameraman Charlie Johnson. Tonight I am reporting live to you, from inside a freight train boxcar where The Flying Dragons are shipping one of the largest drug shipments in US History. As you can see behind me, there are several huge boxes from the China Star Clothing Factory in NY being shipped to Thuy Cleaners in Chicago. At first glance you can see the garments as per the shipping paperwork. However, if we move a few of the garments aside, we find bags of pure cocaine and Crystal Meth. This is only part of the shipment as there are three trailer loads of these boxes on this train".

Charlie zooms in on the labels making sure they are readable to the television audience. Sherry continued on to explain what they've learned up until this point: Kim's experiment, The Saigon Republic, the China Star Clothing Factory, and the invention that conceals the drugs from detection. Charlie is realizing Sherry is a fantastic news reporter; he can't help but notice the spark in her eyes, and the talent she possesses. He says, in his mind, *"She has so much talent that sadly she'd been hiding from her viewers all these years. No doubt these reports will propel her into a tremendous star, and hopefully, lift her spirits."* Charlie fears for Sherry's safety now, more than ever, because there is no turning back due to the simple fact that they are in the middle of something big, real big -- The Flying Dragons' drug business.

"Once again we are reporting live, from inside a boxcar of the Philadelphia, Bethlehem, and New England Freight Company with several hundred pounds of cocaine and Crystal Meth. I am Sherry Mann, street reporter for Eye Witness News, WWNJ Philadelphia and WGN TV Chicago."

As he turns off the camera, Charlie begins congratulating her on a fantastic report. He says in an attempt to lift her spirits, "You are going to be a big star at the end of all this." She just shrugs him off, and he felt challenged realizing that it was going to take nothing short of a miracle to lift the spirits of the most precious person in his life. Unaware at the time, but as soon as the Video ended, the China Star Clothing Factory was raided by the NYPD and the FBI. Holding a search warrant, evidence of the drug shipment left behind was taken, and 15 or so people were arrested, including Aye Lam and his so-called 'Quan-De-Khan' and his posse. Now it's time for Charlie to get rid of their guest, so he walks over to the sleeping beauty, tries to wake him up, but he is still unconscious. So to make sure it takes him a long time to get help, Charlie ties his feet together and his hands behind his back, then pushes him out of the door into a desolate area of northern New Jersey. The warrior tumbles to the grassland and Charlie waves, and using another silly expression of his,

"It's been nice knowing ya. Come back when you're in a hurry," then turns to Sherry and she is laughing out loud. "Do I make you laugh? Did I say something that you find amusing?" Charlie sits down next to her.

"Almost everything you say is strange to me and I find it funny," then she smiles.

"So what's your point, what's your story, what's your angle?" They sit there laughing until they reach the next destination.

At the Crossroads of Terror

Philadelphia Rail Yard:

$\mathcal{T}$he train pulls into the Philadelphia train yard where a new engineer takes the helm. This was Sherry's father's route and where he normally took over the controls. Sherry rode this route many times before. The ride took two days with two engineers taking turns at the controls, to make the trip. Each engineer operated the train in two four-hour shifts since this is a nonstop route. The tension builds as Charlie and Sherry wait to see what they will be facing next. Sherry begins to surmise, her woman's intuition take over, the answer's tragic loss will be discovered here.

"This is it," Sherry says, "My father's route is coming up, and I've got goosebumps in anticipation. Can you sense what I'm experiencing?"

"Err... sense what?" Charlie replies, sounding confused.

"There is a spirit in this boxcar with us, and I can feel it." She is walking slowly around the boxcar, as if she is trying to pin point where it is.

"You are scaring me Sherry. Are you gonna start freaking out on me? I need you," Charlie says, standing by her side.

"No, the spirit is here. Don't worry, I'm okay. Maybe my father's spirit is looking out for us." Then she stops.

"CJ, something tells me we should hide. I have a strong feeling about this, so let's hurry and hide behind those boxes." As soon as they were safely hidden, the boxcar door rolls open and one of the Philadelphia Flying Dragons, Danny, checks on the shipment. He looks around as if nothing was wrong, making no swift movements, and he seems to be unaware that anyone was stationed in the boxcar, so he closes the door and just walks away.

"I believe you're right again, your father's spirit helped us." Charlie stands up and moves over to the door to get a better view. Several gang members are chatting when an Asian train engineer walks up to the boys and laughs alongside of them, as if he were one of them.

"They are calling him Ben Ho. Does that sound familiar?" Charlie asks. "Can you send a text message to my father checking out a Ben Ho who is a train engineer for Philadelphia, Bethlehem, and New

England Freight Company?" Sherry gasps and quickly steps over to the door to curiously peek through the crack. Upon noticing him, she anxiously replies.

"That's Binh Ho, not Ben Ho, he was my father's co- engineer." Then Charlie sees it, they both see it, Binh has the logo of 'The Flying Dragons' on his arm. Charlie looks at Sherry to check her reaction. "I hate every one of those bastards, and he must have been involved in my parent's death." She takes the video camera out and starts filming everyone outside the train. She has tears falling, knowing for sure 'The Flying Dragons' were the monsters who murdered her parents. Charlie is furious and wants to make sure this Nhat-Quo Jeong Kim gets what he deserves. The anger he and Sherry harbor for them is immense, and they strongly bear the desire to avenge the deaths of Chelly and Sherry's mom and dad, the only people she had in her life back then. The boys disperse and Binh Ho climbs aboard the locomotive; within minutes the train begins to roll.

"Can I borrow your phone?" Charlie asks Sherry. "I want to call my dad and tell him what we know and that we are on our way to Kansas City. We are going to need help, lots of it. Our expected arrival is in about 16 hours." Charlie informs his dad of everything, and that they'll need help in Kansas City. He mentions that the shipment is quite large and many gang members with major firearms will be at their destination. His dad assures him plenty of help will be in Kansas City, without letting on he knows the FBI is on their trail every step of the way. Now all they have to do is sit and wait. By now the two of them are so physically and mentally exhausted, they open a box from China Star to make a bed. They made it behind the garage operators at the far end of the boxcar.

As they relax, Charlie begins to think,
"I feel the need to talk about our relationship, but by her lying there with her eyes glazed over, staring off at the roof of the boxcar, it is probably not a good time." Charlie was contemplating whether to be a little selfish and talk or just leave her alone in her deep thoughts. Being insecure, Charlie sometime needs to be recharged, rejuvenated or reassured about personal things. Sherry being in the state she is in, discovering who murdered her parents, he decides to wait.

Slaying the Dragon:

$\mathcal{F}$ifteen hours since the train had started on a course to Philadelphia, when the train begins to slow down, Sherry wonders to herself,

"This is strange, as we still have to travel at least an hour more to reach Kansas City." Charlie is aware of Sherry's horror, and she quickly becomes curious. She opens the sliding door and shouts aloud, "This isn't right. We are slowing down, why?" She is ready to panic, Charlie opens the opposite door and they are heading towards Far East Trucking Company terminal,

"I guess this is where they will be unloading," Charlie says.

Meanwhile at the FBI stakeout in KC, a federal agent Max Harper yells out to several other agents, "Who is out at East Independence?" The Feds expected the train to be unloaded somewhere along the way, so agents were stationed at every other train depot from Cincinnati to KC. They got their answer from Jack Wright, the agent at the Independence train depot, and Jack calls in.

"Max please," Jack says as he is calling in with information.

"Max here," Max replies as he is looking at a computer screen in front of him.

"Max, the train is making an unscheduled stop at the Far East Trucking terminal in East Independence Mo. I ran a check on the trucking company, it is owned by a Chicago corporation. The CEO of that corporation is Jeong Kim.

"Got him, we got Kim-connected boys. Jack, how many men are there?" Max says aloud.

"Just the two of us, Max" Jack hastily replies.

"We'll send backup for you. Do not make a move until backup arrives."

"Will do Max."

Back in the train, Sherry starts the video camera and records the terminal when Charlie says, "We got to hide now." As he closes the door, "We'll have to get into a box. I will cut breathing holes. You get in one, and I will put a box on top. I'll be in a box next to you. Do not get out until I get you, understand? I mean it. Please do not get out," sternly he implores into her eyes.

"Let's do it Stewart," she says with a warm smile. At that point Charlie sensed hope. Somehow they will make it through this. They make a good team together as they are in sync with each other. Charlie helps Sherry into a box and quickly gets into another. Now all they need to do is be patient and wait.

The Dragon falls:

𝒯he darkness and silence waiting for something to happen seemed like an eternity to Charlie and Sherry, although it wasn't too long before sensing being lifted and moved to a different truck. Charlie can assume they are headed to Chicago for Jeong Kim to inspect his goods. Only when they are in route, traveling at a steady pace, does he get out of his box inspects the situation and helps Sherry free herself.

"How well did you manage the trip?" Charlie asks Sherry. She pauses and realizes Charlie is tense and wants to loosen him up a bit,

"Remind me never again to travel coach with you anymore," she fires back, trying to make him laugh, but he is too serious about everything.

"I figure we are headed to Chicago, another 8 hours before we arrive. We'll need to find a place to hide, especially if you do not want to travel coach anymore." He glances over at her and she begins to smile. She comprehends, he is loose. "Kim is only interested in the boxes addressed to Thuy's Cleaners," he says, "We'll need to plan for a hiding spot for before we dock in Chicago." They decide to rearrange the cargo to secure their safety.

At the Crossroads of Terror

Meanwhile, back at Far East Trucking Company:

ℱBI and ATF agents heavily armed, along with arrest and search warrants confiscated the entire shipment, remained behind and arrested Binh Ho, Bao Dai and everyone with a Flying Dragon tattoo on their arm, 23 people. The FBI and ATF were making the biggest drug bust in history, all because of Sherry and Charlie. The President of the United States was informed and is following this bust from the White House.

Charlie and Sherry arrive at the Far East Terminal in Chicago. They are able to hear the guard at the gate tell the driver to pull into dock 23, "They are waiting for you." Charlie grabs hold of Sherry's arm, pulling her close and begins to gaze into her beautiful hazel eyes.

"I want to tell you now, in case something happens to me before I get to say this --" Sherry tries to stop him,

"No CJ, nothing is going to happen." He puts his hand over her mouth, letting her know he needs to continue.

"You somehow captured my heart, somewhere along our journey. I do not understand how I managed to live without you in my life. I realize without you I wasn't living. I was missing something in my life you have given me. I now know it was my heart and my soul you've given. I love you and everything about you." Sherry stops him by putting her hand over his mouth and finally says the words he has been waiting for these last few weeks.

"I love you." They kiss. They break from their kiss and Charlie pulls her behind the boxes at the opposite end from the roll up door.

The door rolls up making a loud noise, Sherry starts trembling from fear. Charlie takes hold of her to calm her, with little success. The last thing they need is for Kim and his gang to find them. The fear of being captured, tortured and killed is overwhelming. At the open door three men are standing on the loading dock, a warehouse worker, Jeong Kim next to a huge man in a suit standing with him. Kim gives the order to another, out of view, "Unload this skid, and deliver it to the secured area for inspection." Kim and the man walk away. The first skid is unloaded, giving Charlie and Sherry enough time to exit. Charlie gives a signal to Sherry and says, "Time for us to get out of here and follow the shipment." They exit the truck and make their way over to the warehouse storage racks opposite the truck. They creep up to the secured area being hidden by boxes in the warehouse. Kim is opening one of the boxes, taking out several of the bags they both suspect is cocaine, and walks into a nearby office. The big guy Kim was with earlier is standing guard outside the door. As Charlie thinks, "How are we going to get past this guy?"

Someone behind them yells, Geu Mahn. Charlie doesn't know the translation, but it means trouble to them. He quickly turns around and sees two guys in their attack stance, snarling. Charlie, in response, gets in one of his from his old boxing days. They both begin to laugh. One of the guys kicks Charlie, feet first, in his chest where he was operated on, knocking Charlie across the aisle into a storage rack, hitting his head hard enough to make him dizzy, before falling to the cement floor. In a blur, Charlie realizes their attention is on Sherry. He becomes terrified to think what they can do to her; he manages to get up and run towards Sherry, pulling the knife from his pocket that he stole from the beast on the train. Charlie gets closer to the attacker as his heart starts to race, and his mind is telling him not to fail. He tackles the guy, while simultaneously pushing the knife into him multiple times yelling, "Die you scum bag, die." Charlie, a little remorseful as blood began spewing out all over him. Now the second guy's fist is coming right at Charlie's face, but manages to roll enough to avoid the full impact. The blow caught Charlie in the mouth, causing him to bleed. Charlie pushes himself up quickly and this guy begins to come feet first. Again Charlie tries to dodge the attacker, but he hit on his left shoulder, knocking him to the floor. Looking up, this guy is coming fast with a strike Charlie believes is deadly. With his heart pounding and their lives on the line, somehow still holding onto the knife, and Sherry yelling, Charlie throws the knife at this SOB, hoping for something positive. The knife lands into his leg and he falls to the floor, before his kick of death. Instinctively, Charlie rushes over to him as he is pulling the knife out of his leg. Charlie kicks his hand and the knife goes flying across the warehouse floor. Charlie leaps onto his body, giving him massive blows to his head, striking this guy with one punch after another, making his head bounce off the cement floor. He wants this bastard to suffer for all the pain they caused. Like the time they were in Chicago and Charlie kept pulling the trigger over and over, shooting Kwan, and seeing his body twitch with each shot. He didn't want to stop here either. He kept pounding him, while his blood from his mouth, nose and eye was spattering everywhere, and his head slamming off the floor. Relating to his past, Charlie was Helmut in rage, pounding Arte, hoping to make all the wrongs right, but it can never be, and all his punches couldn't correct the wrongs. They were just giving him the power to release his anger, the emotions he had inside all these years. In the meantime, Sherry is doing her best to calm him down, trying to get Charlie to stop his rage, the anger busting out from within him, uncontrollably. She continues her plea. The fury he had inside, knowing everything he has learned about these guys, every punch meant something to him: This one is for Chelly, another for Mr. Manley, one for Mrs. Manley, over and over. He wanted to release his anger and rage.

Sherry somehow manages to get Charlie to calm down, in tears, begging him to stop, his brain catching up to reality, comprehending his surroundings. Their mission is still incomplete. He turns to Sherry and realizes he frightened her, as much as the Flying Dragons. He grabs hold of her.

"I hate myself for this, being in an uncontrollable rage and scaring you. This was building inside of me since the day Helmut was executed." In tears, he gives her a hug, knowing he terrified her. "Can you forgive me? I need your forgiveness most of all."

"I forgive you. I know this has been very stressful on the both of us," with the satisfaction of knowing she could calm him down, as they embrace.

"It's time we get to Kim's office," Charlie says, as his mouth is still bleeding and he aches all over. When he stands, the pain in the side of his chest and head are throbbing from the kicks he received from these two beasts.

"Are you alright?" Sherry asks as she helps him to steady himself. Gradually, he moans, "Yes, I have to be." They walk over to the office Kim entered earlier. The huge guy is still standing outside the door. Charlie scans the area and finds a pry bar on an empty forklift nearby. He grabs it and says to Sherry, "Walk slowly past "Herc-u-rock", a term he uses referring to muscle-bound guys. The expression is from a Stone Age cartoon show, when Charlie was a kid. Sherry gives him a strange look when he says one of his silly sayings she doesn't understand or that doesn't make sense.

Sherry walks past Herc-u-rock, he stops her by grabbing her arm. As he grabs her, Charlie whacks him in the back with the pry bar. He doesn't fall, rather he starts to turn around towards Charlie. So he swings again, only this time he gets hit square in the face and then he falls to the floor. Charlie stands over him trying to loosen the tension in this dangerous situation and says,

"How do you feel about that now, fella?" Charlie shouts and Sherry rolls her eyes and has a faint smile on her face. Charlie takes out a gun and hands it to Sherry. The frightened look on her face told him the whole story, the reasons why they need to continue forward and have it end here now.

"Use it only if necessary and please be careful with it. All you have to do is point and shoot," Charlie says with a kiss on her cheek. Charlie takes out a second gun and they enter Kim's office.

Jeong Kim is sitting at his desk, sampling the cocaine. He has a straw in his nose, inhaling the white powder on his desk. They walk in with the guns pointed at Kim's head, the door closes behind them. Mr. Kim, however didn't seem to be alarmed, as if he expected their arrival.

"It's over Nhat-Quo. We know all about you and your sleazy operation. I should blow your rotten head off your shoulders just to get revenge for Chelly's murder!" Charlie shouts angrily, his body begins to tremble in rage with the anger he built up for this guy. Charlie's hand suddenly stings and the gun slams to the floor. He turns and there is another Herc-u-rock, only bigger than the last one, realizing he kicked the gun out of his hand.

"*Oh Crap!*" Charlie's thinking, as he throws Sherry across the room. He turns back around towards Charlie, in fear, "*I know I said I wasn't afraid of the physical abuse, but seeing this guy at this moment, I guess I lied. He's King Kong, a big powerful guy, I'm nothing in comparison. I'm in for some major pain.*" Charlie is concerned as this guy's fist comes flying towards his head like lightning. Charlie can't block it. The force was tremendous. Charlie's head snaps backwards and his body follows. He falls over a chair, his head slams into the wall, then to the floor. Everything around was in a blur, Charlie's head ached like a migraine, cannot move his hand, as though it was paralyzed. Charlie senses him coming again, unable to defend himself. He is forcefully picked up and thrown into the opposite wall. A tooth flies out of his mouth and he falls to the floor again. Blood begins to gush out of

Charlie's mouth, the pain is excruciating beyond anything he has experienced. "*Oh God!*" He is thinking, "I need your help. This guy is much too powerful for me." His heart is pounding, beating throughout his entire body. Charlie opens his eyes and Sherry is on this guy's back. "*What a brave woman she is*," Charlie thinks, and giving him the courage to continue the fight. Charlie becomes infuriated when Sherry is thrown like a rag doll. His heart pounding, like the time he fought Long Ngo, at North Street Garage in Chicago. Charlie moves his head towards Sherry, and the gun is magically lying on the floor next to him. "*Thank you God, you heard my prayer.*" He reaches for the gun and rolls himself as King Kong comes towards him, like the kid at the tree house. Only this guy will actually *kill* with his kick. Through his blood, his sweat, pouring down his face, while his heart is beating unmercifully hard, all the way down to his fingertips, the fear of failure, so he aims and pulls the trigger. He shoots until King Kong falls to the floor, counting the bullets this time, making sure he has at least one bullet left for Kim.

King Kong falls backwards to the floor, almost hitting Sherry on his way down. Relief, when Charlie notes the blood oozing out of his lifeless body. With his mouth bleeding and massive pain all over, Charlie walks over to Sherry and helps her up.

"Thank you," he says, "Thank you for being there for me, my guardian angel. You saved my life once again."

Charlie turns his focus to Kim, now nervous. He knew he was in big trouble, the pupils of his eyes widened through those thick lenses, in those black plastic frames. He is starting to panic with sweat beads forming on his forehead, realizing his bodyguard is no longer going to protect him. Charlie stands proud.

"Looks like you lose yom," with the gun pointed at Kim's head. "You lost it all, the shipment, your freedom, your wealth and most of all, your power. The Dragon has been killed, and you will rot in hell for all the sadistic things you did."

"You're crazy Charlie! You do not have a chance getting out of here alive. My boys will kill you and your kitten as soon as that door opens." Then Kim reaches for his cane.

"Don't even think about picking that up," Charlie yells. "My kitten? Let me introduce you to my kitten. Her name is Sherry Manley. I know you've heard that name before. Manley, remember it?" Charlie is starting to grow angrier, now Sherry gets involved, standing next to him pointing her gun at Kim. He continues, "Tell me who Manley was?"

"Oh yes, the Manleys. Dennis was Binh Ho's co-engineer. It's a shame his wife witness his death, then die herself at the construction site of my Dragon's Den," as he makes a sinister chuckle.

"You son of a bitch!" Sherry yells as she is ready to shoot the bastard. Charlie realizes her mood changed, like Helmut's mood changed before he went ballistic, like Charlie's emotions were spilling out a few minutes ago. She is screaming and cursing at the top of her lungs at him. Charlie needs to react, "I am not going to stare and do nothing this time, no way. I cannot let anything happen to Sherry. I need to calm her down."

"Sherry, you got him where you want him. Put the gun down, please, he is going to pay for all his crimes. I am begging, don't let your anger get the best of you. I won't be able to live if you get arrested for murder, please listen." She is out of control. Someone at the door shouts, "FBI, open up." Then he pleads with her once more, as his heart starts pounding harder. Charlie is afraid she is going to lose it, like Helmut lost it, and says, "I love you, if you love me don't shoot," as the door gets busted open. They are surrounded with agents pointing guns at Sherry and Kim. Charlie keeps negotiating with her. "He will spend the rest of his sorry ass life in prison, being greeted every morning in the shower by a guy named Rosy Gross Berger, or he will be executed in a few years." Charlie is planning to grab the gun from Sherry's arm as she is concentrated on Nhat-Quo Jeong Kim. Her only thought is to kill him, to shoot the bastard dead. "Listen to me," Charlie pleads, "Look around, the FBI is here ready to take him. Don't let them take you away from me too, please, I beg you." Charlie, instead of pleading decides to yell, "Watch out!" breaking Sherry's concentration, and takes the gun away from her.

Now the commotion is all around. The FBI reads Kim his rights. As Kim was walking out in handcuffs he said something nasty to Sherry, "Too bad I didn't get to have you like I had your mother." He made CJ so furious, he punched him so hard he fell to the floor and let out a moan. He got some satisfaction when he saw Kim's mouth bleeding and him on the floor, like a broken man, a sight for sore eyes. But like CJ said earlier, this couldn't make a wrong right, or bring back Sherry's folks, or Chelly. CJ looks up at the agent who was escorting Kim and sees him smile. CJ stares down Kim.

At the Crossroads of Terror

"Rosy Gross Berger is waiting for you pal. You son of a bitch," with Charlie's sinister smile smacked into his face.

At that moment CJ realizes what has just happened and what Sherry and he accomplished today. The Dragon was slain, lives were saved and people will be safer in several cities because of the heroics of their actions. The FBI, ATF, and local police authorities were able to do major damage to the Asian Organized Crime family, the Flying Dragons. With the evidence that was provided through video and audio tapes along with personal statements, 175 gang members were arrested. The fronts of the Flying dragons: the Dragon's Den in Philadelphia, Saigon Republic LLC in Englewood, NJ, the China Star Clothing factory in NY, Thuy' Cleaner's in Chicago and the national Far East Trucking Company terminals were closed down. A warrant for the arrest of Hung Vuong aka the Street Prince, was issued for the murder of Mrs. Chang and her daughter Linh, for arson and extortion. The facts later revealed Mr. Chang was murdered for falling behind on his loan payments to the gang's loan sharking business. When he refused to sign a new fire insurance policy in which Mr. Hung Vuong was the beneficiary, he wrote his death sentence. Later, after Mr. Chang's death, Mrs. Chang signed the policy and within 5 weeks the place was torched with her and her daughter Linh inside. Without the NY, Philadelphia, Chicago and KC sectors, the leadership and revenue that those cities produced, the remaining free gang members will probably go back to being an insignificant local street gang. Back to being a street gang meant the dismemberment of the organization that the trio, Jeong Kim, Hung Vuong and Long Ngo built years earlier. The drug trafficking practically came to a halt as the trucking and rail systems were no longer available to them. With the evidence that Charlie and Sherry provided, future arrest warrants were issued for the street warriors who eventually made it past airport security with the drugs.

The President calls:

𝔚ith his mouth bleeding profusely from losing his tooth, his entire body aching in pain, being smacked against walls and warehouse racks, now in the arms of Sherry, Charlie is braced for anything as FBI agent Richard Diamond walks up to him.

"Could you walk with me, you have an important phone call."

"Who's calling?" Sherry asks.

"The President of the United States, and he wants a few words with you two," then holds out his hand to escort them back into Kim's office.

"Who's better than us?" Charlie proclaims, as Sherry is overtaken, her eyes beginning to water, her every emotion running rabid. They enter the room and are seated in front of Kim's desk. The President is on speaker phone.

"They're here sir," Richard Diamond says as he stands next to the desk.

The President:

"Let me start off by thanking the both of you for your courageous act of bravery. With your help, we were able to make this historic organized crime and drug bust. In no other time in the history of the US has such an undertaking been achieved. With the power of my office as President of the United States, you both will be honored with the highest award any US citizen ever received, The President's Medal of Freedom Award. This award comes with one million dollars to the recipients.

The both of you will also receive the US Citizen of the Year award and be honored at my annual Christmas party in December.

You did a great job in defending our freedom and our country. I will see you next week at your Freedom Award ceremony and reception.

America thanks you, and I thank you. Peace to you both."

"Peace to you, Mr. President," they both said in unison as they turn to each other in amazement.

All at once, the terminal was filled with agents and local police arresting as many as 45 gang members including the Kim's Leadership council. That's when the WGN TV camera crew was on the set. Sherry's boss calls, "I need you to do a live broadcast. This is your time, to take it to the next level," as Sherry walks over to the camera crew and starts to discuss their strategy. Sherry introduces CJ to Steven Bailey, the cameraman, as she grabs hold of the microphone and begins her report.

"Good Afternoon ladies and gentlemen. I am Sherry Mann, street reporter for WWNJ Philadelphia and WGN TV Chicago. I am reporting live from inside the Chicago terminal of The Far East Trucking Company. This is the headquarters of one of the most feared Asian gangs in America, the Flying Dragons. The noises you hear are the sound of the Dragon being slain.

"That's right the Dragon died, with federal agents arresting many of the members of the Flying Dragon's gang members today. The FBI and ATF agents are both at the biggest drug bust in US history," pausing to catch her breath. *"Please once again forgive me how I am dressed. I have been riding a freight train along with Charlie Johnson in pursuit of following the gang's drug shipment.*

"The Leader, Nhat-Quo, which means # 1 soldier, Jeong Kim was arrested for racketeering, drug trafficking, prostitution, rape, and 7 counts of murder. He is being charged with the murders of Michelle Kelly Robinson, Detectives Jim Sweeney and Ralph Inzerillo, Officers Allen Kennedy and Doug Burke.

"The next two murders were committed fourteen years ago, a homicide that hits home for me. This one has been sitting in the cold case files of the Philadelphia PD since 1992. The victims were my parents," as tears start rolling down her cheeks, *"My dear father and mother, Dennis and Marie Manley. At the time of their death they were living in Cherry Hill New Jersey."*

As the broadcast continues, Sherry's television persona is enthralling. The TV audiences in Philly and Chicago are awestruck with her. Sherry explains how she and CJ put themselves in a dangerous situation to stop more violence from happening, how they wore disguises (she explains why her hair is still jet black) and entered Saigon Republic pretending to be a couple looking for a wedding reception hall. How the two of them rode the freight train, jumped into one of the boxes where the drugs were packed to gain access into the Dragon's lair, the Far East Trucking terminal; how CJ took on guys twice his size in order for this massive drug bust to take place.

"Come over here, CJ," she says as he is in shock as to why she is calling him on the set. "Come," as she is waving her hands for him to walk in front of the cameras. Steve turns the camera to Charlie. With no other choice, he waves and smiles at the camera. "Here is the bravest man I know, the man I fell in love with during this shocking and unbelievable adventure."

Now she starts asking CJ questions like she was interviewing him, "How did you feel when you beat the Dragon and won the battle, CJ?" Steve moves the camera towards him. CJ, with his mouth bleeding, thinking how today turned out to be a fabulous day. She called him "CJ" and told thousands of people she loves him. Even a call from the president, Wow! "Who is better than me? No one, not today, nobody except for her," pointing at Sherry, "The woman I love."

CJ begins:

"It was an extensive and tiring excursion. The road home was long. Sherry and I haven't been home since April 17th. Today is July 10th. Other than that, I am elated and walking, or should I say, flying on a cloud. With the help of this lovely lady, we may have prevented more lives from being lost by these true monsters of the midway." Charlie turns towards Sherry and mouths the words, *"me too, I love you."*

Sherry gets a breaking news flash in her ear set,

"I found out that the total arrested on this bust is up to 175 gang members of the Flying Dragons from NY, Kansas City, Philadelphia, and Chicago. The FBI closed down the operations of The Dragon's Den in Philadelphia, Saigon Republic LLC in Englewood, NJ, the China Star Clothing factory in NY, Thuy's Cleaner's in Chicago and all the Far East Trucking Company terminals, until their investigation is complete."

She manages to complete her report, which is making national headlines as the biggest drug bust in US History. Soon millions of Americans will fall in love with the same woman as Charlie has. He said when they started this endeavor he didn't want to make her career with his troubles, but now he is elated for her and he couldn't be happier. He is looking at a woman who paid her dues, in fact more than her dues, to make it. Tomorrow she will be on the front page of every major

[218]

newspaper in America and like CJ, America won't be able to get enough of her.

"Reporting live at the Far East Trucking Company, I am Sherry Mann, on-site street reporter for Eye Witness News, WWNJ Philadelphia and WGN TV Chicago, we are signing off and may God bless you."

Once again, the viewers fall in love with Sherry. This time the phones don't stop ringing for several days, since this was a national news story. The ratings for both stations have jumped through the roof, something they both enjoyed immensely. As Sherry finishes up her broadcast and wrapping up things, saying her goodbyes, CJ walks up to her and says, "It's been a long time since we've been home; can we go home now?" To his surprise Sherry says, "No, I prefer to stay the night, we'll go tomorrow."

"Tomorrow?" Charlie says with a slight pause. "Sherry!" as she puts her hands to his lips to stop him.

"My new boss has given me this," as she waves something in front of his face.

"You have a new boss? Gave you? What was that?" Charlie says as it flashes again in front of his eyes.

"It's something we've started and I think we should finish," as she waves this credit card again.

"I give up, you win. Now I'm really curious," CJ says.

"I win? That's what you say, Charlie? Get a new vocabulary, sir," smiling while shouting. "That's the same thing you told me then, and we didn't finish what we started," Sherry fires back in a rather loud voice. "What?" CJ is now totally confused.

"It's the door key to room 219 at the Holiday Inn on Joliet Road Chicago. You remember, you called it the room with a view?" She gives him one of her looks that drives him absolutely berserk, "Well? Are you coming with me or should I ask Steven Bailey, the cameraman?" She then gives CJ the biggest and warmest smile and uses one of his lines:

"Let's do it Stewart."

CJ, talking to himself aloud, "You know what CJ always says, imitation **is** the best form of flattery." Then he begins to smile and give her the ole Charlie look.

Home at Last

Chapter 12

A Hero's Welcome, the following day:

$\mathcal{U}$pon arrival at the hotel, Charlie and Sherry make their way up to room #219, as if they were young children at a carnival. As they approach the entrance, Sherry turns to Charlie. With intent on his face, he smiles and gestures for her to open the door. Upon entering, Sherry stretches out her arms and lets out a loud sigh of relief, turns to Charlie with a big smile and darts to the rest room. Meanwhile Charlie can't resist the enchanting view from the window and finds himself compelled to gaze out at the indoor pool. In doing so he ponders the thought of becoming intimate with Sherry. In a nervous attempt, he practices in a huge designer mirror hung next to the window. Charlie clears his throat and stares deep into the eyes of his own reflection.

"Sherry, you are blessed with the most beautiful green eyes, and I've fallen in love with you." Suddenly, and quite unexpectedly, Sherry grabs him by the shoulders to turn him around, grabs hold of his chin, and stares deep into his bewildered eyes.

"And you CJ possess the sexiest blue eyes I've ever seen. I'm in love with you."

At that moment, they embrace in a heated kiss. He brought his lips, soft and warm, to hers. As he let the tip of his tongue work her lips apart, he entwined his hands in her hair. She welcomes him in, with inviting thoughts. For a moment, they stood with their mouths locked together. At the end of the kiss, Charlie pulled his hands back from her face.

"You're sure, right? I need you to be completely sure." With the approval of the nod of her head, he began to remove her top and let it drop to the floor, looking into her eyes for her reaction, making sure this was the right time for her. Satisfied with her answer, he unzipped her pants and followed the open path left by the zipper with tiny kisses and touches of his tongue. Sherry moaned in silence as she was lost in the warm tingling of his tongue. When he had finished unzipping Sherry's pants, he let them fall to the floor as he reached around to unhook her bra. He threw it, leaned forward and with his tongue began to massage each of her breasts before he kissed each one. Exercising all the restraint he could, he straightened up and stepped back to enjoy her delicious body. His eyes filled with an uncontrollable desire. He was mesmerized as she stepped out of her underwear. She was an absolute knockout, in Charlie's mind the most beautiful woman he ever laid eyes on.

Now it was Sherry's turn, her chance to explore the body of the man she believed was the man she waited for her entire life. She stepped closer to Charlie, her eyes filled with passion. Once again, she traced light paths along the edge of his lips, down his neck with her fingers. This time, her hands did not stop at his collar; instead, she unbuttoned his shirt. In a provocative fashion, she removed it off his body and let it drop to the floor. Instinctively, he raised his hands to pull her to him, but she stopped him by capturing and pushing his hands back to his side. She proceeded to hook her thumbs under the edge of his t-shirt and worked it up his chest. Her breathing pleasantly tight and her groin throbbing with a desire, she unhooked his pants and drew the zipper down. She freed him of his boxers and delicately kissed his aroused member as Charlie moaned by the pleasure her kiss sent through his body. She let his pants and boxers drop to the floor.

Sherry stood back to enjoy Charlie's body for several seconds. His beautiful eyes, those enticing lips, and his muscular chest. She beheld for the first time his solid member, waiting to deliver them both into bliss. Now they were going to complete what Charlie and Sherry wanted to do for the last several months. It was his sensual body that he presented to her for the first time. Charlie stepped out of his clothes, left down around his ankles. His eyes now burned with the desire of Sherry. He gently caressed her breasts and walked her over to the bed. In a long sigh, she becomes weak, and extremely wet, and tender. He understood the expression on her face while her moans seemed to passionately beckon to him. Sherry, in a flirtatious manner, moves downward, kisses him on the neck and chest, all the way down to his abdomen. Just as he is about to explode, he lifts up to stop, temporarily.

"We've both waited too long for this, and now all I can think of is you and my desire to make passionate love to you. Again I need to make sure you are okay with this." Sherry nods and with his arms around her abdomen and a quick thrust, they were soon in heaven, where they remained in ecstasy for the remainder of the night.

Upon arising, they'd both fallen asleep out of sheer pleasure, Sherry notices the daylight through an opening in the drapes, jumps up and yells, "Oh my God CJ, we are going to be late!"

"Calm down. We'll make the plane. Would you like to shower first?" Charlie replies.

"The heck with that, let's hit the shower together, I'm starved."

They arrive at the airport on time. Once they were seated, they just stared into each other's eyes, and with a kiss they fell asleep head to head. They are awakened by the flight attendant's announcement, "We will be taking off shortly. Please make sure that your seat belt is securely fastened. Thank you." Sherry and Charlie enjoyed a beautiful night together. A night they will remember for a long time. Charlie expected their night together to be good, but never imagined how incredible it could be. He reaches over to Sherry and says,

"I am the luckiest man on earth." In a relaxed manner, he continues, "You are remarkable." She gazes at him with that lovely smile of hers and replies, "My place or yours?"

While holding her hand, he says, "At my place we won't have to turn the bed over to use it." She raises her eyes towards the ceiling and just smiles as the plane comes in for a landing.

The plane reaches the gate and the stewardess makes one more announcement while another one walks up to Sherry and Charlie to ask them to remain in their seats. "Everybody, may I have your attention, we need all passengers to gather your things and walk straight out to the assigned luggage area C55 or to the spectators' area. We have two special guests on board who are going to receive a hero's welcome by the city of Philadelphia." Upon hearing this, Charlie looks over at Sherry and she has tears in her eyes.

"Why are you crying now? This is a good thing, right?" Charlie asks as he begins to wipe the tears from her eyes.

"I am crying from happiness. I am honored to be in the presence of a national hero. You did it. You attempted something and truly did it. I am so proud of you."

"I couldn't have done any of this without you." Charlie replies then turns toward the flight attendant and with a funny expression on his face says, "Who's better than me? I am embracing the love of my life."

A long road home, but somehow Charlie and Sherry arrived. Upon landing at Philadelphia's International Airport, they are greeted by thousands of people, all the local television stations, radio stations and several national stations. Governor Randall Edwards and the Philadelphia Mayor Franklin James were in attendance for the heroes' ceremony. Charlie's parents were seated next to each other by the podium. The special greeting was warm and unexpected as the city of brotherly love gave Sherry and Charlie the love they truly earned.

Another night in Heaven:

𝒜s Sherry is making her thank you speech at the podium to the crowd, she turns to Charlie.

"We should go to 15th Street, Cherry Hill." Charlie knew exactly what she meant, and he begins to smile, thinking about another night in heaven with Sherry at his apartment.

Meanwhile in Los Angeles, Hung Vuong, the street prince, is yelling at the television,

"You'll pay for this!!!!! If it's the last thing I do, the two of you will pay for this!!!!!"

The End

Acknowledgements

I would especially like to thank my family starting with my wife, Camille, who has put up with my moods, my patience or shall I say lack of, and still somehow managed to give me hope and encouragement when I needed it most. I would also like to give thanks to my three girls; Jeanine Marie, Danielle, and Cheri-Lyn, who I am so proud of.

In writing this book, I had to research many subjects virtually unknown to me. So I would like to give special thanks to Wikipedia along with other internet web sites for making my research a little easier. Although this book is fiction, there are many facts we all should be aware of. The victims of a rape and violent gang related crimes are all too real, as I learned from my research. The research took me into the world of violence throughout America. In towns, we all believe to be a safe haven and where people can go to bed with their front doors unlocked. This is an erroneous belief as I learned that violence is everywhere in America today. It's hard to imagine exactly the feeling of being violated, unless you were in the shoes of the victim.

My heart became extremely saddened to go inside the minds and hear from these victims as they relive their most despicable experience as they retold it for all to read. One lady's experience with rape touched my heart like no other as she communicated her story. She is a brave and courageous lady, and it is because of her and others like her, I decided that a portion of the proceeds from this book with be donated to a RAINN (Rape, Abuse & Incest National Network), providing help 24/7 visit their site *www.rainn.org*. Their new 24 hour hotline is providing help to over 1.2 million people through the National Sexual Assault Hotline 800.656.HOPE ~ 800.656.4673.

I would like to give many thanks to the following special people in my life for making of this novel possible because without them, I could not have completed it. Steve Berent, founder of Starmemoirs.com for his keen-eyed editing and proofreading for final edits. Lisa Velarde along with Steve Berent managed to take my original unedited script to create what I would like to think is a masterpiece today. Carl Esposito who, along the way helped in the edits and structure of this novel to get me started in the right direction. Several readers in Texas Alex Ajraz, Steve Schachter, and Larry Laper who have given me the friendship we all need in order to enhance our lives. I also would like to acknowledge some of my readers and reviewers, Erik McKeever of North Dallas, and Mario Puglia for taking the time to read an unedited novel and enlightening me with some helpful and corrective tips. To my daughter Danielle, her artistic creativity and talent, brings this novel to life, by creating such a beautiful book cover.

Some of my teachers and professors who kept their faith in me at times I felt I would not be able to make it, especially, Dr. Ira Lieberman, Mrs. Wolfe, Miss Inzerillo, Mr. Gilmartin, and the late Mr. Sachesman from Brentwood High School in New York.

May God bless everyone who reads this novel, and I hope you feel a portion of the emotions I felt while I was writing this book, to you.

I give you my special wish;

'May each of you live as long as you want, but never want as long as you live. And may each of you live to be a hundred and me a hundred minus a day, so I never know that nice people like you have passed away.'

God Bless - In Italian; 'Il Dio Benedice'

About the Author: Lenny Emanuelli;

Lenny Emanuelli has been a song writer since the late 1960's. He currently holds a master's degree in business finance.

His credits include over forty songs recorded by various artists, and the 1975 musical;

"Dreamin' My Life Away"

'**Simon Sez**' is the next project he is working on. It's a story about Todd Simon, who writes a weekly advice column for a local Baltimore newspaper called "Simon Sez". He is also assigned to cover the news of a serial killer in the area, the Bay Street Killer, who just murdered the fifth victim.

The story is very intense and powerful with many twists and turns and an unexpected ending.

More about RAINN

RAINN (Rape, Abuse & Incest National Network) is the nation's largest anti-sexual assault organization and was named one of "America's 100 Best Charities" by Worth Magazine. RAINN created and operates the National Sexual Assault Hotline (800.656.HOPE) in partnership with over 1,000 local rape crisis centers across the country. In April 2008, RAINN launched the National Sexual Assault Online Hotline, the first secure web-based crisis hotline providing live and anonymous support. These hotlines have helped more than 1.2 million people since 1994. RAINN also carries out programs to prevent sexual assault, help victims and ensure that rapists are brought to justice. For more information about RAINN, please visit rainn.org.

RAINN (Rape, Abuse & Incest National Network)
www.rainn.org
800-656-HOPE ~ 800-656-4673

The facts:

Every 2 minutes another American is sexually assaulted. Almost half of these victims are under 18, and 80% are under 30.

My pledge:

With each and every copy of this book that gets sold a 10% donation will be made to RAINN. I will also be making personal appearances to help education as many as I can about this growing problem within the communities throughout America.

Three ways to reduce your risk of sexual assault

- **Travel in packs**
When you got out, go in a group. Check in with each other & leave together. Don't be isolated with someone you don't know or trust.

- **Trust Your Instincts**
If a situation feels unsafe or uncomfortable, it probably is.

- **Don't feel Obligated**
To do anything you don't want to. "I don't want to" is *always* a good enough reason.

Let's work together and do our part to help as many innocent victims as we can.

Additional Help Hotlines

National Runaway Switchboard
1-800-Runaway | http://www.1800runaway.org
A national number for runaways and youth in Crisis as well as their families ~ We can even help you get home if you want

National Domestic Violence Hotline
1-800-799-SAFE (7233) or 1-800-787-3244 (TTY)
http://www.ndvh.org/
National Toll free hotline for domestic violence problems ~ confidential, 24 hrs Translators available

RAINN - Rape, Abuse, and Incest National Network
1-800-656-HOPE (4673) | http://www.rainn.org/
Toll free, 24 hour confidential hotline for people in abusive situations

(RAINN transfers your call to your local rape crisis center or DV shelter, and picks up the tab for it. You will not get long distance charges, the call will not show up on your phone bill, and it's also free from a payphone.)

National Center for Victims of Crime and National Stalking Resource Center
1-800- FYI-CALL (1-800-394-2255)
http://www.ncvc.org/src/index.html
A resource to help you understand and address stalking and harassment ~ Available M-F, 8:30 am- 8:30 PM EST

Miles Foundation
203-270-7861 | http://www.milesfdn@aol.com
A confidential resource for victims of Interpersonal Violence in the Military

Darkness to Light Hotline
1-866-FOR-LIGHT (367-5444) | http://www.darkness2light.org/
Toll free, confidential, 24 hours hotline for victims of child sexual abuse

Childhelp USA National Child Abuse Hotline
1-800-4- A-CHILD (1-800-422-4453) | http://www.childhelpusa.org/
Toll free, confidential, 24 hr hotline for advice, information and to
clarify options. It is not the same as reporting the abuse. You don't need
to give your name or name of the abuser to talk.

NCMEC –
National Center for Missing and Exploited Children
1-800-THE-LOST (1-800-843-5678) | http://www.missingkids.com/
They also run an alternate database for runaway youth and can help.

Stop It Now!
1-888-PREVENT | http://www.stopitnow.com/
A national helpline for adults who are concerned about inappropriate
sexualized behavior in themselves or people they know ~ Toll free,
confidential M-F 9am-6PM ET

National Center on Elder Abuse
1 (800) 677-1116 | http://www.elderabusecenter.org/
Eldercare Locator- is not a helpline, but rather will direct you to the state
hotline number. They can help you find the right place to report elder
abuse.

Women's Law Initiative
http://www.womenslaw.org/
State-by-state legal information on domestic violence and orders of
protection

American Domestic Violence Crisis Line
From within the USA, dial 1-866-USWOMEN.
From overseas, contact your local AT&T operator and ask to be
connected to 866-USWOMEN
http://www.866uswomen.org/
If you have a safe email, email them anytime at
crisis@866uswomen.org

**International toll free domestic violence crisis line for
American women and children living abroad** from 10:00PM to
6:00 AM, Pacific Standard Time, Monday night through Friday morning
and Tuesdays and Thursdays from 9:00 AM to 1:00 PM. All
communication is confidential.

International Directory of Resources
http://www.hotpeachpages.com
International inventory of hotlines, shelters, refuges, crisis centers and
women's organizations, searchable by country, plus index of domestic
violence resources in over 70 languages.

National Suicide Hotline
1-800-SUICIDE | http://www.hopeline.com/
national hotline for people dealing with depression and suicide, their
friends and family